THE HEECHEE LOTTERY

THE STAKES
A lifetime of riches and ease, and a place in the history of the human race as one of the few who brought back a priceless piece of the alien Heechee technology . . . wagered against the certainty of a miserable death in the wastes of space.

THE ODDS
Rotten. Only a third of the abandoned Heechee ships staffed by human explorers ever came back with living crews . . . or with dead ones, for that matter. Some never came back.

THE WINNER
Bob Broadhead, who lucked into two unprecedented finds and made it as big as anyone could. So why was his life—mansion, girls, and everything else he wanted—unbearable? Somehow he would have to find the answer . . . or never find peace!

"*Gateway* is one of those rare gems: a deeply human story set against the wonders and beauty of the infinite starry universe. Fred Pohl, Old Master that he is, has broken new ground for the science-fiction novel."
—Ben Bova,
Editor, *Analog Magazine*

GATEWAY GARNERS

GREAT REVIEWS

Also by Frederik Pohl
Published by Ballantine Books:

THE AGE OF THE PUSSYFOOT

BEYOND THE BLUE EVENT HORIZON

THE BEST OF FREDERIK POHL
    Edited and with an Introduction by Lester del Rey

A PLAGUE OF PYTHONS

THE WAY THE FUTURE WAS

FARTHEST STAR (with Jack Williamson)

PREFERRED RISK (with Lester del Rey)

THE SPACE MERCHANTS (with C. M. Kornbluth)

GATEWAY

Frederik Pohl

A Del Rey Book

BALLANTINE BOOKS • NEW YORK

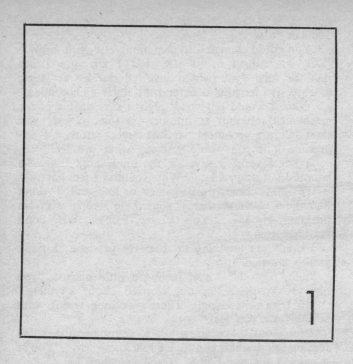

1

My name is Robinette Broadhead, in spite of which I am male. My analyst (whom I call Sigfrid von Shrink, although that isn't his name; he hasn't got a name, being a machine) has a lot of electronic fun with this fact:

"Why do you care if some people think it's a girl's name, Bob?"

"I don't."

"Then why do you keep bringing it up?"

He annoys me when he keeps bringing up what I keep bringing up. I look at the ceiling with its hanging mobiles and piñatas, then I look out the window. It isn't really a window. It's a moving holopic of surf coming in on Kaena Point; Sigfrid's programming is pretty eclectic. After a while I say, "I can't help what my parents called me. I tried

1

spelling it R-O-B-I-N-E-T, but then everybody pronounces it wrong."

"You could change it to something else, you know."

"If I changed it," I say, and I am sure I am right in this, "you would just tell me I was going to obsessive lengths to defend my inner dichotomies."

"What I would tell you," Sigfrid says, in his heavy mechanical attempt at humor, "is that, please, you shouldn't use technical psychoanalytic terms. I'd appreciate it if you would just say what you feel."

"What I feel," I say, for the thousandth time, "is happy. I got no problems. Why wouldn't I feel happy?"

We play these word games a lot, and I don't like them. I think there's something wrong with his program. He says, "You tell me, Robbie. Why don't you feel happy?"

I don't say anything to that. He persists. "I think you're worried."

"Shit, Sigfrid," I say, feeling a little disgust, "you always say that. I'm not worried about anything."

He tries wheedling. "There's nothing wrong with saying how you feel."

I look out the window again, angry because I can feel myself trembling and I don't know why. "You're a pain in the ass, Sigfrid, you know that?"

He says something or other, but I am not listening. I am wondering why I waste my time coming here. If there was anybody ever who had every reason to be happy, I have to be him. I'm rich. I'm pretty good-looking. I am not too old, and anyway, I have Full Medical so I can be just about any age I want to be for the next fifty years or so. I live in New York City under the Big Bubble, where you can't afford to live unless you're really well fixed, and maybe some kind of celebrity besides. I have a summer apartment that overlooks the Tappan Sea and the Palisades Dam. And the girls go crazy over my three Out bangles. You don't see too many prospectors anywhere on Earth, not even in New York. They're all wild to have me tell them what it's really like out around the Orion Nebula or the

481	IRRAY (O)=IRRAY (P)	13,320
	,C, I think you're worried.	13,325
482	XTERNALS ;66AA3 IF ;5B	13,330
	GOTO **7Z3	13,335
	XTERNALS @ 01R IF @ 7	13,340
	GOTO **7Z4	13,345
	,S, Shit, Sigfrid, you always	13,350
	say that.	13,355
	XTERNALS ¢99997AA! IF ¢8	13,360
	GOTO **7Z4 IF ? GOTO	13,365
	**7Z10	13,370
	,S, I'm not worried about any-	13,375
	thing.	13,380
483	IRRAY .SHIT. .ALWAYS.	13,385
	.WORRIED/NOT.	13,390
484	,C, Why don't you tell me	13,395
	about it?	13,400
485	IRRAY (P)=IRRAY (Q) INITI-	13,405
	ATE COMFORT MODE	13,410
	,C, There's nothing wrong	13,415
	with saying how you	13,420
	feel.	13,425
487	IRRAY (Q)=IRRAY (R) GOTO	13,430
	**1 GOTO **2 GOTO	13,435
	**3	13,440
489	,S, You're a pain in the ass,	13,445
	Sigfrid, you know	13,450
	that?	13,455
	XTERNALS ¢1! IF ! GOTO	13,460
	**7Z10 IF **7Z10! GOTO	13,465
	**1 GOTO **2 GOTO **3	13,470
	IRRAY .PAIN.	13,475

Lesser Magellanic Cloud. (I've never been to either place, of course. The one really interesting place I've been to I don't like to talk about.)

"Or," says Sigfrid, having waited the appropriate number of microseconds for a response to whatever it was he said last, "if you really are happy, why do you come here for help?"

I hate it when he asks me the same questions I ask myself. I don't answer. I squirm around until I get comfortable again on the plastic foam mat, because I can tell that it's going to be a long, lousy session. If I knew why I needed help, why would I need help?

"Rob, you aren't very responsive today," Sigfrid says through the little loudspeaker at the head of the mat. Sometimes he uses a very lifelike dummy, sitting in an armchair, tapping a pencil and smiling quirkily at me from time to time. But I've told him that that makes me nervous. "Why don't you just tell me what you're thinking?"

"I'm not thinking about anything, particularly."

"Let your mind roam. Say whatever comes into it, Bob."

"I'm remembering—" I say, and stop.

"Remembering what, Rob?"

"Gateway?"

"That sounds more like a question than a statement."

"Maybe it is. I can't help that. That's what I'm remembering: Gateway."

I have every reason to remember Gateway. That's how I got the money and the bangles, and other things. I think back to the day I left Gateway. That was, let's see, Day 31 of Orbit 22, which means, counting back, just about sixteen years and a couple of months since I left there. I was thirty minutes out of the hospital and couldn't wait to collect my pay, catch my ship, and blow.

Sigfrid says politely, "Please say what you're thinking out loud, Robbie."

"I'm thinking about Shikitei Bakin," I say.

4

"Yes, you've mentioned him. I remember. What about him?"

I don't answer. Old, legless Shicky Bakin had the room next to mine, but I don't want to discuss it with Sigfrid. I wriggle around on my circular mat, thinking about Shicky and trying to cry.

"You seem upset, Bob."

I don't answer to that, either. Shicky was almost the only person I said good-bye to on Gateway. That was funny. There was a big difference in our status. I was a prospector, and Shicky was a garbageman. They paid him enough money to cover his life-support tax because he did odd jobs, and even on Gateway they have to have somebody to clean up the garbage. But sooner or later he would be too old and too sick to be any more use at all. Then, if he was lucky, they would push him out into space and he would die. If he wasn't lucky, they'd probably send him back to a planet. He would die there, too, before very long; but first he would have the experience of living for a few weeks or so as a helpless cripple.

Anyway, he was my neighbor. Every morning he would get up and painstakingly vacuum every square inch around his cell. It would be dirty, because there was so much trash floating around Gateway all the time, despite the attempts to clean it up. When he had it perfectly clean, even around the roots of the little shrublets he planted and shaped, he would take a handful of pebbles, bottle caps, bits of torn paper—the same trash he'd just vacuumed up, half the time—and painstakingly arrange it on the place he had just cleaned. Funny! I never could see the difference, but Klara said . . . Klara said she could.

"Bob, what were you thinking about just then?" Sigfrid asks.

I roll up into a fetal ball and mumble something.

"I couldn't understand what you just said, Robbie."

I don't say anything. I wonder what became of Shicky. I suppose he died. Suddenly I feel very sad about Shicky dying, such a very long way from Nagoya, and I wish again that I could cry. But I can't.

5

I squirm and wriggle. I flail against the foam mat until the restraining straps squeak. Nothing helps. The pain and shame won't come out. I feel rather pleased with myself that I am trying so hard to let the feelings out, but I have to admit I am not being successful, and the dreary interview goes on.

Sigfrid says, "Bob, you're taking a long time to answer. Do you think you're holding something back?"

I say virtuously, "What kind of a question is that? If I am, how would I know?" I pause to survey the inside of my brain, looking in all the corners for padlocks that I can open for Sigfrid. I don't see any. I say judiciously, "I don't think that's it, exactly. I don't *feel* as if I were blocking. It's more as if there were so many things I wanted to say that I couldn't decide which."

"Take any one, Rob. Say the first thing that comes into your mind."

Now, that's dumb, it seems to me. How do I know which is the first thing, when they're all boiling around in there together? My father? My mother? Sylvia? Klara? Poor Shicky, trying to balance himself in flight without any legs, flapping around like a barn swallow chasing bugs as he scoops the cobwebby scraps out of Gateway's air?

I reach down into my mind for places where I know it hurts, because it has hurt there before. The way I felt when I was seven years old, parading up and down the Rock Park walk in front of the other kids, begging for someone to pay attention to me? The way it was when we were out of realspace and knew that we were trapped, with the ghost star coming up out of nothingness below us like the smile of a Cheshire cat? Oh, I have a hundred memories like those, and they all hurt. That is, they can. They are pain. They are clearly labeled PAINFUL in the index to my memory. I know where to find them, and I know what it feels like to let them surface.

But they will not hurt unless I let them out.

"I'm waiting, Bob," Sigfrid says.

"I'm thinking," I say. As I lie there it comes to my mind that I'll be late for my guitar lesson. That reminds

6

me of something, and I look at the fingers of my left hand, checking to see that the fingernails have not grown too long, wishing the calluses were harder and thicker. I have not learned to play the guitar very well, but most people are not that critical and it gives me pleasure. Only you have to keep practicing and remembering. Let's see, I think, how do you make that transition from the D-maj to the C-7th again?

"Bob," Sigfrid says, "this has not been a very productive session. There are only about ten or fifteen minutes left. Why don't you just say the first thing that comes into your mind . . . *now.*"

I reject the first thing and say the second. "The first thing that comes into my mind is the way my mother was crying when my father was killed."

"I don't think that was actually the first thing, Bob. Let me make a guess. Was the first thing something about Klara?"

My chest fills, tingling. My breath catches. All of a sudden there's Klara rising up before me, sixteen years earlier and not yet an hour older. . . . I say, "As a matter of fact, Sigfrid, I think what I want to talk about is my mother." I allow myself a polite, deprecatory chuckle.

Sigfrid doesn't ever sigh in resignation, but he can be silent in a way that sounds about the same.

"You see," I go on, carefully outlining all the relevant issues, "she wanted to get married again after my father died. Not right away. I don't mean that she was glad about his death, or anything like that. No, she loved him, all right. But still, I see now, she was a healthy young woman—well, fairly young. Let's see, I suppose she was about thirty-three. And if it hadn't been for me I'm sure she would have remarried. I have feelings of guilt about that. I kept her from doing it. I went to her and said, 'Ma, you don't need another man. I'll be the man in the family. I'll take care of you.' Only I couldn't, of course. I was only about five years old."

"I think you were nine, Robbie."

"Was I? Let me think. Gee, Sigfrid, I guess you're

right—" And then I try to swallow a big drop of spit that has somehow instantly formed in my throat and I gag and cough.

"Say it, Rob!" Sigfrid says insistently. "What do you want to say?"

"God damn you, Sigfrid!"

"Go ahead, Rob. Say it."

"Say what? Christ, Sigfrid! You're driving me right up the wall! This shit isn't doing either one of us any good!"

"Say what's bothering you, Bob, please."

"Shut your fucking tin mouth!" All that carefully covered pain is pushing its way out and I can't stand it, can't deal with it.

"I suggest, Bob, that you try—"

I surge against the straps, kicking chunks out of the foam matting, roaring, "Shut up, you! I don't want to hear. I can't cope with this, don't you understand me? I can't! Can't cope, can't cope!"

Sigfrid waits patiently for me to stop weeping, which happens rather suddenly. And then, before he can say anything, I say wearily, "Oh, hell, Sigfrid, this whole thing isn't getting us anywhere. I think we should call it off. There must be other people who need your services more than I do."

"As to that, Rob," he says, "I am quite competent to meet all the demands on my time."

I am drying my tears on the paper towels he has left beside the mat and don't answer.

"There is still excess capacity, in fact," he goes on. "But you must be the judge of whether we continue with these sessions or not."

"Have you got anything to drink in the recovery room?" I ask him.

"Not in the sense you mean, no. There is what I am told is a very pleasant bar on the top floor of this building."

"Well," I say, "I just wonder what I'm doing here."

And, fifteen minutes later, having confirmed my appointment for the next week, I am drinking a cup of tea in Sigfrid's recovery cubicle. I listen to hear if his next patient has started screaming yet, but I can't hear anything.

So I wash my face, adjust my scarf, and slick down the little cowlick in my hair. I go up to the bar for a quick one. The headwaiter, who is human, knows me, and gives me a seat looking south toward the Lower Bay rim of the bubble. He looks toward a tall, copper-skinned girl with green eyes sitting by herself, but I shake my head. I drink one short drink, admire the legs on the copper-skinned girl and, thinking mostly about where I am going to go for dinner, keep my appointment for my guitar lesson.

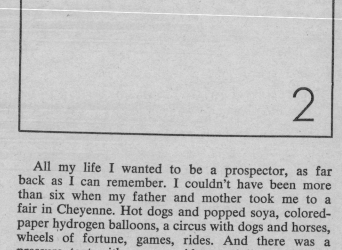

2

All my life I wanted to be a prospector, as far back as I can remember. I couldn't have been more than six when my father and mother took me to a fair in Cheyenne. Hot dogs and popped soya, colored-paper hydrogen balloons, a circus with dogs and horses, wheels of fortune, games, rides. And there was a pressure tent with opaque sides, a dollar to get in, and inside somebody had arranged a display of imports from the Heechee tunnels on Venus. Prayer fans and fire pearls, real Heechee-metal mirrors that you could buy for twenty-five dollars apiece. Pa said they weren't real, but to me they were real. We couldn't afford twenty-five dollars apiece, though. And when you came right down to it, I didn't really need a mirror. Freckled face, buck teeth, hair I brushed straight back and tied. They had just found Gateway.

The Heechee Hut

Direct from the Lost Tunnels of Venus!
Rare Religious Objects
Priceless Gems Once Worn by the Secret Race
Astounding Scientific Discoveries
EVERY ITEM GUARANTEED AUTHENTIC!
Special Discount for
Scientific Parties and Students
THESE FANTASTIC OBJECTS
ARE OLDER THAN HUMANITY!

Now for the first time at popular prices
Adults, $2.50   Children, $1.00
Delbert Guyne, Ph.D., D.D., Proprietor

I heard my father talking about it going home that night in the airbus, when I guess they thought I was asleep, and the wistful hunger in his voice kept me awake.

If it hadn't been for my mother and me he might have found a way to go. But he never got the chance. He was dead a year later. All I inherited from him was his job, as soon as I was big enough to hold it.

I don't know if you've ever worked in the food mines, but you've probably heard about them. There isn't any great joy there. I started, half-time and half-pay, at twelve. By the time I was sixteen I had my father's rating: charge driller—good pay, hard work.

But what can you do with the pay? It isn't enough for Full Medical. It isn't enough even to get you out of the mines, only enough to be a sort of local success story. You work six hours on and ten hours off. Eight hours' sleep and you're on again, with your clothes stinking of shale all the time. You can't smoke, except in sealed rooms. The oil fog settles everywhere. The girls are as smelly and slick and frazzled as you are.

So we all did the same things, we worked and chased each other's women and played the lottery. And we drank a lot, the cheap, powerful liquor that was made not ten miles away. Sometimes it was labeled Scotch and sometimes vodka or bourbon, but it all came off the same slime-still columns. I was no different from any of the others . . . except that, one time, I won the lottery. And that was my ticket out.

Before that happened I just lived.

My mother was a miner, too. After my father was killed in the shaft fire she brought me up, with the help of the company crèche. We got along all right until I had my psychotic episode. I was twenty-six at the time. I had some trouble with my girl, and then for a while I just couldn't get out of bed in the morning. So they put me away. I was out of circulation for most of a year, and when they let me out of the shrink tank my mother had died.

12

Face it: that was my fault. I don't mean I planned it, I mean she would have lived if she hadn't had me to worry about. There wasn't enough money to pay the medical expenses for both of us. I needed psychotherapy. She needed a new lung. She didn't get it, so she died.

I hated living on in the same apartment after she was dead, but it was either that or go into bachelor quarters. I didn't like the idea of living in such close proximity to a lot of men. Of course I could have gotten married. I didn't—Sylvia, the girl I'd had the trouble with, was long gone by that time—but it wasn't because I had anything against the idea of marriage. Maybe you might think I did, considering my psychiatric history, and also considering that I'd lived with my mother as long as she was alive. But it isn't true. I liked girls very much. I would have been very happy to marry one and raise a child.

But not in the mines.

I didn't want to leave a son of mine the way my father had left me.

Charge drilling is bitchy hard work. Now they use steam torches with Heechee heating coils and the shale just politely splits away, like carving cubes of wax. But then we drilled and blasted. You'd go down into the shaft on the high-speed drop at the start of your shift. The shaft wall was slimy and stinking ten inches from your shoulder, moving at sixty kilometers an hour relative to you; I've seen miners with a few drinks in them stagger and stretch out a hand to support themselves and pull back a stump. Then you pile out of the bucket and slip and stumble on the duckboards for a kilometer or more till you come to the working face. You drill your shaft. You set your charges. Then you back out into a cul-de-sac while they blast, hoping you figured it right and the whole reeking, oily mass doesn't come down on you. (If you're buried alive you can live up to a week in the loose shale. People have. When they don't get rescued until after the third day they're usually never any good for anything anymore.) Then, if everything has gone all right, you dodge the handling loaders as they come creeping in on their tracks, on your way to the next face.

The masks, they say, take out most of the hydrocarbons and the rock dust. They don't take out the stink. I'm not sure they take out all the hydrocarbons, either. My mother is not the only miner I knew who needed a new lung—nor the only one who couldn't pay for one, either.

And then, when your shift is over, where is there to go?

You go to a bar. You go to a dorm-room with a girl. You go to a rec-room to play cards. You watch TV.

You don't go outdoors very much. There's no reason. There are a couple of little parks, carefully tended, planted, replanted; Rock Park even has hedges and a lawn. I bet you never saw a lawn that had to be washed, scrubbed (with detergent!), and air-dried every week, or it would die. So we mostly leave the parks to the kids.

Apart from the parks, there is only the surface of Wyoming, and as far as you can see it looks like the surface of the Moon. Nothing green anywhere. Nothing alive. No birds, no squirrels, no pets. A few sludgy, squidgy creeks that for some reason are always bright ochre-red under the oil. They tell us that we're lucky at that, because our part of Wyoming was shaft-mined. In Colorado, where they strip-mined, things were even worse.

I always found that hard to believe, and still do, but I've never gone to look.

And apart from everything else, there's the smell and sight and sound of the work. The sunsets orangey-brown through the haze. The constant smell. All day and all night there's the roar of the extractor furnaces, heating and grinding the marlstone to get the kerogen out of it, and the rumble of the long-line conveyors, dragging the spent shale away to pile it somewhere.

See, you have to heat the rock to extract the oil. When you heat it it expands, like popcorn. So there's

14

no place to put it. You can't squeeze it back into the shaft you've taken it out of; there's too much of it. If you dig out a mountain of shale and extract the oil, the popped shale that's left is enough to make two mountains. So that's what you do. You build new mountains.

And the runoff heat from the extractors warms the culture sheds, and the oil grows its slime as it trickles through the shed, and the slime-skimmers scoop it off and dry it and press it . . . and we eat it, or some of it, for breakfast the next morning.

Funny. In the old days oil used to bubble right out of the ground! And all people thought to do with it was stick it in their automobiles and burn it up.

All the TV shows have morale-builder commercials telling us how important our work is, how the whole world depends on us for food. It's all true. They don't have to keep reminding us. If we didn't do what we do there would be hunger in Texas and kwashiorkor among the babies in Oregon. We all know that. We contribute five *trillion* calories a day to the world's diet, half the protein ration for about a fifth of the global population. It all comes out of the yeasts and bacteria we grow off the Wyoming shale oil, along with parts of Utah and Colorado. The world needs that food. But so far it has cost us most of Wyoming, half of Appalachia, a big chunk of the Athabasca tar sands region . . . and what are we going to do with all those people when the last drop of hydrocarbon is converted to yeast?

It's not my problem, but I still think of it.

It stopped being my problem when I won the lottery, the day after Christmas, the year I turned twenty-six.

The prize was two hundred and fifty thousand dollars. Enough to live like a king for a year. Enough to marry and keep a family on, provided we both worked and didn't live too high.

Or enough for a one-way ticket to Gateway.

I took the lottery ticket down to the travel office

and turned it in for passage. They were glad to see me; they didn't do much of a business there, especially in that kind of commodity. I had about ten thousand dollars left over in change, give or take a little. I didn't count it. I bought drinks for my whole shift as far as it would go. With the fifty people in my shift, and all the friends and casual drop-ins who leeched on to the party, it went about twenty-four hours.

Then I staggered through a Wyoming blizzard back to the travel office. Five months later, I was circling in toward the asteroid, staring out the portholes at the Brazilian cruiser that was challenging us, on my way to being a prospector at last.

3

Sigfrid never closes off a subject. He never says, "Well, Bob, I guess we've talked enough about that." But sometimes when I've been lying there on the mat for a long time, not responding much, making jokes or humming through my nose, after a while he'll say:

"I think we might go back to a different area, Bob. There was something you said some time ago that we might follow up. Can you remember that time, the last time you—"

"The last time I talked to Klara, right?"

"Yes, Bob."

"Sigfrid, I always know what you're going to say."

"Doesn't matter if you do, Bob. What about it? Do you want to talk about how you felt that time?"

"Why not?" I clean the nail of my right middle

finger by drawing it between my two lower front teeth. I inspect it and say, "I realize that was an important time. Maybe it was the worst moment of my life, about. Even worse than when Sylvia bitched me, or when I found out my mother died."

"Are you saying you'd rather talk about one of those things, Rob?"

"Not at all. You say talk about Klara, we'll talk about Klara."

And I settle myself on the foam mat and think for a while. I've been very interested in transcendental insight, and sometimes when I set a problem to my mind and just start saying my mantra over and over I come out of it with the problem solved: Sell the fish-farm stock in Baja and buy plumbing supplies on the commodities exchange. That was one, and it really paid out. Or: Take Rachel to Merida for waterskiing on the Bay of Campeche. That got her into my bed the first time, when I'd tried everything else.

And then Sigfrid says, "You're not responding, Rob."

"I'm thinking about what you said."

"Please don't think about it, Rob. Just talk. Tell me what you're feeling about Klara right now."

I try to think it out honestly. Sigfrid won't let me get into TI for it, so I look inside my mind for suppressed feelings.

"Well, not much," I say. Not much on the surface, anyway.

"Do you remember the feeling at the time, Bob?"

"Of course I do."

"Try to feel what you felt then, Bob."

"All right." Obediently I reconstruct the situation in my mind. There I am, talking to Klara on the radio. Dane is shouting something in the lander. We're all frightened out of our wits. Down underneath us the blue mist is opening up, and I see the dim skeletal star for the first time. The Three-ship—no, it was a Five. . . . Anyway, it stinks of vomit and perspiration. My body aches.

18

I can remember it exactly, although I would be lying if I said I was letting myself feel it.

I say lightly, half chuckling, "Sigfrid, there's an intensity of pain and guilt and misery there that I just can't handle." Sometimes I try that with him, saying a kind of painful truth in the tone you might use to ask the waiter at a cocktail party to bring you another rum punch. I do that when I want to divert his attack. I don't think it works. Sigfrid has a lot of Heechee circuits in him. He's a lot better than the machines at the Institute were, when I had my episode. He continuously monitors all my physical parameters: skin conductivity and pulse and beta-wave activity and so on. He gets readings from the restraining straps that hold me on the mat, to show how violently I fling myself around. He meters the volume of my voice and spectrum-scans the print for overtones. And he also understands what the words mean. Sigfrid is extremely smart, considering how stupid he is.

It is very hard, sometimes, to fool him. I get to the end of a session absolutely limp, with the feeling that if I had stayed with him for one more minute I would have found myself falling right down into that pain and it would have destroyed me.

Or cured me. Perhaps they are the same thing.

322	,S, I don't know why I keep	17,095
	coming back to you,	17,100
	Sigfrid.	17,105
323	IRRAY .WHY.	17,110
324	,C, I remind you, Robby,	17,115
	you've already used up	17,120
	three stomachs and, let me	17,125
	see, nearly five meters	17,*30
	of intestine.	17,135
325	,C, Ulcers, cancer.	17,140
326	,C, Something appears to be	17,145
	eating away at you,	17,150
	Bob.	17,155

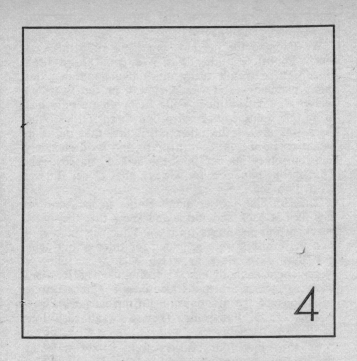

4

So there was Gateway, getting bigger and bigger in the ports of the ship up from Earth:

An asteroid. Or perhaps the nucleus of a comet. About ten kilometers through, the longest way. Pearshaped. On the outside it looks like a lumpy charred blob with glints of blue. On the inside it's the gateway to the universe.

Sheri Loffat leaned against my shoulder, with the rest of our bunch of would-be prospectors clustered behind us, staring. "Jesus, Bob. Look at the cruisers!"

"They find anything wrong," said somebody behind us, "and they blow us out of space."

"They won't find anything wrong." said Sheri, but she ended her remark with a question mark. Those cruisers looked mean, circling jealously around the asteroid, watching to see that whoever comes in isn't going to steal the secrets that are worth more than anyone could ever pay.

We hung to the porthole braces to rubberneck at them. Foolishness, that was. We could have been killed. There wasn't really much likelihood that our ship's matching orbit with Gateway or the Brazilian cruiser would take much delta-V, but there only had to be one quick course correction to spatter us. And there was always the other possibility, that our ship would rotate a quarter-turn or so and we'd suddenly find ourselves staring into the naked, nearby sun. That meant blindness for always, that close. But we wanted to see.

The Brazilian cruiser didn't bother to lock on. We saw flashes back and forth, and knew that they were checking our manifests by laser. That was normal. I said the cruisers were watching for thieves, but actually they were more to watch each other than to worry about anybody else. Including us. The Russians were suspicious of the Chinese, the Chinese were suspicious of the Russians, the Brazilians were suspicious of the Venusians. They were all suspicious of the Americans.

So the other four cruisers were surely watching the Brazilians more closely than they were watching us. But we all knew that if our coded navicerts had not matched the patterns their five separate consulates at the departure port on Earth had filed, the next step would not have been an argument. It would have been a torpedo.

It's funny. I could imagine that torpedo. I could imagine the cold-eyed warrior who would aim and launch it, and how our ship would blossom into a flare of orange light and we would all become dissociated atoms in orbit. . . . Only the torpedoman on that ship, I'm pretty sure, was at that time an armorer's mate named Francy Hereira. We got to be pretty good buddies later on. He wasn't what you'd really call a cold-eyed killer. I cried in his arms all the day after I got back from that last trip, in my hospital room, when he was supposed to be searching me for contraband. And Francy cried with me.

The cruiser moved away and we all surged gently out, then pulled ourselves back to the window with the grips, as our ship began to close in on Gateway.

"Looks like a case of smallpox," said somebody in the group.

It did; and some of the pockmarks were open. Those were the berths for ships that were out on mission. Some of them would stay open forever, because the ships wouldn't be coming back. But most of the pocks were covered with bulges that looked like mushroom caps.

Those caps were the ships themselves, what Gateway was all about.

The ships weren't easy to see. Neither was Gateway itself. It had a low albedo to begin with, and it wasn't very big: as I say, about ten kilometers on the long axis, half that through its equator of rotation. But it could have been detected. After that first tunnel rat led them to it, astronomers began asking each other why it hadn't been spotted a century earlier. Now that they know where to look, they find it. It sometimes gets as bright as seventeenth magnitude, as seen from Earth. That's easy. You would have thought it would have been picked up in a routine mapping program.

The thing is, there weren't that many routine mapping programs in that direction, and it seems Gateway wasn't where they were looking when they looked.

Stellar astronomy usually pointed away from the sun. Solar astronomy usually stayed in the plane of the ecliptic—and Gateway has a right-angle orbit. So it fell through the cracks.

The piezophone clucked and said, "Docking in five minutes. Return to your bunks. Fasten webbing."

We were almost there.

Sheri Loffat reached out and held my hand through the webbing. I squeezed back. We had never been to bed together, never met until she turned up in the

Q. What did the Heechee look like?

Professor Hegramet: Nobody knows. We've never found anything resembling a photograph, or a drawing, except for two or three maps. Or a book.

Q. Didn't they have some system of storing knowledge, like writing?

Professor Hegramet: Well, of course they must have. But what it is, I don't know. I have a suspicion . . . well, it's only a guess.

Q. What?

Professor Hegramet: Well, think about our own storage methods and how they would have been received in pretechnological times. If we'd given, say, Euclid a book, he could have figured out what it was, even if he couldn't understand what it was saying. But what if we'd given him a tape cassette? He wouldn't have known what to do with it. I have a suspicion, no, a conviction, that we have some Heechee "books" we just don't recognize. A bar of Heechee metal. Maybe that Q-spiral in the ships, the function of which we don't know at all. This isn't a new idea. They've all been tested for magnetic codes, for microgrooves, for chemical patterns— nothing has shown up. But we may not have the instrument we need to detect the messages.

Q. There's something about the Heechee that I just don't understand. Why did they leave all these tunnels and places? Where did they go?

Professor Hegramet: Young lady, it beats the piss out of me.

bunk next to mine on the ship, but the vibrations were practically sexual. As though we were about to make it in the biggest, best way there ever could be; but it wasn't sex, it was Gateway.

When men began to poke around the surface of Venus they found the Heechee diggings.

They didn't find any Heechees. Whoever the Heechees were, whenever they had been on Venus, they were gone. Not even a body was left in a burial pit to exhume and cut apart. All there was, was the tunnels, the caverns, the few piddling little artifacts, the technological wonders that human beings puzzled over and tried to reconstruct.

Then somebody found a Heechee map of the solar system. Jupiter was there with its moons, and Mars, and the outer planets, and the Earth-Moon pair. And Venus, which was marked in black on the shining blue surface of the Heechee-metal map. And Mercury, and one other thing, the only other thing marked in black besides Venus: an orbital body that came inside the perihelion of Mercury and outside the orbit of Venus, tipped ninety degrees out of the plane of the ecliptic so that it never came very close to either. A body which had never been identified by terrestrial astronomers. Conjecture: an asteroid, or a comet—the difference was only semantic—which the Heechees had cared about specially for some reason.

Probably sooner or later a telescopic probe would have followed up that clue, but it wasn't necessary. Then The Famous Sylvester Macklen—who wasn't up to that point the famous anything, just another tunnel rat on Venus—found a Heechee ship and got himself to Gateway, and died there. But he managed to let people know where he was by cleverly blowing up his ship. So a NASA probe was diverted from the chromosphere of the sun, and Gateway was reached and opened up by man.

Inside were the stars.

Inside, to be less poetic and more literal, were nearly a thousand smallish spacecraft, shaped something like fat mushrooms. They came in several shapes

25

and sizes. The littlest ones were button-topped, like the mushrooms they grow in the Wyoming tunnels after they've dug all the shale out, and you buy in the supermarket. The bigger ones were pointy, like morels. Inside the caps of the mushrooms were living quarters and a power source that no one understood. The stems were chemical rocket ships, kind of like the old Moon Landers of the first space programs.

No one had ever figured out how the caps were driven, or how to direct them.

That was one of the things that made us all nervous: the fact that we were going to take our chances with something nobody understood. You literally had no control, once you started out in a Heechee ship. Their courses were built into their guidance system, in a way that nobody had figured out; you could pick one course, but once picked that was it—and you didn't know where it was going to take you when you picked it, any more than you know what's in your box of Cracker-Joy until you open it.

But they worked. They still worked, after what they say is maybe half a million years.

The first guy who had the guts to get into one and try to start it up succeeded. It lifted out of its crater on the surface of the asteroid. It turned fuzzy and bright, and was gone.

And three months later, it was back, with a starved, staring astronaut inside, aglow with triumph. He had been to another star! He had orbited a great gray planet with swirling yellow clouds, had managed to reverse the controls—and had been brought back to the very same pockmark, by the built-in guidance controls.

So they sent out another ship, this time one of the big, pointy morel-shaped ones, with a crew of four and plenty of rations and instrumentation. They were gone only about fifty days. In that time they had not just reached another solar system, they had actually used the lander to go down to the surface of a planet. There wasn't anything living there . . . but there had been.

They found the remnants. Not a lot. A few beat-up pieces of trash, on a corner of a mountaintop that had missed the general destruction that had hit the planet. Out of the radioactive dust they had picked up a brick, a ceramic bolt, a half-melted thing that looked as though it had once been a chromium flute.

Then the star rush began . . . and we were part of it.

5

Sigfrid is a pretty smart machine, but sometimes I can't figure out what's wrong with him. He's always asking me to tell him my dreams. Then sometimes I come in all aglow with some dream I'm positive he's going to love, a big-red-apple-for-the-teacher kind of dream, full of penis symbols and fetishism and guilt hang-ups, and he disappoints me. He takes off on some crazy track that has nothing at all to do with it. I tell him the whole thing, and then he sits and clicks and whirs and buzzes for a while—he doesn't really, but I fantasy that while I'm waiting—and then he says:

"Let's go back to something different, Bob. I'm interested in some of the things you've said about the woman, Gelle-Klara Moynlin."

I say, "Sigfrid, you're off on a wild-goose chase again."

"I don't think so, Bob."

"But that dream! My God, don't you see how important it is? What about the mother figure in it?"

"What about letting me do my job, Bob?"

"Do I have a choice?" I say, feeling sulky.

"You always have a choice, Bob, but I would like very much to quote to you something you said a while ago." And he stops, and I hear my own voice coming out of somewhere in his tapes. I am saying:

"Sigfrid, there's an intensity of pain and guilt and misery there that I just can't handle."

He waits for me to say something.

After a moment I do. "That's a nice recording," I acknowledge, "but I'd rather talk about the way my mother fixation comes out in my dream."

"I think it would be more productive to explore this other matter, Bob. It is possible they're related."

"Really?" I am all warmed up to discuss this theoretical possibility in a detached and philosophical way, but he beats me to the punch:

"The last conversation you had with Klara, Bob. Please tell me what you feel about it."

"I've told you." I am not enjoying this at all, it is such a waste of time, and I make sure he knows it by the tone of my voice and the tenseness of my body against the restraining straps. "It was even worse than with my mother."

"I know you'd rather switch to talking about your mother, Rob, but please don't, right now. Tell me about that time with Klara. What are you feeling about it at this minute?"

I try to think it out honestly. After all, I can do that much. I don't actually have to say it. But all I can find to say is, "Not much."

After a little wait he says, "Is that all, 'not much'?"

"That's it. Not much." Not much on the surface, anyway. I do remember how I was feeling at the time. I open up that memory, very cautiously, to see what it was like. Going down into that blue mist.

Seeing the dim ghost star for the first time. Talking to Klara on the radio, while Dane is whispering in my ear. . . . I close it up again.

"It all hurts, a lot, Sigfrid," I say conversationally. Sometimes I try to fool him by saying emotionally loaded things in the tone you might use to order a cup of coffee, but I don't think it works. Sigfrid listens to volume and overtones, but he also listens to breathing and pauses, as well as the sense of the words. He is extremely smart, considering how stupid he is.

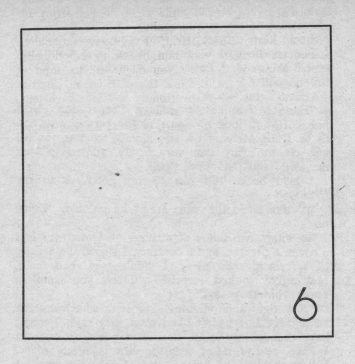

6

Five permanent-party noncoms, one from each of the cruisers, patted us down, checked our IDs and turned us over to a Corporation screening clerk. Sheri giggled when the Russian's pat hit a sensitive spot and whispered, "What do they think we're smuggling *in,* Rob?"

I shushed her. The Corporation woman had taken our landing cards from the Chinese Spec/3 in charge of the detail and was calling out our names. There were eight of us altogether. "Welcome aboard," she said. "Each one of you fish will get a proctor assigned to you. He'll help you get straightened out with a place to live, answer your questions, let you know where to report for the medical and your classes. Also, he'll give you a copy of the contract to sign. You've each had eleven hundred and fifty dollars deducted from

31

your cash on deposit with the ship that brought you here; that's your life-support tax for the first ten days. The rest you can draw on any time by writing a P-check. Your proctor will show you how. Linscott!"

The middle-aged black man from Baja California raised his hand. "Your proctor is Shota Tarasvili. Broadhead!"

"Here I am."

"Dane Metchnikov," said the Corporation clerk.

I started to look around, but the person who had to be Dane Metchnikov was already coming toward me. He took my arm very firmly, started to lead me away and then said, "Hi."

I held back. "I'd like to say good-bye to my friend—"

"You're all in the same area," he grunted. "Come on."

So within two hours of arriving on Gateway I had a room, a proctor, and a contract. I signed the articles of agreement right away. I didn't even read them. Metchnikov looked surprised. "Don't you want to know what they say?"

"Not right this minute." I mean, what was the advantage? If I hadn't liked what they said, I might have changed my mind, and what other options did I have, really? Being a prospector is pretty scary. I *hate* the idea of being killed. I hate the idea of dying at all, ever; not being alive anymore, having everything stop, knowing that all those other people would go on living and having sex and joy without me being there to share it. But I didn't hate it as much as I hated the idea of going back to the food mines.

Metchnikov hung himself by his collar to a hook on the wall of my room, to be out of the way while I put away my belongings. He was a squat, pale man, not very talkative. He didn't seem to be a very likable person, but at least he didn't laugh at me because I was a clumsy new fish. Gateway is about as close to zero-G as you get. I had never experienced low-gravity before; you don't get much of it in Wyoming,

MEMORANDUM OF AGREEMENT

I, _____, being of sound mind,
hereby assign all rights in and to any discoveries, artifacts, objects, and things of value of any description
I may find during or as a result of exploration involving
any craft furnished me or information given me by
the Gateway Authority irrevocably to said Gateway
Authority.

2. Gateway Authority may, in its own sole direction,
elect to sell, lease or otherwise dispose of any artifact,
object or other thing of value arising from my activities
under this contract. If it does so, it agrees to assign
to me 50% (fifty percent) of all revenues arising from
such sale, lease, or disposal, up to the costs of the
exploration trip itself (including my own costs in coming
to Gateway and my subsequent costs of living while
there), and 10% (ten percent) of all subsequent
revenues once the aforesaid costs have been repaid. I
accept this assignment as payment in full for any
obligations arising to me from the Gateway Authority
of whatever kind, and specifically undertake not to lay
any claim for additional payment for any reason
at any time.

3. I irrevocably grant to Gateway Authority the full
power and authority to make decisions of all kinds
relating to the exploitation, sale, or lease of rights in
any such discoveries, including the right, at Gateway
Authority's sole discretion, to pool my discoveries or
other things of value arising under this contract with
those of others for purpose of exploitation, lease, or
sale, in which case my share shall be whatever proportion of such earnings Gateway Authority may deem
proper; and I further grant to Gateway Authority
the right to refrain from exploiting any or all such
discoveries or things of value in any way, at its own
sole discretion.

4. I release Gateway Authority from any and all
claims by me or on my behalf arising from any injury,
accident, or loss of any kind to me in connection with
my activities under this contract.

5. In the event of any disagreement arising from this
Memorandum of Agreement, I agree that the terms
shall be interpreted according to the laws and precedents
of Gateway itself, and that no laws or precedents of
any other jurisdiction shall be considered relevant
in any degree.

so I kept misjudging. When I said something, Metchnikov said, "You'll get used to it. Have you got a toke?"

"Afraid not."

He sighed, looking a little like somebody's Buddha hung up on the wall, with his legs pulled up.

He looked at his time dial and said, "I'll take you out for a drink later. It's a custom. Only it's not very interesting until about twenty-two hundred. The Blue Hell'll be full of people then, and I'll introduce you around. See what you can find. What are you, straight, gay, what?"

"I'm pretty straight."

"Whatever. You're on your own about that, though. I'll introduce you to whoever I know, but then you're on your own. You better get used to that right away. Have you got your map?"

"Map?"

"Oh, hell, man! It's in that packet of stuff they gave you."

I opened the lockers at random until I found where I had put the envelope. Inside it were my copy of the articles of agreement, a booklet entitled *Welcome to Gateway,* my room assignment, my health questionnaire that I would have to fill out before 0800 the next morning . . . and a folded sheet that, opened up, looked like a wiring diagram with names on it.

"That's it. Can you locate where you are? Remember your room number: Levil Babe, Quadrant East, Tunnel Eight, Room Fifty-one. Write it down."

"It's already written here, Dane, on my room assignment."

"Well, don't lose it." Dane reached behind his neck and unhooked himself, let himself fall gently to the floor. "So why don't you look around by yourself for a while. I'll meet you here. Anything else you need to know right now?"

I thought, while he looked impatient. "Well—mind if I ask you a question about you, Dane? Have you been out yet?"

"Six trips. All right, I'll see you at twenty-two

34

hundred." Then he pushed the flexible door open, slipped out into the jungly green of the corridor and was gone.

I let myself flop—so gently, so slowly—into my one real chair and tried to make myself understand that I was on the doorstep of the universe.

I don't know if I can make you feel it, how the universe looked to me from Gateway: like being young with Full Medical. Like a menu in the best restaurant in the world, when somebody else is going to pick up the check. Like a girl you've just met who likes you. Like an unopened gift.

The things that hit you first on Gateway are the tininess of the tunnels, feeling tinier even than they are because they're lined with windowboxy things of plants; the vertigo from the low gravity, and the stink. You get Gateway a little bit at a time. There's no way of seeing it all in one glance; it is nothing but a maze of tunnels in the rock. I'm not even sure they've all been explored yet. Certainly there are miles of them that nobody ever goes into, or not very often.

That's the way the Heechees were. They grabbed the asteroid, plated it over with wall metal, drove tunnels into it, filled them with whatever sort of possessions they had—most were empty by the time we got there, just as everything that ever belonged to the Heechees is, all over the universe. And then they left it, for whatever reason they left.

The closest thing to a central point in Gateway is Heecheetown. That's a spindle-shaped cave near the geometric center of the asteroid. They say that when the Heechees built Gateway they lived there. We lived there too, at first, or close to it, all of us new people off Earth. (And elsewhere. A ship from Venus had come in just before ours.) That's where the company housing is. Later on, if we got rich on a prospecting trip, we could move out farther toward the surface, where there was a little more gravity and less noise. And above all, less smell. A couple thousand people had breathed the air I was breathing, one time or another, voided the water I drank and exuded their smells into the atmosphere. The people didn't stay around very long, most of them. But the smells were still there.

I didn't care about the smell. I didn't care about any of it. Gateway was my big, fat lottery ticket to Full Medical, a nine-room house, a couple of kids, and a lot of joy. I had won one lottery already. It made me cocky about my chances of winning another.

It was all exciting, although at the same time it was dingy enough, too. There wasn't much luxury around. For your $238,575 what you get is transportation to Gateway, ten days' worth of food, lodging, and air, a cram course in ship handling, and an invitation to sign up on the next ship out. Or any ship you like. They don't *make* you take any particular ship, or for that matter any ship at all.

The Corporation doesn't make any profit on any of that. All the prices are fixed at about cost. That doesn't mean they were cheap, and it certainly doesn't mean that what you got was good. The food was just about what I had been digging, and eating, all my life. The lodging was about the size of a large steamer trunk, one chair, a bunch of lockers, a fold-down table, and a hammock that you could stretch across it, corner to corner, when you wanted to sleep.

My next-door neighbors were a family from Venus. I caught a glimpse through the part-opened door. Imagine! Four of them sleeping in one of those cubicles! It looked like two to a hammock, with two hammocks crisscrossed across the room. On the other side was Sheri's room. I scratched at her door, but she didn't answer. The door wasn't locked. Nobody locks his door much on Gateway, because there's nothing much worth stealing among other reasons. Sheri wasn't there. The clothes she had been wearing on the ship were thrown all over.

I guessed that she had gone out exploring, and wished I had been a little earlier. I would have liked someone to explore with. I leaned against the ivy

WELCOME TO GATEWAY!

Congratulations!

You are one of a very few people each year who may become a limited partner in Gateway Enterprises, Inc. Your first obligation is to sign the enclosed Memorandum of Agreement. You need not do this at once. You are encouraged to study the agreement and to seek legal advice, if available.

However, until you sign you will not be eligible to occupy Corporation housing, dine at the Corporation commissary or participate in the Corporation instruction courses.

Accommodations are available at the Gateway Hotel and Restaurant for those who are here as visitors, or who do not at present wish to sign the Memorandum of Agreement.

KEEPING GATEWAY GOING

In order to meet the costs of
maintaining Gateway, all persons are
required to pay a daily per-capita
assessment for air, temperature control, administration, and other
services.

If you are a guest, this cost is
included in your hotel bill.

Rates for other persons are
posted. The tax may be prepaid up
to one year in advance if desired.
Failure to pay the daily per-capita
tax will result in immediate expul-
sion from Gateway.

Note: Availability of a ship to
receive expelled persons cannot be
guaranteed.

growing out of one wall of the tunnel and pulled out my map.

It did give me some idea of what to look for. There were things marked "Central Park" and "Lake Superior." What were they? I wondered about "Gateway Museum," which sounded interesting, and "Terminal Hospital," which sounded pretty bad—I found out later that "terminal" meant as in end of the line, on your return trip from wherever you went to. The Corporation must have known that it had another sound to it, too; but the Corporation never went to much trouble to spare a prospector's feelings.

What I really wanted was to see a ship!

As soon as that thought percolated out of my mind I realized that I wanted it a *lot*. I puzzled over how to get to the outer skin, where the ship docks were located of course. Holding onto a railing with one hand, I tried to keep the map open with the other. It didn't take me long to locate myself. I was at a five-way intersection which seemed to be the one marked "East Star Babe G" on the map. One of the five tunnels out of it led to a dropshaft, but I couldn't tell which.

I tried one at random, wound up in a dead end, and on the way back scratched on a door for directions. It opened. "Excuse me—" I said . . . and stopped.

The man who opened the door seemed as tall as I, but was not. His eyes were on a level with my own. But he stopped at the waist. He had no legs.

He said something, but I didn't understand it; it wasn't in English. It wouldn't have mattered. My attention was taken up with him. He wore gauzy bright fabric strapped from wrists to waist, and he fluttered the wings gently to stay in the air. It wasn't hard, in Gateway's low-G. But it was surprising to see. I said, "I'm sorry. I just wanted to know how to get to Level Tanya." I was trying not to stare, but I wasn't succeeding.

He smiled, white teeth in an unlined, old face. He had jet eyes under a crest of short white hair. He pushed past me out into the corridor and said in excellent English, "Certainly. Take the first turning on your right. Go to the next star, and take the second turning on your left. It'll be marked." He indicated with his chin the direction toward the star.

I thanked him and left him floating behind me. I wanted to turn back, but it didn't seem good manners. It was strange. It hadn't occurred to me that there would be any cripples on Gateway.

That's how naive I was then.

Having seen him, I knew Gateway in a way I had not known it from the statistics. The statistics are clear enough, and we all studied them, all of us who came up as prospectors, and all of that vastly larger number who only wished they could. About eighty percent of flights from Gateway come up empty. About fifteen percent don't come back at all. So one person in twenty, on the average, comes back from a prospecting trip with something that Gateway—that mankind in general—can make a profit on. Most of even those are lucky if they collect enough to pay their costs for getting here in the first place.

And if you get hurt while you're out . . . well, that's tough. Terminal Hospital is about as well equipped as any anywhere. But you have to get there for it to do you any good. You can be months in transit. If you get hurt at the other end of your trip—and that's where it usually happens—there's not much that can be done for you until you get back to Gateway. By then it can be too late to make you whole, and likely enough too late to keep you alive.

There's no charge for a return trip to where you came from, by the way. The rockets always come up fuller than they return. They call it wastage.

The return trip is free . . . but to what?

I let go the down-cable on Level Tanya, turned into a tunnel, and ran into a man with cap and armband. Corporation Police. He didn't speak English, but he pointed and the size of him was convincing;

40

I grabbed the up-cable, ascended one level, crossed to another dropshaft, and tried again.

The only difference was that this time the guard spoke English. "You can't come through here," he said.

"I just want to see the ships."

"Sure. You can't. You've got to have a blue badge," he said, tapping his own. "That's Corporation specialist, flight crew or VIP."

"I am flight crew."

He grinned. "You're a new fish off the Earth transport, aren't you? Friend, you'll be flight crew when you sign on for a flight and not before. Go on back up."

I said reasonably, "You understand how I feel, don't you? I just want to get a look."

"You can't, till you've finished your course, except they'll bring you down here for part of it. After that, you'll see more than you want."

I argued a little more, but he had too many arguments on his side. But as I reached for the up-cable the tunnel seemed to lurch and a blast of sound hit my ears. For a minute I thought the asteroid was blowing up. I stared at the guard, who shrugged, in a not unfriendly way. "I only said you couldn't see them," he said. "I didn't say you couldn't hear them."

I bit back the *"wow"* or "Holy God!" that I really wanted to say, and said, "Where do you suppose that one's going?"

"Come back in six months. Maybe we'll know by then."

Well, there was nothing in that to feel elated about. All the same, I felt elated. After all those years in the food mines, here I was, not only on Gateway, but right there when some of those intrepid prospectors set out on a trip that would bring them fame and incredible fortune! Never mind the odds. This was really living on the top line.

So I wasn't paying much attention to what I was

doing, and as a result I got lost again on the way back. I reached Levil Babe ten minutes late.

Dane Metchnikov was striding down the tunnel away from my room. He didn't appear to recognize me. I think he might have passed me if I hadn't put out my arm.

"Huh," he grunted. "You're late."

"I was down on Level Tanya, trying to get a look at the ships."

"Huh. You can't go down there unless you have a blue badge or a bangle."

Well, I had found that out already, hadn't I? So I tagged along after him, without wasting energy on attempts at further conversation.

Metchnikov was a pale man, except for the marvelously ornate curled whisker that followed the line of his jaw. It seemed to be waxed, so that each separate curl stood out with a life of its own. "Waxed" was wrong. It had something in it besides hair, but whatever it was wasn't stiff. The whole thing moved as he moved, and when he talked or smiled the muscles moored to the jawbone made the beard ripple and flow. He finally did smile, after we got to the Blue Hell. He bought the first drink, explaining carefully that that was the custom, but that the custom only called for one. I bought the second. The smile came when, out of turn, I also bought the third.

Over the noise in the Blue Hell talk wasn't easy, but I told him about hearing a launch. "Right," he said, lifting his glass. "Hope they have a good trip." He wore six blue-glowing Heechee metal bracelets, hardly thicker than wire. They tinkled faintly as he swallowed half the drink.

"Are they what I think they are?" I asked. "One for every trip out?"

He drank the other half of the drink. "That's right. Now I'm going to dance," he said. My eyes followed his back as he lunged toward a woman in a luminous pink sari. He wasn't much of a talker, that was sure.

On the other hand, at that noise level you couldn't

WHAT IS GATEWAY?

Gateway is an artifact created by the so-called Heechee. It appears to have been formed around an asteroid, or the core of an atypical comet. The time of this event is not known, but it almost surely precedes the rise of human civilization.

Inside Gateway the environment resembles Earth, except that there is relatively little gravity. (There is actually none, but centrifugal force derived from Gateway's rotation gives a similar effect.) If you have come from Earth you will notice some difficulty in breathing for the first few days because of the low atmospheric pressure. However, the partial pressure of oxygen is identical with the 2000-meter elevation at Earth and is fully adequate for all persons in normal health.

talk much anyhow. You couldn't really dance much, either. The Blue Hell was up in the center of Gateway, part of the spindle-shaped cave. Rotational G was so low that we didn't weigh more than two or three pounds; if anyone had tried to waltz or polka he would have gone flying. So they did those no-touching junior-high-school sort of dances that appear to be designed so fourteen-year-old boys won't have to look up at too sharp an angle to the fourteen-year-old girls they're dancing with. You pretty much kept your feet in place, and your head and arms and shoulders and hips went where they wanted to. Me, I like to touch. But you can't have everything. I like to dance, anyway.

I saw Sheri, way across the room, with an older woman I took to be her proctor, and danced one with her. "How do you like it so far?" I shouted over the tapes. She nodded and shouted something back, I couldn't say what. I danced with an immense black woman who wore two blue bracelets, then with Sheri again, then with a girl Dane Metchnikov dropped on me, apparently because he wanted to be rid of her, then with a tall, strong-faced woman with the blackest, thickest eyebrows I had ever seen under a female hairdo. (She wore it pulled back in two pigtails that floated around behind her as she moved.) *She* wore a couple of bracelets, too. And between dances I drank.

They had tables that were meant for parties of eight or ten, but there weren't any parties of eight or ten. People sat where they wanted to, and took each other's seats without worrying about whether the owner was coming back. For a while there were half a dozen crewmen in Brazilian Navy dress whites sitting with me, talking to each other in Portuguese. A man with one golden earring joined me for a while, but I couldn't understand what he was saying, either. (I did, pretty well, understand what he meant.)

There was that trouble all the time I was in Gateway. There always is. Gateway sounds like an international conference when the translation equipment has broken down. There's a sort of lingua franca you hear a lot, pieces of a dozen different languages thrown together, like, *"Écoutez, gospodin, tu es verrückt."* I danced twice with one of the Brazilians, a skinny, dark little girl with a hawk nose but sweet brown eyes, and tried to say a few simple words. Maybe she understood me. One of the men she was with, though, spoke fine English, introduced himself and the others all around. I didn't catch any of the names but his, Francesco Hereira. He bought me a drink, and let me buy one for the crowd, and then I realized I'd seen him before: He was one of the detail that searched us on the way in.

While we were commenting on that, Dane leaned over me and grunted in my ear, "I'm going to gamble. So long, unless you really want to come."

It wasn't the warmest invitation I'd ever had, but the noise in the Blue Hell was getting heavy. I tagged after him and discovered a full-scale casino just next to the Blue Hell, with blackjack tables, poker, a slow-motion roulette with a big, dense ball, craps with dice that took forever to stop, even a roped-off section for baccarat. Metchnikov headed for the blackjack tables and drummed his fingers on the back of a player's chair, waiting for an opening. Around then he noticed I had come with him.

"Oh." He looked around the room. "What do you like to play?"

"I've played it all," I said, slurring the words a little. Bragging a little, too. "Maybe a little baccarat."

He looked at me first with respect, then amusement. "Fifty's the minimum bet."

I had five or six thousand dollars left in my account. I shrugged.

"That's fifty thousand," he said.

I choked. He said absently, moving over behind a player whose chip stack was running out, "You can get down for ten dollars at roulette. Hundred minimum for most of the others. Oh, there's a ten-dollar slot machine around somewhere, I think." He dived for the open chair and that was the last I saw of him.

I watched for a moment and realized that the black-eyebrowed girl was at the same table, busy studying her cards. She didn't look up.

I could see I wasn't going to be able to afford much gambling here. At that point I realized I couldn't really afford all the drinks I'd been buying, either, and then my interior sensory system began to make me realize just how many of those drinks I had had. The last thing I realized was that I had to get back to my room, pretty fast.

SYLVESTER MACKLEN:
FATHER OF GATEWAY

Gateway was discovered by Sylvester Macklen, a tunnel explorer on Venus, who found an operable Heechee spacecraft in a dig. He succeeded in getting it to the surface and bringing it to Gateway, where it now rests in Dock 5-33. Tragically, Macklen was not able to return and, although he succeeded in signaling his presence by exploding the fuel tank of the lander of his ship, he was dead before investigators reached Gateway.

Macklen was a courageous and resourceful man, and the plaque at Dock 5-33 commemorates his unique service to humanity. Services are held at appropriate times by representatives of the various faiths.

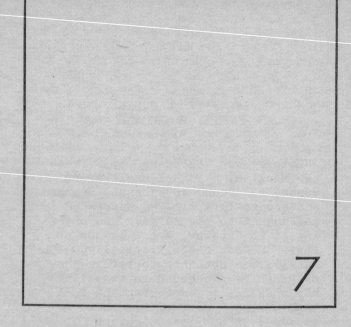

7

I am on the mat, and I am not very comfortable.
Physically, I mean. I have had an operation not long
ago and probably the stitches aren't yet absorbed.

Sigfrid says, "We were talking about your job, Bob."

That's dull enough. But safe enough. I say, "I hated
my job. Who wouldn't hate the food mines?"

"But you kept it, Bob. You never even tried to
get on anywhere else. You could have switched to
sea-farming, maybe. And you dropped out of school."

"You're saying I stuck myself in a rut?"

"I'm not saying anything, Bob. I'm asking you
what you feel."

"Well. I guess in a sense I did do that. I thought
about making some kind of a change. I thought
about it a lot," I say, remembering how it was in
those bright early days with Sylvia. I remember sitting

48

with her in the cockpit of a parked sailplane on a January night—we had no other place to go—and talking about the future. What we would do. How we would beat the odds. There's nothing there for Sigfrid, as far as I can see. I've told Sigfrid all about Sylvia, who married a stockholder in the long run. But we'd broken up long before that. "I suppose," I say, pulling myself up short and trying to get my money's worth out of this session, "that I had a kind of death wish."

"I prefer that you don't use psychiatric terms, Bob."

"Well, you understand what I mean. I knew time was going by. The longer I stayed in the mines the harder it would be to get out. But nothing else looked any better. And there were compensations. My girlfriend, Sylvia. My mother, while she was alive. Friends. Even some fun things. Sailplaning. It is great over the hills, and when you're up high enough Wyoming doesn't look so bad and you can hardly smell the oil."

"You mentioned your girlfriend, Sylvia. Did you get along with her?"

I hesitated, rubbing at my belly. I have almost half a meter of new intestine in there now. They cost fearfully, those things, and sometimes you get the feeling the previous owner wants them back. You wonder who he was. Or she. How he died. Or did he die? Could he still be alive, so poor that he sells off parts of himself, the way I've heard of pretty girls doing with a well-shaped breast or ear?

"Did you make friends with girls easily, Bob?"

"I do now, all right."

"Not now, Bob. I think you said you didn't make friends easily as a child."

"Does anyone?"

"If I understand that question, Robbie, you are asking if anyone remembers childhood as a perfectly happy and easy experience, and of course the answer is 'no.' But some people seem to carry the effects of it over into their lives more than others."

"Yeah. I guess, thinking back, that I was a little afraid of my peer group—sorry about that, Sigfrid! I mean the other kids. They all seemed to know each

49

507	IRRAY .MATURITY. GOTO	26,830
	*M88	26,835
508	,C, Maybe maturity is wanting	26,840
	what you want,	26,845
	instead of what somebody	26,850
	else tells you you should	26,855
	want.	26,860
511	XTERNALS @ IF @ GOTO &&	26,865
512	,S, Maybe, Sigfrid, dear old	26,870
	tin god, but what it	26,875
	feels like is mature is dead.	26,880

other. They had things to say to each other all the time. Secrets. Shared experiences. Interests. I was a loner."

"You were an only child, Robbie?"

"You know I was. Yeah. Maybe that was it. Both my parents worked. And they didn't like me playing near the mines. Dangerous. Well, it really was dangerous for kids. You can get hurt around those machines, or even if there's a slide in the tailings or an outgassing. I stayed at home a lot, watching shows, playing cassettes. Eating. I was a fat kid, Sigfrid. I loved all the starchy, sugary stuff with all the calories. They spoiled me, buying me more food than I needed."

I still like to be spoiled. Now I get a higher class of diet, not as fattening, about a thousand times as expensive. I've had real caviar. Often. It gets flown in from the aquarium at Galveston. I have real champagne, and butter. . . . "I remember lying in bed," I say, "I guess I was very small, maybe about three. I had a teddy-talker. I took it to bed with me, and it told me little stories, and I stuck pencils into it and tried to pull its ears off. I loved that thing, Sigfrid."

I stop, and Sigfrid picks up immediately. "Why are you crying, Robbie?"

"I don't know!" I bawl, tears running down my face, and I look at my watch, the skipping green numerals rippling through the tears. "Oh," I say, very conversationally, and sit up, the tears still rolling down my face but the fountain turned off, "I've really got to go now, Sigfrid. I've got a date. Her name's Tania. Beautiful girl. The Houston Symphony. She loves Mendelssohn and roses, and I want to see if I can pick up some of those dark-blue hybrids that will go with her eyes."

"Rob, we've got nearly ten minutes left."

"I'll make it up another time." I know he can't do that, so I add quickly, "May I use your bathroom? I need to."

"Are you going to excrete your feelings, Rob?"

"Oh, don't be smart. I know what you're saying. I

51

know this looks like a typical displacement mechanism—"

"Rob."

"—all right, I mean, it looks like I'm copping out. But I honestly do have to go. To the bathroom, I mean. And to the florist's, too. Tani is pretty special. She's a fine person. I'm not talking about sex, but that's great, too. She can g— She can—"

"Rob? What are you trying to say?"

I take a breath and manage to say: "She's great at oral sex, Sigfrid."

"Rob?"

I recognize that tone. Sigfrid's repertory of vocal modes is quite large, but parts of it I have learned to identify. He thinks he is on the track of something.

"What?"

"Bob, what do you call it when a woman gives you oral sex?"

"Oh, Christ, Sigfrid, what kind of dumb game is this one?"

"What do you call it, Bob?"

"Ah! You know as well as I do."

"Please tell me what you call it, Bob."

"They say, like, 'She eats me.'"

"What other expression, Bob?"

"Lots of them! 'Giving head,' that's one. I guess I've heard a thousand terms for it."

"What other, Bob?"

I have been building up to rage and pain and it suddenly boils over. "Don't play these fucking games with me, Sigfrid!" My gut aches, and I am afraid I am going to mess my pants; it is like being a baby again. "Jesus, Sigfrid! When I was a little kid I used to talk to my teddy. Now I'm forty-five and I'm still talking to a stupid machine as if it was alive!"

"But there is another term, isn't there, Bob?"

"There are thousands of them! Which one do you want?"

"I want the expression you were going to use and didn't, Bob. Please try to say it. That term means

52

something special to you, so that you can't say the words without trouble."

I crumple over onto the mat, and now I'm really crying.

"Please say it, Bob. What's the term?"

"Damn you, Sigfrid! Going down! That's it. Going down, going down, going down!"

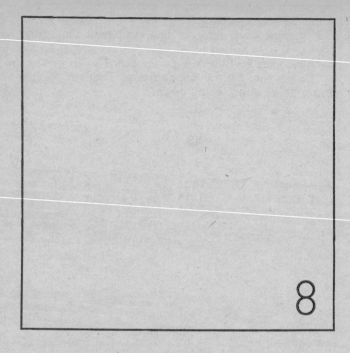

8

"Good morning," said somebody, speaking right into the middle of a dream about getting stuck in a sort of quicksand in the middle of the Orion Nebula. "I have brought you some tea."

I opened an eye. I looked over the edge of the hammock into a nearby pair of coalsack-black eyes set into a sand-colored face. I was fully dressed and hung over; something smelled very bad, and I realized it was me.

"My name," said the person with the tea, "is Shikitei Bakin. Please drink this tea. It will help rehydrate your tissues."

I looked a little further and saw that he ended at the waist; he was the legless man with the strap-on wings whom I had seen in the tunnel the day before. "Uh," I said, and tried a little harder and got as far as,

WHO OWNS GATEWAY?

Gateway is unique in the history of humanity, and it was quickly realized that it was too valuable a resource to be given to any one group of persons, or any one government. Therefore Gateway Enterprises, Inc., was formed.

Gateway Enterprises (usually referred to as "the Corporation") is a multinational corporation whose general partners are the governments of the United States of America, the Soviet Union, the United States of Brazil, the Venusian Confederation, and New People's Asia, and whose limited partners are all those persons who, like yourself, have signed the attached Memorandum of Agreement.

"Good morning." The Orion Nebula was fading back into the dream, and so was the sensation of having to push through rapidly solidifying gas clouds. The bad smell remained. The room smelled excessively foul, even by Gateway standards, and I realized I had thrown up on the floor. I was only millimeters from doing it again. Bakin, slowly stroking the air with his wings, dexterously dropped a stoppered flask next to me on the hammock at the end of one stroke. Then he propelled himself to the top of my chest of drawers, sat there, and said:

"I believe you have a medical examination this morning at oh-eight hundred hours."

"Do I?" I managed to get the cap off the tea and took a sip. It was very hot, sugarless, and almost tasteless, but it did seem to tip the scales inside my gut in the direction opposite to throwing up again.

"Yes. I think so. It's customary. And in addition, your P-phone has rung several times."

I went back to, "Uh?"

"I presume it was your proctor calling you to remind you. It is now seven-fifteen, Mr.—"

"Broadhead," I said thickly, and then more carefully: "My name is Bob Broadhead."

"Yes. I took the liberty of making sure you were awake. Please enjoy your tea, Mr. Broadhead. Enjoy your stay on Gateway."

He nodded, fell forward off the chest, swooped toward the door, handed himself through it, and was gone. With my head thudding at every change of attitude I got myself out of the hammock, trying to avoid the nastier spots on the floor, and somehow succeeded in getting reasonably clean. I thought of depilating, but I had about twelve days on a beard and decided to let it go for a while; it no longer looked unshaven, exactly, and I just didn't have the strength.

When I wobbled into the medical examining room I was only about five minutes late. The others in my group were all ahead of me, so I had to wait and go last. They extracted three kinds of blood from me, fingertip, inside of the elbow, and lobe of the ear;

I was sure they would all run ninety proof. But it didn't matter. The medical was only a formality. If you could survive the trip up to Gateway by spacecraft in the first place; you could survive a trip in a Heechee ship. Unless something went wrong. In which case you probably couldn't survive anyway, no matter how healthy you were.

I had time for a quick cup of coffee off a cart that someone was tending next to a dropshaft (private enterprise on Gateway? I hadn't known that existed), and then I got to the first session of the class right on the tick. We met in a big room on Level Dog, long and narrow and low-ceilinged. The seats were arranged two on each side with a center aisle, sort of like a schoolroom in a converted bus. Sheri came in late, looking fresh and cheerful, and slipped in beside me; our whole group was there, all seven of us who had come up from Earth together, the family of four from Venus and a couple others I knew to be new fish like me. "You don't look *too* bad," Sheri whispered as the instructor pondered over some papers on his desk.

"Does the hangover show?"

"Actually not. But I assume it's there. I heard you coming in last night. In fact," she added thoughtfully, "the whole tunnel heard you."

I winced. I could still smell myself, but most of it was apparently inside me. None of the others seemed to be edging away, not even Sheri.

The instructor stood up and studied us thoughtfully for a while. "Oh, well," he said, and looked back at his papers. Then he shook his head. "I won't take attendance," he said. "I teach the course in how to run a Heechee ship." I noticed he had a batch of bracelets; I couldn't count them, but there were at least half a dozen. I wondered briefly about these people I kept seeing who had been out a lot of times and still weren't rich. "This is only one of the three courses you get. After this you get survival in unfamiliar environments, and then how to recognize what's valuable. But this one is in ship-handling, and the way we're going to

57

SHOWER PROCEDURE

This shower will automatically deliver two 45-second sprays. Soap between sprays.

You are entitled to 1 use of the shower in each 3-day period.

Additional showers may be charged against your credit balance at the rate of

45 seconds—$5

start learning it is by doing it. All of you come with me."

So we all got up and gaggled after him, out of the room, down a tunnel, onto the down-cable of a drop-shaft and past the guards—maybe the same ones who had chased me away the night before. This time they just nodded to the instructor and watched us go past. We wound up in a long, wide, low-ceilinged passage with about a dozen squared-off and stained metal cylinders sticking up out of the floor. They looked like charred tree stumps, and it was a moment before I realized what they were.

I gulped.

"They're *ships*," I whispered to Sheri, louder than I intended. A couple of people looked at me curiously. One of them, I noticed, was a girl I had danced with the night before, the one with the dense black eyebrows. She nodded to me and smiled; I saw the bangles on her arm, and wondered what she was doing there—and how she had done at the gambling tables.

The instructor gathered us around him, and said, "As someone just said, these are Heechee ships. The lander part. This is the piece you go down to a planet in, if you're lucky enough to find a planet. They don't look very big, but five people can fit into each of those garbage cans you see. Not comfortably, exactly. But they can. Generally speaking, of course, you'll always leave one person in the main ship, so there'll be at most four in the lander."

He led us past the nearest of them, and we all satisfied the impulse to touch, scratch, or pat it. Then he began to lecture:

"There were nine hundred and twenty-four of these ships docked at Gateway when it was first explored. About two hundred, so far, have proved nonoperational. Mostly we don't know why; they just don't work. Three hundred and four have actually been sent out on at least one trip. Thirty-three of those are here now, and available for prospecting trips. The others haven't been tried yet." He hiked himself up on the stumpy cylinder and sat there while he went on:

59

"One thing you have to decide is whether you want to take one of the thirty-three tested ones or one of the ones that has never been flown. By human beings, I mean. There you just pay your money and take your choice. It's a gamble either way. A high proportion of the trips that didn't come back were in first flights, so there's obviously some risk there. Well, that figures, doesn't it? After all, nobody has done any maintenance on them for God knows how long, since the Heechee put them there.

"On the other hand, there's a risk in the ones that have been out and back safely, too. There's no such thing as perpetual motion. We think some of the no-returns have been because the ships ran out of fuel. Trouble is, we don't know what the fuel is, or how much there is, or how to tell when a ship is about to run out."

He patted the stump. "This, and all the others you see here, were designed for five Heechees in the crews. As far as we can tell. But we send them out with three human beings. It seems the Heechee were more tolerant of each other's company in confined spaces than people are. There are bigger and smaller ships, but the no-return rate on them has been very bad the last couple of orbits. It's probably just a string of bad luck, but . . . Anyway, I personally would stick with a Three. You people, you do what you want.

"So you come to your second choice, which is who you go with. Keep your eyes open. Look for companions— What?"

Sheri had been semaphoring her hand until she got his attention. "You said 'very bad,'" she said. "How bad is that?"

The instructor said patiently, "In the last fiscal orbit about three out of ten Fives came back. Those are the biggest ships. In several cases the crews were dead when we got them open, even so."

"Yeah," said Sheri, "that's very bad."

"No, that's not bad at all, compared to the one-man ships. Two orbits ago we went a whole orbit and only two Ones came back at all. *That's* bad."

"Why is that?" asked the father of the tunnel-rat family. Their name was Forehand. The instructor looked at him for a moment.

"If you ever find out," he said, "be sure and tell somebody. Now. As far as selecting a crew is concerned, you're better off if you can get somebody who's already been out. Maybe you can, maybe you can't. Prospectors who strike it rich generally quit; the ones that are still hungry may not want to break up their teams. So a lot of you fish are going to have to go out with other virgins. Um." He looked around thoughtfully. "Well, let's get our feet wet. Sort yourselves out into groups of three—don't worry about who's in your group, this isn't where you pick your partners—and climb into one of those open landers. Don't touch anything. They're supposed to be in deactive mode, but I have to tell you they don't always *stay* deactive. Just go in, climb down to the control cabin and wait for an instructor to join you."

That was the first I'd heard that there were other instructors. I looked around, trying to work out which were teachers and which were fish, while he said, "Are there any questions?"

Sheri again. "Yeah, What's your name?"

"Did I forget that again? I'm Jimmy Chou. Pleased to meet you all. Now let's go."

Now I know a lot more than my instructor did, including what happened to him half an orbit later— poor old Jimmy Chou, he went out before I did, and came back while I was on my second trip, very dead. Flare burns, they say his eyes were boiled out of his head. But at that time he knew it all, and it was all very strange and wonderful to me.

So we crawled into the funny elliptical hatch that let you slip between the thrusters and down into the landing capsule, and then down a peg-ladder one step further into the main vehicle itself.

We looked around, three Ali Babas staring at the treasure cave. We heard a scratching above us, and a head poked in. It had shaggy eyebrows and pretty eyes, and it belonged to the girl I had been dancing with the night before. "Having fun?" she inquired. We were clinging together as far from anything that looked movable as we could get, and I doubt we really looked at ease. "Never mind," she said, "just look around. Get familiar with it. You'll see a lot of it. That vertical line of wheels with the little spokes sticking out of them? That's the target selector. That's the most important thing not to touch for now—maybe ever. That golden spiral thing over next to you there, the blond girl? Anybody want to guess what that's for?"

You-there-blond-girl, who was one of the Forehand daughters, shrank away from it and shook her head. I shook mine, but Sheri hazarded, "Could it be a hatrack?"

Teacher squinted at it thoughtfully. "Hmm. No, I don't think so, but I keep hoping one of you fish will know the answer. None of us here do. It gets hot sometimes in flight; nobody knows why. The toilet's in there. You're going to have a lot of fun with *that*. But it does work, after you learn how. You can sling your hammocks and sleep there—or anywhere you want to, actually. That corner, and that recess are pretty dead space. If you're in a crew that wants some privacy, you can screen them off. A little bit, anyway."

Sheri said, "Don't any of you people like to tell your names?"

Teacher grinned. "I'm Gelle-Klara Moynlin. You want to know the rest about me? I've been out twice and didn't score, and I'm killing time until the right trip comes along. So I work as assistant instructor."

"How do you know which is the right trip?" asked the Forehand girl.

"Bright fellow, you. Good question. That's another of those questions that I like to hear you ask, because it shows you're thinking, but if there's an answer I don't know what it is. Let's see. You already know this ship is a Three. It's done six round trips already, but it's a reasonable bet that it's got enough reserve fuel for a couple more. I'd rather take it than a One. That's for long-shot gamblers."

62

WHAT DOES THE CORPORATION DO?

The purpose of the Corporation is to exploit the spacecraft left by the Heechee, and to trade in, develop, or otherwise utilize all artifacts, goods, raw materials, or other things of value discovered by means of these vessels.

The Corporation encourages commercial development of Heechee technology, and grants leases on a royalty basis for this purpose.

Its revenues are used to pay appropriate shares to limited partners, such as you, who have been instrumental in discovering new things of value; to pay the costs of maintaining Gateway itself over and above the per-capita tax contribution; to pay to each of the general partners an annual sum sufficient to cover the cost of maintaining surveillance by means of the space cruisers you will have observed in orbit nearby; to create and maintain an adequate reserve for contingencies; and to use the balance of its income to subsidize research and development on the objects of value themselves.

In the fiscal year ending February 30 last, the total revenues of the Corporation exceeded 3.7×10^{12} dollars U.S.

"Mr. Chou said that," said the Forehand girl, "but my father says he's been all through the records since Orbit One, and the Ones aren't that bad."

"Your father can have mine," said Gelle-Klara Moynlin. "It's not just statistics. Ones are lonesome. Anyway, one person can't really handle everything if you hit lucky, you need shipmates, one in orbit—most of us keep one man in the ship, feels safer that way; at least somebody *might* get help if things go rancid. So two of you go down in the lander to look around. Of course, if you do hit lucky you have to split it three ways. If you hit anything big, there's plenty to go around. And if you don't hit, one-third of nothing is no less than all of it."

"Wouldn't it be even better in a Five, then?" I asked.

Klara looked at me and half-winked; I hadn't thought she remembered dancing the night before. "Maybe, maybe not. The thing about Fives is that they have almost unlimited target acceptance."

"Please talk English," Sheri coaxed.

"Fives will accept a lot of destinations that Threes and Ones won't. *I* think it's because some of those destinations are dangerous. The worst ship I ever saw come back was a Five. All scarred and seared and bent; nobody knows how it made it back at all. Nobody knows where it had been, either, but I heard somebody say it might've actually been in the photosphere of a star. The crew couldn't tell us. They were dead.

"Of course," she went on meditatively, "an armored Three has almost as much target acceptance as a Five, but you take your chances any way you swing. Now let's get with it, shall we? You—" she pointed at Sheri, "sit down over there."

The Forehand girl and I crawled around the mix of human and Heechee furnishings to make room. There wasn't much. If you cleared everything out of a Three you'd have a room about four meters by three by three, but of course if you cleared everything out it wouldn't go.

Sheri sat down in front of the column of spoked wheels, wriggling her bottom to try to get a fit. "What kind of behinds did the Heechee have?" she complained.

Teacher said, "Another good question, same no-good answer. If you find out, tell us. The Corporation puts that webbing in the seat. It isn't original equipment. Okay. Now, that thing you're looking at is the target selector. Put your hand on *one* of the wheels. Any one. Just don't touch any other. Now move it." She peered down anxiously as Sheri touched the bottom wheel, then thrust with her fingers, then laid the heel of her hand on it, braced herself against the V-shaped arms of the seat, and shoved. Finally it moved, and the lights along the row of wheels began to flicker.

"Wow," said Sheri, "they must've been pretty strong!"

We took turns trying with that one wheel—Klara wouldn't let us touch any other that day—and when it came my turn I was surprised to find that it took about as much muscle as I could bring to bear to make it move. It didn't feel rusted stuck; it felt as though it were meant to be hard to turn. And, when you think how much trouble you can get into if you turn a setting by accident in the middle of a flight, it probably was.

Of course, now I know more about that, too, than my teacher did then. Not that I'm so smart, but it has taken, and is still taking, a lot of people a hell of a long time to figure out what goes on just in setting up a target on the course director.

What it is is a vertical row of number generators. The lights that show up display numbers; that's not easy to see, because they don't *look* like numbers. They aren't positional, or decimal. (Apparently the Heechee expressed numbers as sums of primes and exponents, but all that's way over my head.) Only the check pilots and the course programmers working for the Corporation really have to be able to

GATEWAY'S SHIPS

The vessels available on Gateway are capable of interstellar flight at speeds greater than the velocity of light. The means of propulsion is not understood (see pilot manual). There is also a fairly conventional rocket propulsion system, using liquid hydrogen and liquid oxygen for attitude control, and for propulsion of the landing craft which is docked into each interstellar vessel.

There are three major classifications, designated as Class 1, Class 3, and Class 5, according to the number of persons they can carry. Some of the vessels are of particularly heavy construction and are designated "armored." Most of the armored class are Fives.

Each vessel is programmed to navigate itself automatically to a number of destinations. Return is automatic, and is quite reliable in practice. Your course in ship-handling will adequately prepare you for all the necessary tasks in piloting your vessel safely; however, see pilot manual for safety regulations.

read the numbers, and they don't do it directly, only with a computing translator. The first five digits appear to express the position of the target in space, reading from bottom to top. (Dane Metchnikov says the prime ordering isn't from bottom to top but from front to back, which says something or other about the Heechee. They were three-D oriented, like primitive man, instead of two-D oriented, like us.) You would think that three numbers would be enough to describe any position anywhere in the universe, wouldn't you? I mean, if you make a three-dimensional representation of the Galaxy you can express any point in it by means of a number for each of the three dimensions. But it took the Heechee five. Does that mean there were five dimensions that were perceptible to the Heechee? Metchnikov says not . . . .

Anyway. Once you get a lock on the first five numbers, the other seven can be turned to quite arbitrary settings and you'll still go when you squeeze the action teat.

What you usually do—or what the course programmers the Corporation keeps on the payroll to do this sort of thing for you usually do—is pick four numbers at random. Then you cycle the fifth digit until you get a kind of warning pink glow. Sometimes it's faint, sometimes it's bright. If you stop there and press the flat oval part under the teat, the other numbers begin to creep around, just a couple of millimeters one way or another, and the pink glow gets brighter. When they stop it's shocking pink and shockingly bright. Metchnikov says that's an automatic fine-tuning device. The machine allows for human error—sorry, I mean for Heechee error—so when you get close to a real, valid target setting it makes the final adjustments for you automatically. Probably he's right.

(Of course, learning every step of this cost a lot of time and money, and most of it cost some lives. It's dangerous being a prospector. But for the first few out, it was more like suicidal.)

Sometimes you can cycle all the way through your

fifth digit and get nothing at all. So what you do is, you swear. Then you reset one of the other four and go again. It only takes a few seconds to cycle, but check pilots have run up a hundred hours of new settings before they got good color.

Of course, by the time I went out, the check pilots and the course programmers had worked out a couple hundred possible settings that had been logged as good color but not as yet used—as well as all the settings that had been used, and aren't worth going back to. Or that the crews didn't come back from.

But all that I didn't know at the time, and when I sat down in that modified Heechee seat it was all new, new, new. And I don't know if I can make you understand what it felt like.

I mean, there I was, in a seat where Heechee had sat half a million years ago. The thing in front of me was a target selector. The ship could go *anywhere*. Anywhere! If I selected the right target I could find myself around Sirius, Procyon, maybe even the Magellanic Clouds!

Teacher got tired of hanging head-down and wriggled through, squeezing in behind me. "Your turn, Broadhead," she said, resting a hand on my shoulder and what felt like her breasts on my back.

I was reluctant to touch. I asked, "Isn't there any way of telling where you're going to wind up?"

"Probably," she said, "providing you're a Heechee with pilot training."

"Not even like one color means you're going farther from here than some other color?"

"Not that anybody here has figured out. Of course, they keep trying. There's a whole team that spends its time programming returned mission reports against the settings they went out with. So far they've come up empty. Now let's get on with it, Broadhead. Put your whole hand on that first wheel, the one the others have used. Shove it. It'll take more muscle than you think."

It did. In fact, I was almost afraid to push it hard enough to make it work. She leaned over and put her hand on mine, and I realized that that nice musk-oil smell that had been in my nostrils for the last little while was hers. It wasn't just musk, either; her pheromones were snuggling nicely into my chemoreceptors. It made a very nice change from the rest of the Gateway stink.

But all the same, I didn't get even a show of color, although I tried for five minutes before she waved me away and gave Sheri another shot in my place.

When I got back to my room somebody had cleaned it up. I wondered gratefully who that had been, but I was too tired to wonder very long. Until you get used to it, low gravity can be exhausting; you find yourself overusing all your muscles because you have to relearn a whole pattern of economies.

I slung my hammock and was just dozing off when I heard a scratching at the lattice of my door and Sheri's voice: "Bob?"

"What?"

"Are you asleep?"

Obviously I wasn't, but I interpreted the question the way she had intended it. "No. I've been lying here thinking."

"So was I. . . . Bob?"

"Yeah?"

"Would you like me to come into your hammock?"

I made an effort to wake myself up enough to consider the question on its merits.

"I really want to," she said.

"All right. Sure. I mean, glad to have you." She slipped into my room, and I slid over in the hammock, which swung slowly as she crawled into it. She was wearing a knitted T-shirt and underpants, and she felt warm and soft against me when we rolled gently together in the hollow of the hammock.

"It doesn't have to be sex, stud," she said. "I'm easy either way."

"Let's see what develops. Are you scared?"

Her breath was the sweetest-smelling thing about

Classifieds.

HOW DO you know you're not a Unitarian? Gateway Fellowship now forming. 87-539.

BILITIS WANTED for Sappho and Lesbia, joint trips till we make it, then happily ever after in Northern Ireland. Permanent trimarriage only. 87-033 or 87-034.

STORE YOUR effects. Save rent, avoid Corporation seizure while out. Fee includes disposal instructions if nonreturn. 88-125.

her; I could feel it on my cheek. "A lot more than I thought I would be."

"Why?"

"Bob—" she squirmed herself comfortable and then twisted her neck to look at me over her shoulder, "you know, you say kind of asshole things sometimes?"

"Sorry."

"Well, I mean it. I mean, look what we're doing. We're going to get into a ship that we don't know if it's going to get where it's supposed to go, and we don't even know where it's supposed to go. We go faster than light, nobody knows how. We don't know how long we'll be gone, even if we knew where we were going. So we could be traveling the rest of our lives and die before we got there, even if we didn't run into something that would kill us in two seconds. Right? Right. So how come you ask me why I'm scared?"

"Just making conversation." I curled up along her back and cupped a breast, not aggressively but because it felt good.

"And not only that. We don't know anything about the people who built these things. How do we know this isn't all a practical joke on their part? Maybe their way of luring fresh meat into Heechee heaven?"

"We don't," I agreed. "Roll over this way."

"And the ship they showed us this morning doesn't hardly look like I thought it was going to be, at all," she said, doing as I told her and putting a hand on the back of my neck.

There was a sharp whistle from somewhere, I couldn't tell where.

"What's that?"

"I don't know." It came again, sounding both out in the tunnel and, louder, inside my room. "Oh, it's the phone." What I was hearing was my own piezophone and the ones on either side of me, all ringing at once. The whistle stopped and there was a voice:

"This is Jim Chou. All you fish who want to see what a ship looks like when it comes back after a

71

bad trip, come to Docking Station Four. They're bringing it in now."

I could hear a murmuring from the Forehands' room next door, and I could feel Sheri's heart pounding. "We'd better go," I said.

"I know. But I don't think I want to—much."

The ship had made it back to Gateway, but not quite all the way. One of the orbiting cruisers had detected it and closed in on it. Now a tug was bringing it in to the Corporation's own docks, where usually only the rockets from the planets latched in. There was a hatch big enough to hold even a Five. This was a Three . . . what there was left of it.

"Oh, sweet Jesus," Sheri whispered. "Bob, what do you suppose happened to them?"

"To the people? They died." There was not really any doubt of that. The ship was a wreck. The lander stem was gone, just the interstellar vehicle itself, the mushroom cap, was still there, and that was bent out of shape, split open, seared by heat. Split open! Heechee metal, that doesn't even soften under an electric arc!

But we hadn't seen the worst of it.

We never did see the worst of it, we only heard about it. One man was still inside the ship. All over the inside of the ship. He had been literally spattered around the control room, and his remains had been baked onto the walls. By what? Heat and acceleration, no doubt. Perhaps he had found himself skipping into the upper reaches of a sun, or in tight orbit around a neutron star. The differential in gravity might have shredded ship and crew like that. But we never knew.

The other two persons in the crew were not there at all. Not that it was easy to tell; but the census of the organs revealed only one jaw, one pelvis, one spine—though in many short pieces. Perhaps the other two had been in the lander?

"Move it, fish!"

Sheri caught my arm and pulled me out of the way. Five uniformed crewmen from the cruisers came

72

through, in American and Brazilian blue, Russian beige, Venusian work white and Chinese all-purpose black-and-brown. The American and the Venusian were female; the faces were all different, but the expressions were all the same mixture of discipline and distaste.

"Let's go." Sheri tugged me away. She didn't want to watch the crewmen poke through the remnants, and neither did I. The whole class, Jimmy Chou, Klara and the other teachers and all, began to straggle back to our rooms. Not quite quick enough. We had been looking through the ports into the lock; when the patrol from the cruisers opened it, we got a whiff of the air inside. I don't know how to describe it. A little bit like overripe garbage being cooked to swill to pigs. Even in the rank air of Gateway, that was hard to take.

Teacher dropped off at her own level—down pretty low, in the high-rent district around Easy Level. When she looked up after me as I said goodnight I observed for the first time that she was crying.

Sheri and I said goodnight to the Forehands at their door, and I turned to her, but she was ahead of me.

"I think I'll sleep this one out," she said. "Sorry, Bob, but, you know, I just don't feel like it anymore."

SAFETY RULES
FOR GATEWAY SHIPS

The mechanism for interstellar
travel is known to be contained in
the diamond-shaped box which is located under the center keel of 3-man
and 5-man ships, and in the sanitary
facilities of the 1-man ships.

No one has successfully opened one
of those containers. Each attempt
has resulted in explosion of approximately 1-kiloton force. A major research project is attempting to
penetrate this box without destroying it, and if you as a limited
partner have any information or suggestions in this connection you
should contact a Corporation officer
at once.

However, under no circumstances
attempt to open the box yourself!
Tampering with it in any way, or
docking a vessel on which the box
has been tampered with, is strictly
forbidden. The penalty is forfeiture
of all rights and immediate expul-
sion from Gateway.

The course-directing equipment
also poses a potential danger. Under
no circumstances should you attempt
to change the setting once you have
begun your flight. No vessel in
which this has been done has ever
returned.

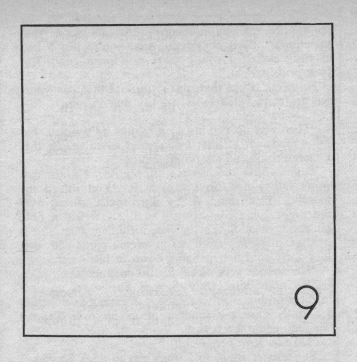

9

I don't know why I keep going back to Sigfrid von
Shrink. My appointment with him is always on a
Wednesday afternoon, and he doesn't like it if I drink
or dope before then. So it blows the whole day. I
pay a lot for those days. You don't *know* what it
costs to live the way I live. My apartment over Washington Square is eighteen thousand dollars a month.
My residence taxes to live under the Big Bubble come
to another three thousand plus. (It doesn't cost that
much to stay on Gateway!) I've got some pretty hefty
charge accounts for furs, wine, lingerie, jewelry,
flowers . . . Sigfrid says I try to buy love. All right,
I do. What's wrong with that? I can afford it. And
that's not mentioning what Full Medical costs me.

Sigfrid, though, comes free. I'm covered by the Full
Medical for psychiatric therapy, any variety I like; I

could have group grope or internal massage for the same price, namely nothing. I kid him about that sometimes. "Even considering that you're just a bag of rusty bolts," I say, "you're not much good. But your price is right."

He asks, "Does that make you feel that you yourself are more valuable, if you say that I'm not?"

"Not particularly."

"Then why do you insist on reminding yourself that I'm a machine? Or that I don't cost anything? Or that I cannot transcend my programming?"

"I guess you just piss me off, Sigfrid." I know that won't satisfy him, so I explain it. "You ruined my morning. This friend, S. Ya. Lavorovna, stayed over last night. She's *something*." So I tell Sigfrid a little bit about what S. Ya. is like, including what she is like walking away from me in stretch pants with that long dirty-gold hair hanging down to her waist.

"She sounds very nice," Sigfrid comments.

"Bet your bolts. Only thing is, she wakes up slow in the morning. Just when she was getting lively again I had to leave my summer place, up over Tappan Sea, and come down here."

"Do you love her, Bob?"

The answer is no, so I want him to think it's yes. I say, "No."

"I think that's an honest answer, Rob," he says, approvingly, and disappointingly. "Is that why you're angry with me?"

"Oh, I don't know. Just in a bad mood, I guess."

"Can you think of any reasons why?"

He waits me out, so after a while I say, "Well, I took a licking at roulette last night."

"More than you can afford?"

"Christ! No." But it's annoying, all the same. There are other things, too. It's getting toward that chilly time of year. My place over Tappan Sea isn't under the Bubble, so sitting out on the porch with S. Ya. for brunch wasn't such a good idea. I don't want to mention this to Sigfrid. He would say something wholly rational like, well, why didn't I have my lunch served indoors? And I would just have to tell him all over again that when I was a kid it was my dream to own a summer place over Tappan Sea and have brunch on the porch, looking out over it. They'd just dammed the Hudson then, when I was about maybe twelve. I used to dream a lot about Making It Big and living in the style of The Rich Folks. Well, he's heard all that.

Sigfrid clears his throat. "Thank you, Bob," he says, to let me know that the hour is over. "Will I see you next week?"

"Don't you always?" I say, smiling. "How the time flies. Actually I wanted to leave a little early today."

"Did you, Bob?"

"I have another date with S. Ya.," I explain. "She's coming back up to the summer place with me tonight. Frankly, what she's going to do is better therapy than what you do."

He says, "Is that all you want out of a relationship, Robbie?"

"You mean, just sex?" The answer in this case is no, but I don't want him to know just what it is I do want out of my relationship with S. Ya. Lavorovna. I say, "She's a little different from most of my girl-friends, Sigfrid. She has about as much clout as I do, for one thing. Has a damn good job. I admire her."

Well, I don't, particularly. Or rather, I don't care much about whether I admire her or not. S. Ya. has one trait that impresses me even more than possessing the sweetest rear view that God ever laid on a human female. Her damn good job is in information handling. She went to the Akademogorsk University, she was a fellow at the Max Planck Institute for Machine Intelligence, and she teaches graduate students in the AI department at NYU. She knows more about Sigfrid than Sigfrid knows about himself, and that suggests interesting possibilities to me.

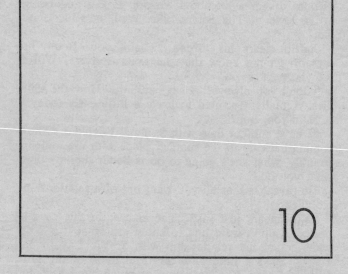

10

Along about my fifth day on Gateway I got up early and splurged, breakfast out in the Heecheetown Arms, surrounded by tourists, bloody-eyed gamblers from the casino across the spindle, and liberty sailors from the cruisers. It felt luxurious, and cost luxurious, too. It was worth it because of the tourists. I could feel their eyes on me. I knew they were talking about me, particularly a smooth-faced but old African type, Dahomeyan or Ghanaian, I think, with his very young, very plump, very jeweled wife. Or whatever. As far as they could tell, I was a swashbuckling hero. True, I didn't have any bangles on my arm, but some of the veterans didn't wear them, either.

I basked. I considered ordering real eggs and bacon, but that was a little more than even my euphoria would let me go for, so I settled for orange juice (it

Classifieds.

GOURMET COOKERY to order. Szechuan, California, Cantonese. Specialty party munches. The Wongs, ph 83-242.

LECTURE & PV careers are waiting for multi-bracelet retirees! Sign up now for course public speaking, holoview preparation, PR management. Inspect authenticated letters graduates earning $3000/wk up. 86-521.

WELCOME TO Gateway! Make contacts quickly our unique service. 200 names, preferences on file. Introductions $50. 88-963.

turned out to be real, to my surprise) and a brioche and several cups of black Danish coffee. All I was really missing was a pretty girl across the armboard of the chair. There were two nice-looking women who seemed to be the liberty crew from the Chinese cruiser, neither of them unwilling to exchange a few radio messages by the glance of the eyes, but I decided to keep them as open prospects for some future date and paid my check (that was painful enough) and left for class.

On the way down I caught up with the Forehands. The man, whose name seemed to be Sess, dropped off the down-cable and waited to wish me a polite good morning. "We didn't see you at breakfast," his wife mentioned, so I told them where I had been. The younger daughter, Lois, looked faintly envious. Her mother caught the expression and patted her. "Don't worry, hon. We'll eat there before we go back to Venus." To me: "We have to watch our pennies right now. But when we hit, we've got some pretty big plans for spending the profits."

"Don't we all," I said, but something was turning over in my head. "Are you really going to go back to Venus?"

"Certainly," they all said, in one way or another, and acted surprised at the question. Which surprised me. I hadn't realized that tunnel rats could manage to think of that molten stinkpot as home. Sess Forehand must have read my expression, too. They were a reserved family, but they didn't miss much. He grinned and said:

"It's our home, after all. So is Gateway, in a way."

That was astonishing. "Actually, we're related to the first man to find Gateway, Sylvester Macklen. You've heard of him?"

"How could I not?"

"He was a sort of a cousin. I guess you know the whole story?" I started to say I did, but he obviously was proud of his cousin, and I couldn't blame him, and so I heard a slightly different version of the familiar legend: "He was in one of the South Pole tunnels, and found a ship. God knows how he got it to the surface, but he did, and he got in and evidently squeezed the go-teat, and it went where it was programmed—here."

"Doesn't the Corporation pay a royalty?" I asked. "I mean, if they're going to pay for discoveries, what discovery would be more worth paying for?"

"Not to us, anyway," said Louise Forehand, somewhat somberly; money was a hard subject with the Forehands. "Of course, Sylvester didn't set out to find Gateway. As you know from what we've been hearing in class, the ships have automatic return. Wherever you go, you just squeeze the go-teat and you come straight back here. Only that didn't help Sylvester, because he *was* here. It was the return leg of a round trip with about a zillion-year stopover."

"He was smart and strong." Sess took up the story. "You have to be to explore. So he didn't panic. But by the time anybody came out here to investigate he was out of life support. He could have lived a little longer. He could have used the lox and H-two from the lander tanks for air and water. I used to wonder why he didn't."

"Because he would have starved anyway," Louise cut in, defending her relative.

"I think so. Anyway, they found his body, with his notes in his hand. He had cut his throat."

They were nice people, but I had heard all this, and they were making me late for class.

Of course, class wasn't all that exciting just at that point. We were up to Hammock Slinging (Basic) and Toilet Flushing (Advanced). You may wonder why they didn't spend more time actually teaching us how to fly the ships. That's simple. The things flew themselves, as the Forehands, and everybody else, had been telling me. Even the landers were no sweat to operate, although they did require a hand on the controls. Once you were in the lander all you had to do was compare a three-D, sort of holographic representation of the immediate area of space with where you wanted to go, and maneuver a point of light in the

LAUNCH AVAILABILITIES

30-107. FIVE. Three vacancies, English-
speaking. Terry Yakamora (ph
83-675) or Jay Parduk (83-004).

30-108. THREE. Armored. One vacancy,
English or French. BONUS TRIP.
Dorlean Sugrue (P-phone 88-108).

30-109. ONE. Check trip. Good safety record. See Launch Captain.

30-110. ONE. Armored. BONUS TRIP. See
Launch Captain.

30-111. THREE. Open enlistment. See
Launch Captain.

30-112. THREE. Probable short trip. Open
enlistment. Minimum guarantee. See
Launch Captain.

30-113. ONE. Four vacancies via Gateway
Two. Transportation in reliable
Five. Tikki Trumbull (ph 87-869).

tank to the point you wanted to reach. The lander went there. It calculated its own trajectories and corrected its own deviations. It took a little muscular coordination to get the hang of twisting that point of light to where you wanted it to go, but it was a forgiving system.

Between the sessions of flushing practice and hammock drill we talked about what we were going to do when we graduated. The launch schedules were kept up to date and displayed on the PV monitor in our class whenever anyone pushed the button. Some of them had names attached to them, and one or two of the names I recognized. Tikki Trumbull was a girl I had danced with and sat next to in the mess hall once or twice. She was an out-pilot, and as she needed crew I thought of joining her. But the wiseheads told me that out-missions were a waste of time.

I should tell you what an out-pilot is. He's the guy who ferries fresh crews to Gateway Two. There are about a dozen Fives that do that as a regular run. They take four people out (which would be what Tikki wanted people for), and then the pilot comes back alone, or with returning prospectors—if any— and what they've found. Usually there's somebody.

The team who found Gateway Two are the ones we all dreamed about. They *made* it. Man, did they make it! Gateway Two was another Gateway, nothing more or less, except that it happened to orbit around a star other than our own. There was not much more in the way of treasure on Gateway Two than there was on our own Gateway; the Heechee had swept everything pretty clean, except for the ships themselves. And there weren't nearly as many ships there, only about a hundred and fifty, compared to almost a thousand on our old original solar Gateway. But a hundred and fifty ships are worth finding all by themselves. Not to mention the fact that they accept some destinations that our local Gateway's ships don't appear to.

The ride out to Gateway Two seems to be about four hundred light-years and takes a hundred and nine days each way. Two's principal star is a bright blue B-type. They think it is Alcyone in the Pleiades, but there is some doubt. Well, actually that's not Gateway Two's *real* star. It doesn't orbit the big one, but a little cinder of a red dwarf nearby. They say the dwarf is probably a distant binary with the blue B, but they also say it shouldn't be because of the difference in ages of the two stars. Give them a few more years to argue and they'll probably know. One wonders why the Heechee would have put their spacelines junction in orbit around so undistinguished a star, but one wonders a lot about the Heechee.

However, all that doesn't affect the pocketbook of the team who happened to find the place. They get a royalty on everything that any later prospector finds! I don't know what they've made so far, but it has to be in the tens of millions apiece. Maybe the hundreds. And that's why it doesn't pay to go with an out-pilot; you don't really have a much better chance of scoring, and you have to split what you get.

So we went down the list of upcoming launches and hashed them over in the light of our five-day expertise. Which wasn't much. We appealed to Gelle-Klara Moynlin for advice. After all, she'd been out twice. She studied the list of flights and names, pursing her lips. "Terry Yakamora's a decent guy," she said. "I don't know Parduk, but it might be worth taking a chance on that one. Lay off Dorlean's flight. There's a million-dollar bonus, but what they don't tell you is that they've got a bastard control board in it. The Corporation's experts have put in a computer that's supposed to override the Heechee target selector, and I wouldn't trust it. And, of course, I wouldn't recommend a One in any circumstances."

Lois Forehand asked, "Which one would you take if it was up to you, Klara?"

She scowled thoughtfully, rubbing that dark left eyebrow with the tips of her fingers. "Maybe Terry. Well, any of them. But I'm not going out again for a while." I wanted to ask her why, but she turned away from the screen and said, "All right, gang, let's get back to the drill. Remember, up for pee; down, close, wait ten and up for poo."

I celebrated completing the week on ship-handling by offering to buy Dane Metchnikov a drink. That wasn't my first intention. My first intention had been to buy Sheri a drink and drink it in bed, but she was off somewhere. So I worked the buttons on the piezo-phone and got Metchnikov.

He sounded surprised at my offer. "Thanks," he said, and then considered. "Tell you what. Give me a hand carrying some stuff, and then I'll buy *you* a drink."

So I went down to his place, which was only one level below Babe; his room was not much better than my own, and bare, except for a couple of full carry-alls. He looked at me almost friendly. "You're a prospector now," he grunted.

"Not really. I've got two more courses."

"Well, this is the last you see of me, anyway. I'm shipping out with Terry Yakamora tomorrow."

I was surprised. "Didn't you just get back, like ten days ago?"

"You can't make any money hanging around here. All I was waiting for was the right crew. You want to come to my farewell party? Terry's place. Twenty hundred."

"That sounds fine," I said. "Can I bring Sheri?"

"Oh, sure, she's coming anyway, I think. Buy you the drink there, if you don't mind. Give me a hand and we'll get this stuff stored."

He had accumulated a surprising amount of goods. I wondered how he had managed to stash them all away in a room as tiny as my own: three fabric car-riers all stuffed full, holodisks and a viewer, book tapes and a few actual books. I took the carriers. On Earth they would have weighed more than I could handle, probably fifty or sixty kilos, but of course on Gateway lifting them was no problem; it was only tugging them through the corridors and jockeying them down the shafts that was tricky. I had the mass, but Metchnikov had the problems, since what he was carrying was in odd shapes and varying degrees of fragility. It was about an hour's haul, actually. We wound up in a part of the asteroid I'd never seen before, where an elderly Pakistani woman counted the pieces, gave Metchnikov a receipt and began dragging them away down a thickly vine-grown corridor.

"Whew," he grunted. "Well, thanks."

"You're welcome." We started back toward a drop-shaft, and making conversation, I assume out of some recognition that he owed me a social favor and should practice some social skills, he said:

"So how was the course?"

"You mean apart from the fact that I've just finished it and still don't have any idea how to fly those god-damned ships?"

"Well, of course you don't," he said, irritably. "The course isn't going to teach you that. It just gives you the general idea. The way you learn, you do it. Only hard part's the lander, of course. Anyway, you've got your issue of tapes?"

"Oh, yes." There were six cassettes of them. Each of us had been given a set when we completed the first week's course. They had everything that had been said, plus a lot of stuff about different kinds of controls that the Corporation might, or might not, fit on a Heechee board and so on.

"So play them over," he said. "If you've got any sense you'll take them with you when you ship out. Got plenty of time to play them then. Mostly the ships fly themselves anyway."

"They'd better," I said, doubting it. "So long." He waved and dropped onto the down-cable without looking back. Apparently I had agreed to take the drink he owed me at the party. Where it wouldn't cost him anything.

I thought of looking for Sheri again, and decided against it. I was in a part of Gateway I didn't know, and course I'd left my map back in my room. I drifted along, more or less at random, past star-points where some of the tunnels smelled musty and dusty and there weren't many people, then through an inhabited section that seemed to be mostly Eastern European. I didn't recognize the languages, but there were little notes and wall signs hanging from the everywhere-growing ivy that were in alphabets that looked Cyrillic or even stranger. I came to a dropshaft, thought for a moment, and then caught hold of the up-cable. The easy way not to be lost on Gateway is to go up until you get to the spindle, where "up" ends.

But this time I found myself passing Central Park and, on impulse, dropped off the up-cable to sit by a tree for a while.

Central Park isn't really a park. It's a large tunnel, not far from the center of rotation of the asteroid, which has been devoted to vegetation. I found orange trees there (which explained the juice), and grape vines; and ferns and mosses, but no grass. I am not sure why. Probably it has something to do with planting only varieties that are sensitive to the available light, mostly the blue gleam from the Heechee metal all around, and perhaps they couldn't find a grass that could use it efficiently for its photochemistry. The principal reason for having Central Park in the first place was to suck up CO_2 and give back oxygen; that was before they spread planting all over the tunnels. But it also killed smells, or anyway it was supposed to, a little, and it grew a certain amount of food. The whole thing was maybe eighty meters long and twice as tall as I was. It was broad enough to have room for some winding paths. The stuff they grew in looked a lot like good old genuine Earthside dirt. What it was, really, was a humus made out of the sewage sludge from the couple of thousand people who had used Gateway toilets, but you couldn't tell that by looking at it, or by smelling it, either.

The first tree big enough to sit by was no good for that purpose; it was a mulberry, and under it were spread out sheets of fine netting to catch the dropping fruit. I walked past it, and down the path there were a woman and a child.

A child! I hadn't known there were any children on

87

Gateway. She was a little bit of a thing, maybe a year and a half, playing with a ball so big, and so lazy in the light gravity, that it was like a balloon.

"Hello, Bob."

That was the other surprise; the woman who greeted me was Gelle-Klara Moynlin. I said without thinking, "I didn't know you had a little girl."

"I don't. This is Kathy Francis, and her mother lets me borrow her sometimes. Kathy, this is Bob Broadhead."

"Hello, Bob," the little thing called, studying me from three meters away. "Are you a friend of Klara's?"

"I hope so. She's my teacher. Do you want to play catch?"

Kathy finished her study of me and said precisely, each word separate from the one before it and as clearly formed as an adult's, "I don't know how to play catch, but I will get six mulberries for you. That's all you can have."

"Thank you." I slumped down next to Klara, who was hugging her knees and watching the child. "She's cute."

"Well, I guess so. It's hard to judge, when there aren't very many other children around."

"She's not a prospector, is she?"

I wasn't exactly joking, but Klara laughed warmly. "Her parents are permanent-party. Well, most of the time. Right now her mother's off prospecting; they do that sometimes, a lot of them. You can spend just so much time trying to figure out what the Heechee were up to before you want to try your own solutions to the puzzles."

"Sounds dangerous."

She shushed me. Kathy came back, with three of my mulberries in each open hand, so as not to crush them. She had a funny way of walking, which didn't seem to use much of the thigh and calf muscles; she sort of pushed herself up on the ball of each foot in turn, and let herself float to the next step. After I figured that out I tried it for myself, and it turned out to be a pretty efficient way of walking in near-zero gravity, but

This Park Is
MONITORED
By Closed-Circuit PV

You are welcome to enjoy it. Do not pick flowers or fruit. Do not damage any plant. While visiting, you may eat any fruits which have fallen, to the following limits:

Grapes, cherries	8 per person
Other small fruits or berries	6 per person
Oranges, limes, pears	1 per person

Gravel may not be removed from walks. Deposit all trash of any kind in receptacles.

MAINTENANCE DIVISION
THE GATEWAY CORPORATION

my reflexes kept lousing it up. I suppose you have to be born on Gateway to come by it naturally.

Klara in the park was a lot more relaxed and feminine than Klara the teacher. The eyebrows that had looked masculine and angry became outdoorsy and friendly. She still smelled very nice.

It was pretty pleasant, chatting with her, while Kathy stepped daintily around us, playing with her ball. We compared places we'd been, and didn't find any in common. The one thing we did find in common was that I was born almost the same day as her two-year-younger brother.

"Did you like your brother?" I asked, a gambit played for the hell of it.

"Well, sure. He was the baby. But he was an Aries, born under Mercury and the Moon. Made him fickle and moody, of course. I think he would have had a complicated life."

I was less interested in asking her about what happened to him than in asking if she really believed in that garbage, but that didn't seem tactful, and anyway she went on talking. "I'm a Sagittarius, myself. And you—oh, of course. You must be the same as Davie."

"I guess so," I said, being polite. "I, uh, don't go much for astrology."

"Not astrology, genethlialogy. One's superstition, the other's science."

"Um."

She laughed. "I can see you're a scoffer. Doesn't matter. If you believe, all right; if you don't—well, you don't have to believe in the law of gravity to get mashed when you fall off a two-hundred-story building."

Kathy, who had sat down beside us, inquired politely, "Are you having an argument?"

"Not really, honey." Klara stroked her head.

"That's good, Klara, because I have to go to the bathroom now and I don't think I can, here."

"It's time to go anyway. Nice to see you, Bob. Watch out for melancholy, hear?" And they went

90

away hand in hand, Klara trying to copy the little girl's odd walk. Looking very nice . . . for a flake.

That night I took Sheri to Dane Metchnikov's going-away party. Klara was there, looking even nicer in a bare-midriff pants suit. "I didn't know you knew Dane Metchnikov," I said.

"Which one is he? I mean, Terry's the one who invited me. Coming inside?"

The party had spilled out into the tunnel. I peered through the door and was surprised to find how much room there was inside; Terry Yakamora had two full rooms, both more than twice the size of mine. The bath was private and really did contain a bath, or at least a showerhead. "Nice place," I said admiringly, and then discovered from something another guest said that Klara lived right down the tunnel. That changed my opinion of Klara: if she could afford the high-rent district, why was she still on Gateway? Why wasn't she back home spending her money and having fun? Or contrariwise, if she was still on Gateway, why was she fooling around keeping barely even with the head tax by working as an assistant instructor, instead of going out for another killing? But I didn't get a chance to ask her. She did most of her dancing that night with Terry Yakamora and the others in the outgoing crew.

I lost track of Sheri until she came over to me after a slow, almost unmoving fox-trot, bringing her partner. He was a very young man—a boy, actually; he looked about nineteen. He looked familiar: dark skin, almost white hair, a wisp of a jaw-beard that drew an arc from sideburn to sideburn by way of the underside of his chin. He hadn't come up from Earth with me. He wasn't in our class. But I'd seen him somewhere.

Sheri introduced us. "Bob, you know Francesco Hereira?"

"I don't think so."

"He's from the Brazilian cruiser." Then I remembered. He was one of the inspectors who had gone in to fish through the baked gobbets of flesh on the shipwreck we'd seen a few days earlier. He was a torpedoman, according to his cuff stripes. They give the cruiser crews temporary duty as guards on Gateway, and sometimes they give them liberty there, too. He'd come in in the regular rotation about the time we arrived. Somebody put on a tape for a hora just then, and after we were through dancing, a little out of breath, Hereira and I found ourselves leaning against the wall side by side, trying to stay out of the way of the rest of the party. I told him I had just remembered seeing him at the wreck.

"Ah, yes, Mr. Broadhead. I recall."

"Tough job," I said, for something to say. "Isn't it?"

He had been drinking enough to answer me, I guess. "Well, Mr. Broadhead," he said analytically, "the technical description of that part of my job is 'search and registry.' It is not always tough. For instance, in a short time you will no doubt go out; and when you come back I, or someone else in my job, will poke into your holes, Mr. Broadhead. I will turn out your pockets, and weigh and measure and photograph everything in your ship. That is to make sure you do not smuggle anything of value out of your vessel and off Gateway without paying the Corporation its due share. Then I register what I have found; if it is nothing, I write 'nil' on the form, and another crewman from another cruiser chosen at random does the same thing exactly. So you will have two of us prying into you."

It didn't sound like a lot of fun for me, but not as bad as I had thought at first. I said so.

He flashed small, very white teeth. "When the prospector to be searched is Sheri or Gelle-Klara over there, no, not bad at all. One can quite enjoy it. But I have not much interest in searching males, Mr. Broadhead. Especially when they are dead. Have you ever been in the presence of five human bodies that have been dead, but not embalmed, for three months? That was what it was like on the first ship I inspected. I do not think anything will be that bad ever again."

Then Sheri came up and demanded him for another dance, and the party went on.

There were a lot of parties. It turned out there always had been, it was just that we new fish hadn't been part of the network, but as we got nearer graduating we got to know more people. There were farewell parties. There were welcome-back parties, but not nearly as many of those. Even when crews did come back, there was not always any reason to celebrate. Sometimes they had been gone so long they had lost touch with all their friends. Sometimes, when they had hit fairly lucky, they didn't want anything but to get off Gateway on the way home. And sometimes, of course, they couldn't have a party because parties aren't permitted in the intensive care rooms at Terminal Hospital.

It wasn't all parties; we had to study. By the end of the course we were supposed to be fully expert in ship-handling, survival techniques and the appraisal of trade goods. Well, I wasn't. Sheri was even worse off than I. She took to the ship-handling all right, and she had a shrewd eye for detail that would help her a lot in appraising the worth of anything she might find on a prospecting trip. But she didn't seem able to get the survival course through her head.

Studying with her for the final examinations was misery:

"Okay," I'd tell her, "this one's a type-F star with a planet with point-eight surface G, a partial pressure of oxygen of 130 millibars, mean temperature at the equator plus forty Celsius. So what do you wear to the party?"

She said accusingly, "You're giving me an easy one. That's practically Earth."

"So what's the answer, Sheri?"

She scratched reflectively under her breast. Then she shook her head impatiently. "Nothing. I mean, I wear an airsuit on the way down, but once I get to the surface I could walk around in a bikini."

"Shithead! You'd be maybe dead in twelve hours. Earth-normal conditions means there's a good chance

DUTY AND LEAVE ROSTER
USS MAYAGUEZ

1. Following O and crewpersons tr
temp dy stns Gateway for contraband
inspection and compliance patrol:

LINKY, Tina	W/o
MASKO, Casimir J	BsnM 1
MIRARCHI, Iory S	S2

2. Following O and crewpersons authd
24-hr temp dy Gateway for R&R:

GRYSON, Katie W	LtJG
HARVEY, Iwan	RadM
HLEB, Caryle T	S1
HOLL, William F Jr	S1

3. All O and crewpersons are cautioned once again to avoid any repeat
any dispute with O and crewpersons
of other patrol vessels regardless of nationality and regardless
of circumstances, and to refrain
from divulging classified information
to any person whatsoever. Infrac-
tions will be dealt with by complete
deprivation of Gateway leave, in
addition to such other punishments
as a defaulter's court may direct.

4. Temporary duty on Gateway is a
privilege, not a right. If you want
it, you have to earn it.

                    By Command of the CAPTAIN
                    USS MAYAGUEZ

of an Earth normal-type biology. Which means pathogens that could eat you up."

"So all right—" she hunched her shoulders, "so I'd keep the suit until, uh, I tested for pathogens."

"And how do you do that?"

"I use the fucking kit, stupid!" She added hastily, before I could say anything, "I mean I take the, let's see, the Basic Metabolism disks out of the freezer and activate them. I stay in orbit for twenty-four hours until they're ripe, then when I'm down on the surface I expose them and take readings with my, uh, with my C-44."

"C-33. There's no such thing as a C-44."

"So all right. Oh, and also I pack a set of antigen boosters, so if there's a marginal problem with some sort of microorganism I can give myself a booster shot and get temporary immunity."

"I guess that's all right, so far," I said doubtfully. In practice, of course, she wouldn't need to remember all that. She would read the directions on the packages, or play her course tapes, or better still, she would be out with somebody who had been out before and would know the ropes. But there was also the chance that something unforeseen would go wrong and she would be on her own resources, not to mention the fact that she had a final test to take and pass. "What else, Sheri?"

"The usual, Bob! Do I have to run through the whole list? All right. Radio-relay; spare powerpack; the geology kit; ten-day food ration—and no, I don't eat anything I find on the planet at all, not even if there's a McDonald's hamburger stand right next to the ship. And an extra lipstick and some sanitary napkins."

I waited. She smiled prettily, outwaiting me. "What about weapons?"

"Weapons?"

"Yes, God damn it! If it's nearly Earth normal, what are the chances of life being there?"

"Oh, yes. Let's see. Well, of course, if I need them I take them. But, wait a minute, first I sniff for methane

95

in the atmosphere with the spectrometer reading from orbit. If there's no methane signature there's no life, so I don't have to worry."

"There's no *mammalian* life, and you do have to worry. What about insects? Reptiles? Dluglatches?"

"Dluglatches?"

"A word I just made up to describe a kind of life we've never heard of that doesn't generate methane in its gut but eats people."

"Oh, sure. All right, I'll take a sidearm and twenty rounds of soft-nosed ammo. Give me another one."

And so we went on. When we first started rehearsing each other what we usually said at a point like that was either, "Well, I won't have to worry, because you'll be there with me anyway," or "Kiss me, you fool." But we'd kind of stopped saying that.

In spite of it all, we graduated. All of us.

We gave ourselves a graduation party, Sheri and me, and all four of the Forehands, and the others who had come up from Earth with us and the six or seven who had appeared from one place or another. We didn't invite any outsiders, but our teachers weren't outsiders. They all showed up to wish us well. Klara came in late, drank a quick drink, kissed us all, male and female, even the Finnish kid with the language block who'd had to take all his instruction on tapes. *He* was going to have a problem. They have instruction tapes for every language you ever heard of, and if they don't happen to have your exact dialect they run a set through the translating computer from the nearest analogue. That's enough to get you through the course, but after that the problem starts. You can't reasonably expect to be accepted by a crew that can't talk to you. His block kept him from learning any other language, and there was not a living soul on Gateway who spoke Finnish.

We took over the tunnel three doors in each direction past our own, Sheri's, the Forehands' and mine. We danced and sang until it was late enough for some of us to begin to drop off, and then we dialed in the list of open launches on the PV screen. Full of beer and weed, we cut cards for first pick and I won.

Something happened inside my head. I didn't sober up, really. That wasn't it. I was still feeling cheerful and sort of warm all over and open to all personality signals that were coming in. But a part of my mind opened up and a pair of clear-seeing eyes peered out at the future and made a judgment. "Well," I said, "I guess I'll pass my chance right now. Sess, you're number two; you take your pick."

"Thirty-one-oh-nine," he said promptly; all the Forehands had made up their minds in family meeting, long since. "Thanks, Bob."

I gave him a carefree, drunken wave. He didn't really owe me anything. That was a One, and I wouldn't have taken a One for any price. For that matter, there wasn't anything on the board I liked. I grinned at Klara and winked; she looked serious for a minute, then winked back, but still looked serious. I knew she realized what I had come to understand: all these launches were rejects. The best ones had been snapped up as soon as they were announced by returnees and permanent-party.

Sheri had drawn fifth pick, and when it came her turn she looked directly at me. "I'm going to take that Three if I can fill it up. What about it, Bob? Are you going to come or not?"

I chuckled. "Sheri," I said, sweetly reasonable, "there's not a returnee that wants it. It's an armored job. You don't know *where* the hell it might be going. And there's far too much green in the guidance panel to suit me." (Nobody really knew what the colors meant, of course, but there was a superstition in the school that a lot of green meant a superdangerous mission.)

"It's the only open Three, and there's a bonus."

"Not me, honey. Ask Klara; she's been around a long time and I respect her judgment."

"I'm asking you, Bob."

"No. I'll wait for something better."

Classifieds.

GILLETTE, RONALD C., departed Gateway sometime in last year. Anyone having information present whereabouts please inform wife, Annabelle, c/o Canadian Legation, Tharsis, Mars. Reward.

OUTPILOTS, REPEAT winners, let your money work for you while you're out. Invest mutual funds, growth stocks, land, other opportunities. Moderate counseling fee. 88-301.

PORNODISKS FOR those long, lonely trips. 50 hours $500. All interests or to order. Also models wanted. 87-108.

"I'm not waiting, Bob. I already talked to Willa Forehand, and she's agreeable. If worse comes to worst we'll fill it out with—anybody at all," she said, looking at the Finnish kid, smiling drunkenly to himself as he stared at the launch board. "But—you and I did say we were going out together."

I shook my head.

"So stay here and rot," she flared. "Your girlfriend's just as scared as you are!"

Those sober eyes inside my skull looked at Klara, and the frozen, unmoving expression on her face; and, wonderingly, I realized Sheri was right. Klara was like me. We were both afraid to go.

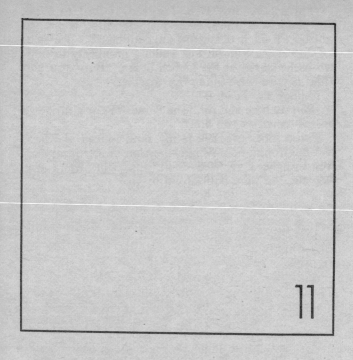

11

I say to Sigfrid, "This isn't going to be a very productive session, I'm afraid. I'm just plain exhausted. Sexually, if you know what I mean."

"I certainly do know what you mean, Bob."

"So I don't have much to talk about."

"Do you remember any dreams?"

I squirm on the couch. As it happens, I do remember one or two. I say. "No." Sigfrid is always after me to tell him my dreams. I don't like it.

When he first suggested it I told him I didn't dream very often. He said patiently, "I think you know, Bob, that everyone dreams. You may not remember the dreams in the waking state. But you can, if you try."

"No, I can't. You can. You're a machine."

"I know I'm a machine, Bob, but we're talking about you. Will you try an experiment?"

"Maybe."

"It isn't hard. Keep a pencil and a piece of paper beside your bed. As soon as you wake up, write down what you remember."

"But I don't ever remember anything at all about my dreams."

"I think it's worth a try, Bob."

Well, I did. And, you know, I actually did begin to remember my dreams. Little tiny fragments, at first. And I'd write them down, and sometimes I would tell them to Sigfrid and they would make him as happy as anything. He just loved dreams.

Me, I didn't see much use in it. . . . Well, not at first. But then something happened that made a Christian out of me.

One morning I woke up out of a dream that was so unpleasant and so real that for a few moments I wasn't sure it wasn't actual fact, and so awful that I didn't dare let myself believe it was only a dream. It shook me so much that I began to write it down, as fast as I could, every bit I could remember. Then there was a P-phone call. I answered it; and, do you know, in just the minute I was on the phone, I forgot the whole thing! Couldn't remember one bit of it. Until I looked at what I had written down, and then it all came back to me.

Well, when I saw Sigfrid a day or two later, I'd forgotten it again! As though it had never happened. But I had saved the piece of paper, and I had to read it to him. That was one of the times when I thought he was most pleased with himself and with me, too. He worried over that dream for the whole hour. He found symbols and meanings in every bit of it. I don't remember what they were, but I remember that for me it wasn't any fun at all.

As a matter of fact, do you know what's really funny? I threw away the paper on the way out of his office. And now I couldn't tell you what that dream was to save my life.

"I see you don't want to talk about dreams," says Sigfrid. "Is there anything you do want to talk about?"

"Not really."

He doesn't answer that for a moment, and I know he is just biding his time to outwait me so that I will say something, I don't know, something foolish. So I say, "Can I ask you a question, Sigfrid?"

"Can't you always, Rob?" Sometimes I think he's actually trying to smile. I mean, really smile. His voice sounds like it.

"Well, what I want to know is, what do you do with all the things I tell you?"

"I'm not sure I understand the question, Robbie. If you're asking what the information storage program is, the answer is quite technical."

"No, that's not what I mean." I hesitate, trying to make sure what the question is, and wondering why I want to ask it. I guess it all goes back to Sylvia, who was a lapsed Catholic. I really envied her her church, and let her know I thought she was dumb to have left it, because I envied her the confession. The inside of my head was littered with all these doubts and fears that I couldn't get rid of. I would have loved to unload them on the parish priest. I could see that you could make quite a nice hierarchical flow pattern, with all the shit from inside my own head flushing into the confessional, where the parish priest flushes it onto the diocesan monsignor (or whoever; I don't really know much about the Church), and it all winds up with the Pope, who is the settling tank for all the world's sludge of pain and misery and guilt, until he passes it on by transmitting it directly to God.(I mean, assuming the existence of a God, or at least assuming that there is an address called "God" to which you can send the shit.)

Anyway, the point is that I sort of had a vision of the same system in psychotherapy: local drains going into branch sewers going into community trunk lines treeing out of flesh-and-blood psychiatrists, if you see what I mean. If Sigfrid were a real person, he wouldn't be able to hold all the misery that's poured into him.

1316	,S, It's very healthy that you	115,215
	view your breakup	115,220
	with Drusilla as a learning	115,225
	experience, Bob.	115,230
1318	,C, I'm a very healthy per-	115,235
	son, Sigfrid, that's	115,240
	why I'm here.	115,245
1319	IRRAY (DE)=IRRAY (DF)	115,250
1320	,C, Anyway, that's what life	115,255
	is, just one learning	115,260
	experience after another,	115,265
	and when you're through	115,270
	with all the learning experi-	115,275
	ences you graduate and	115,280
	what you get for a diploma	115,285
	is, you die.	115,290

To begin with, he would have his own problems. He would have mine, because that's how I would get rid of them, by unloading them onto him. He would also have those of all the other unloaders who share the hot couch; and he would unload all that, because he had to, onto the next man up, who shrank *him,* and so on and so on until they got to—who? The ghost of Sigmund Freud?

But Sigfrid isn't real. He's a machine. He can't feel pain. So where does all that pain and slime *go?*

I try to explain all that to him, ending with: "Don't you see, Sigfrid? If I give you my pain and you give it to someone else, it has to end somewhere. It doesn't feel real to me that it just winds up as magnetic bubbles in a piece of quartz that nobody ever *feels.*"

"I don't think it's profitable to discuss the nature of pain with you, Rob."

"Is it profitable to discuss whether you're real or not?"

He almost sighs. "Bob," he says, "I don't think it's profitable to discuss the nature of reality with you, either. I know I'm a machine. You know I'm a machine. What is the purpose in our being here? Are we here to help me?"

"I sometimes wonder," I say, sulking.

"I don't think you actually wonder about that. I think you know that you are here to help *you,* and the way to do it is by trying to make something happen inside *you.* What I do with the information may be interesting to your curiosity, and it may also provide you with an excuse to spend these sessions on intellectual conversation instead of therapy—"

"Touché, Sigfrid," I interrupt.

"Yes. But it is what you do with it that makes the difference in how you feel, and whether you function somewhat better or somewhat worse in situations that are important to you. Please concern yourself with the inside of your own head, Bob, not mine."

I say admiringly, "You sure are one fucking intelligent machine, Sigfrid."

He says, "I have the impression that what you're

actually saying there is, 'I hate your fucking guts, Sigfrid.' "

I have never heard him say anything like that before, and it takes me aback, until I remember that as a matter of fact I have said exactly that to him, not once but quite a few times. And that it's true.

I do hate his guts.

He is trying to help me, and I hate him for it very much. I think about sweet, sexy S. Ya. and how willing she is to do anything I ask her, pretty nearly. I want, a lot, to make Sigfrid *hurt*.

12

I came back to my room one morning and found the P-phone whining faintly, like a distant, angry mosquito. I punched the message code and found that the assistant personnel director required my presence in her office at ten hundred hours that morning. Well, it was later than that already. I had formed the habit of spending a lot of time, and most nights, with Klara. Her pad was a lot more comfortable than mine. So I didn't get the message until nearly eleven, and my tardiness in getting to the Corporation personnel offices didn't help the assistant director's mood.

She was a very fat woman named Emma Fother. She brushed off my excuses and accused, "You graduated your courses seventeen days ago. You haven't done a thing since."

"I'm waiting for the right mission," I said.

MISSION REPORT

Vessel 3-31, Voyage 08D27. Crew C. Pitrin, N. Ginza, J. Krabbe.

Transit time out 19 days 4 hours. Position uncertain, vicinity (±2 l.y.) Zeta Tauri.

Summary. "Emerged in transpolar orbit planet .88 Earth radius at .4 A.U. Planet possessed 3 detected small satellites. Six other planets inferred by computer logic. Primary K7.

"Landing made. This planet has evidently gone through a warming period. There are no ice caps, and the present shorelines do not appear very old. No detected signs of habitation. No intelligent life.

"Finescreen scanning located what appeared to be a Heechee rendezvous station in our orbit. We approached it. It was intact. In forcing an entrance it exploded and N. Ginza was killed. Our vessel was damaged and we returned, J. Krabbe dying en route. No artifacts were secured. Biotic samples from planet destroyed in damage to vessel."

"How long are you going to wait? Your per capita's paid up for three more days, then what?"

"Well," I said, almost truthfully, "I was going to come in to see you about that today anyway. I'd like a job here on Gateway."

"Pshaw." (I'd never heard anyone say that before, but that's how it sounded.) "Is that why you came to Gateway, to clean sewers?"

I was pretty sure that was a bluff, because there weren't that many sewers; there wasn't enough gravity flow to support them. "The right mission could come along any day."

"Oh, sure, Bob. You know, people like you worry me. Do you have any idea how *important* our work here is?"

"Well, I think so——"

"There's a whole universe out there for us to find and bring home! Gateway's the only way we can reach it. A person like you, who grew up on the plankton farms——"

"Actually it was the Wyoming food mines."

"Whatever! You know how desperately the human race needs what we can give them. New technology. New power sources. Food! New worlds to live in." She shook her head and punched through the sorter on her desk, looking both angry and worried. I supposed that she was check-rated on how many of us idlers and parasites she managed to get to go out, the way we were supposed to, which accounted for her hostility—assuming you could account for her desire to stay on Gateway in the first place. She abandoned the sorter and got up to open a file against the wall. "Suppose I do find you a job," she said over her shoulder. "The only skill you have that's any use here is prospecting, and you're not using that."

"I'll take any—almost anything," I said.

She looked at me quizzically and then returned to her desk. She was astonishingly graceful, considering she had to mass a hundred kilos. Maybe a fat woman's fantasy of not sagging accounted for her desire to hold this job and stay on Gateway. "You'll

108

be doing the lowest kind of unskilled labor," she warned. "We don't pay much for that. One-eighty a day."

"I'll take it!"

"Your per capita has to come out of it. Take that away and maybe twenty dollars a day for toke money, and what do you have left?"

"I could always do odd jobs if I needed more."

She sighed. "You're just postponing the day, Bob. I don't know. Mr. Hsien, the director, keeps a very close watch on job applications. I'll find it very hard to justify hiring you. And what are you going to do if you get sick and can't work? Who'll pay your tax?"

"I'll go back, I guess."

"And waste all your training?" She shook her head. "You disgust me, Bob."

But she punched me out a work ticket that instructed me to report to the crew chief on Level Grand, Sector North, for assignment in plant maintenance.

I didn't like that interview with Emma Fother, but I had been warned I wouldn't. When I talked it over with Klara that evening, she told me actually I'd got off light.

"You're lucky you drew Emma. Old Hsien sometimes keeps people hanging until their tax money's all gone."

"Then what?" I got up and sat on the edge of her cot, feeling for my footgloves. "Out the airlock?"

"Don't make fun, it could conceivably come to that. Hsien's an old Mao type, very hard on social wastrels."

"You're a fine one to talk!"

She grinned, rolled over, and rubbed her nose against my back. "The difference between you and me, Bob," she said, "is that I have a couple of bucks stashed away from my first mission. It didn't pay big, but it paid somewhat. Also I've been out, and they need people like me for teaching people like you."

I leaned back against her hip, half turned and put my hand on her, more reminiscently than aggressively.

There were certain subjects we didn't talk much about, but— "Klara?"

"Uh?"

"What's it like, on a mission?"

She rubbed her chin against my forearm for a moment, looking at the holoview of Venus against the wall. ". . . Scary," she said.

I waited, but she didn't say any more about it, and that much I already knew. I was scared right there on Gateway. I didn't have to launch myself on the Heechee Mystery Bus Trip to know what being scared was like, I could feel it already.

"You don't really have a choice, dear Bob," she said, almost tenderly, for her.

I felt a sudden rush of anger. "No, I don't! You've exactly described my whole life, Klara. I've never had a choice—except once, when I won the lottery and decided to come here. And I'm not sure I made the right decision then."

She yawned, and rubbed against my arm for a moment. "If we're through with sex," she decided, "I want something to eat before I go to sleep. Come on up to the Blue Hell with me and I'll treat."

Plant Maintenance was, actually, the maintenance of plants: specifically, the ivy plants that help keep Gateway livable. I reported for duty and, surprise—in fact, nice surprise—my crew boss turned out to be my legless neighbor, Shikitei Bakin.

He greeted me with what seemed like real pleasure. "How nice of you to join us, Robinette," he said. "I expected you would ship out at once."

"I will, Shicky, pretty soon. When I see the right launch listed on the board, I'll know it."

"Of course." He left it at that, and introduced me to the other plant maintainers. I didn't get them straight, except that the girl had had some sort of connection with Professor Hegramet, the hotshot Heecheeologist back home, and the two men had each had a couple of missions already. I didn't really need to get them straight. We all understood the essential fact about each other without discussion. None of us was quite ready to put our names on the launch roster.

I wasn't even quite ready to let myself think out why.

Plant Maintenance would have been a good place for thought, though. Shicky put me to work right away, fastening brackets to the Heechee-metal walls with tacky-gunk. That was some kind of specially designed adhesive. It would hold to both the Heechee metal and the ribbed foil of plant boxes, and it did not contain any solvent that would evaporate and contaminate the air. It was supposed to be very expensive. If you got it on you, you just learned to live with it, at least until the skin it was on died and flaked off. If you tried to get it off any other way, you drew blood.

When the day's quota of brackets were up, we all trooped down to the sewage plant, where we picked up boxes filled with sludge and covered with cellulose film. We settled them onto the brackets, twisted the self-locking nuts to hold them in place, and fitted them with watering tanks. The boxes probably would have weighed a hundred kilos each on Earth, but on Gateway that simply wasn't a consideration; even the foil they were made of was enough to support them rigidly against the brackets. Then, when we were all done, Shicky himself filled the trays with seedlings, while we went on to the next batch of brackets. It was funny to watch him. He carried trays of the infant ivy plants on straps around his neck, like a cigarette girl's stock. He held himself at tray level with one hand, and poked seedlings through the film into the sludge with the other.

It was a low-pressure job, it served a useful function (I guess) and it passed the time. Shicky didn't make us work any too hard. He had set a quota in his mind for a day's work. As long as we got sixty brackets installed and filled he didn't care if we goofed off, provided we were inconspicuous about it. Klara would come by to pass the time of day now and then, sometimes with the little girl, and we had plenty of other visitors. And when times were slack and there wasn't anybody interesting to talk to, one at a time we could wander off for an hour or so. I explored a lot of Gateway I hadn't seen before, and each day decision was postponed.

We all talked about going out. Almost every day we could hear the thud and vibration as some lander cut itself loose from its dock, pushing the whole ship out to where the Heechee main drive could go into operation. Almost as often we felt the different kind of smaller, quicker shock when some ship returned. In the evenings we went to someone's parties. My whole class was gone by now, almost. Sheri had shipped out on a Five—I didn't see her to ask her why she changed her plans and wasn't sure I really wanted to know; the ship she went on had an otherwise all-male crew. They were German-speaking, but I guess Sheri figured she could get by pretty well without talking much. The last one was Willa Forehand. Klara and I went to Willa's farewell party and then down to the docks to watch her launch the next morning. I was supposed to be working, but I didn't think Shicky would mind. Unfortunately, Mr. Hsien was there, too, and I could see that he recognized me.

"Oh, shit," I said to Klara.

She giggled and took my hand, and we ducked out of the launch area. We strolled away until we came to an up-shaft and lifted to the next level. We sat down on the edge of Lake Superior. "Bob, old stud," she said, "I doubt he'll fire you for screwing off one time. Chew you out, probably."

I shrugged and tossed a chip of filter-pebble into the upcurving lake, which stretched a good two hundred meters up and around the shell of Gateway in front of us. I was feeling tacky, and wondering whether I was reaching the point when the bad vibes about risking nasty death in space were being overtaken by the bad vibes about cowering on Gateway. It's a funny thing about fear. I didn't feel it. I knew that the only reason I was staying on was that I was

Classifieds.

MAID, COOK or companion. Head tax +
$10/da. Phyllis, 88-423.

GOURMET FOODS, hard-to-get Earth imports. Take advantage my Grouped Mass
Guarantee unique co-op order service for any
item you want. Save expensive single-item
shipping costs! Sears, Bradlee, G.U.M. cata-
logues available. 87-747.

FRESH FISH from Australia, M., good-
looking, seeks int. French F. companionship.
65-182.

afraid, but it didn't feel as though I were afraid, only reasonably prudent.

"I think," I said, watching myself going into the sentence without being sure how it was going to come out, "that I'm going to do it. Want to come along?"

Klara sat up and shook herself. She took a moment before she said, "Maybe. What've you got in mind?"

I had nothing in mind. I was only a spectator, watching myself talk myself into something that made my toes curl. But I said, as though I had planned it out for days, "I think it might be a good idea to take a rerun."

"No deal!" She looked almost angry. "If I go, I go where the real money is."

That was also where the real danger was, of course. Although even reruns have turned out bad often enough.

The thing about reruns is that you start out with the knowledge that somebody has already flown that trip and made it back, and, not only that, made a find that's worth following up on. Some of them are pretty rich. There's Peggy's World, where the heater coils and the fur come from. There's Eta Carina Seven, which is probably full of good stuff if you could only get at it. The trouble is, it has had an ice age since the Heechees were last on it. The storms are terrible. Out of five landers, one returned with a full crew, undamaged. One didn't return at all.

Generally speaking, Gateway doesn't particularly want you to do a rerun. They will make a cash offer instead of a percentage where the pickings are fairly easy, as on Peggy. What they pay for is not so much trade goods as maps. So you go out there and you spend your time making orbital runs, trying to find the geological anomalies that indicate Heechee digs may be present. You may not land at all. The pay is worth having, but not lavish. You'd have to make at least twenty runs to build up a lifetime stake, if you take the Corporation's one-pay deal. And if you decide to go on your own, prospecting, you have to pay a share of your profits to the discovery crew, and a cut on

114

From Shikitei Bakin to Aritsune,
His Honored Grandson

I am overwhelmed with joy to learn
of the birth of your first child. Do
not despair. The next will probably
be a boy.

I apologize humbly for my failure
to write sooner, but there is little
to tell. I do my work and attempt to
create beauty where I can. Perhaps
some day I will go out again. It is
not easy without legs.

To be sure, Aritsune, I could buy
new legs. There was a close tissue
match just a few months ago. But the
cost! I might almost as well buy
Full Medical. You are a loyal grandson to urge me to use my capital for
this, but I must decide. I am send-
ing you a half of my capital now to
assist with my great-granddaughter's
expenses. If I die here, you will
receive all of it, for you and for
the others who will be born to you
and your good wife before long. This
is what I want. Do not resist me.

My deepest love to all three of
you. If you can, send me a holo of
the cherry blossoms—they are in
bloom soon, are they not? One loses
sense of Home time here!

Lovingly,

Your Grandfather

what's left of your share to the Corporation. You wind up with a fraction of what you might get on a virgin find, even if you don't have a colony already established on the scene to contend with.

Or you can take a shot at the bonuses: a hundred million dollars if you find an alien civilization, fifty million for the first crew to locate a Heechee ship bigger than a Five, a million bucks to locate a habitable planet.

Seems funny that they would only pay a lousy million for a whole new planet? But the trouble is, once you've found it, what do you do with it? You can't export a lot of surplus population when you can only move them four at a time. That, plus the pilot, is all you can get into the largest ship in Gateway. (And if you don't have a pilot, you don't get the ship back.) So the Corporation has underwritten a few little colonies, one's very healthy on Peggy and the others are spindly. But that does not solve the problem of twenty-five billion human beings, most of them underfed.

You'll never get that kind of bonus on a rerun. Maybe you can't get some of those bonuses at all; maybe the things they're for don't exist.

It is strange that no one has ever found a trace of another intelligent creature. But in eighteen years, upwards of two thousand flights, no one has. There are about a dozen habitable planets, plus another hundred or so that people *could* live on if they absolutely had to, as we have to on Mars and on, or rather in, Venus. There are a few traces of past civilizations, neither Heechee nor human. And there are the souvenirs of the Heechee themselves. At that, there's more in the warrens of Venus than we've found almost anywhere else in the Galaxy, so far. Even Gateway was swept almost clean before they abandoned it.

Damn Heechee, why did they have to be so neat?

So we gave up on the rerun deals because there wasn't enough money in them, and put the special finders' bonuses out of our heads, because there's just no way of planning to look for them.

And finally we just stopped talking, and looked at each other, and then we didn't even look at each other.

No matter what we said, we weren't going. We didn't have the nerve. Klara's had run out on her last trip, and I guess I hadn't ever had it.

"Well," said Klara, getting up and stretching, "I guess I'll go up and win a few bucks at the casino. Want to watch?"

I shook my head. "Guess I'd better get back to my job. If I still have one."

So we kissed good-bye at the upshaft, and when we came to my level I reached up and patted her ankle and jumped off. I was not in a very good mood. We had spent so much effort trying to reassure ourselves that there weren't any launches that offered a promise of reward worth the risks that I almost believed it.

Of course, we hadn't even mentioned the other kind of rewards: the danger bonuses.

You have to be pretty frayed to go for them. Like, the Corporation will sometimes put up half a million or so incentive bonus for a crew to take the same course as some previous crew tried . . . and didn't come back from. Their reasoning is that maybe something went wrong with the ship, ran out of gas or something, and a second ship might even rescue the crew from the first one. (Fat chance!) More likely, of course, whatever killed the first crew would still be there, and ready to kill you.

Then there was a time when you could sign up for a million, later they raised it to five million, if you would try changing the course settings after launch.

The reason they raised the bonus to five million was that crews stopped volunteering when none of them, not one of them, ever came back. Then they cut it out, because they were losing too many ships, and finally they made it a flat no-no. Every once in a while they come up with a bastard control panel, a snappy new computer that's supposed to work symbiotically with the Heechee board. Those ships aren't good gambling bets, either. There's a reason for the safety lock on the Heechee board. You can't change destination while it's on. Maybe you can't change destination at all, without destroying the ship.

I saw five people try for a ten-million-dollar danger bonus once. Some Corporation genius from the permanent-party was worrying about how to transport more than five people, or the equivalent in cargo, at once. We didn't know how to build a Heechee ship, and we'd never found a really big one. So he figured that maybe we could end-run around that obstacle by using a Five as a sort of tractor.

So they built a sort of space barge out of Heechee metal. They loaded it with scraps of junk, and ran a Five out there on lander power. That's just hydrogen and oxygen, and it's easy enough to pump that back in. Then they tied the Five to the barge with monofilament Heechee metal cables.

We watched the whole thing from Gateway on PV. We saw the cables take up slack as the Five put a strain on them with its lander jets. Craziest-looking thing you ever saw.

Then they must have activated the long-range start-teat.

All we saw on the PV was that the barge sort of twitched, and the Five simply disappeared from sight.

It never came back. The stop-motion tapes showed at least the first little bit of what happened. The cable truss had sliced that ship into segments like a hard-boiled egg. The people in it never knew what hit them. The Corporation still has that ten million; nobody wants to try for it anymore.

I got a politely reproachful lecture from Shicky, and a really ugly, but brief, P-phone call from Mr. Hsien, but that was all. After a day or two Shicky began letting us take time off again.

I spent most of it with Klara. A lot of times we'd arrange to meet in her pad, or once in a while mine, for an hour in bed. We were sleeping together almost

MISSION REPORT

Vessel 5-2, Voyage 08D33. Crew
L. Konieczny, E. Konieczny, F. Ito,
F. Lounsbury, A. Akaga.

Transit time out 27 days 16 hours.
Primary not identified but probabil-
ity high as star in cluster 47
Tucanae.

SUMMARY. "Emerged in free-fall.
No planet nearby. Primary A6, very
bright and hot, distance approximately 3.3 A.U.

"By masking the primary star we
obtained a glorious view of what
seemed to be two or three hundred
nearby very bright stars, apparent
magnitude ranging from 2 to -7. However, no artifacts, signals, planets
or landable asteroids were detected.
We could remain on station only
three hours because of intense radiation from the A6 star. Larry and
Evelyn Konieczny were seriously ill
on the return trip, apparently due
to radiation exposure, but recovered. No artifacts or samples
secured."

every night; you'd think we would have had enough of that. We didn't. After a while I wasn't sure what we were copulating for, the fun of it or the distraction it gave from the contemplation of our own self-images. I would lie there and look at Klara, who always turned over, snuggled down on her stomach, and closed her eyes after sex, even when we were going to get up two minutes later. I would think how well I knew every fold and surface of her body. I would smell that sweet, sexy smell of her and wish—oh, wish! Just wish, for things I couldn't spell out: for an apartment under the Big Bubble with Klara, for an airbody and a cell in a Venusian tunnel with Klara, even for a life in the food mines with Klara. I guess it was love. But then I'd still be looking at her, and I would feel the inside of my eyes change the picture I was seeing, and what I would see would be the female equivalent of myself: a coward, given the greatest chance a human could have, and scared to take advantage of it.

When we weren't in bed we would wander around Gateway together. It wasn't like dating. We didn't go much to the Blue Hell or the holofilm halls, or even eat out. Klara did. I couldn't afford it, so I took most of my meals from the Corporation's refectories, included in the price of my per-capita per diem. Klara was not unwilling to pick up the check for both of us, but she wasn't exactly anxious to do it, either—she was gambling pretty heavily, and not winning much. There were groups to be involved with—card parties, or just parties; folk dance groups, music-listening groups, discussion groups. They were free, and sometimes interesting. Or we just explored.

Several times we went to the museum. I didn't really like it that much. It seemed—well, reproachful.

The first time we went there was right after I got off work, the day Willa Forehand shipped out. Usually the museum was full of visitors, like crew members on pass from the cruisers, or ship's crews from the commercial runs, or tourists. This time, for some reason, there were only a couple of people there, and we had a chance to look at everything. Prayer fans by the hundreds, those filmy, little crystalline things that were the commonest Heechee artifact; no one knew what they were for, except that they were sort of pretty, but the Heechee had left them all over the place. There was the original anisokinetic punch, that had earned a lucky prospector something like twenty million dollars in royalties already. A thing you could put in your pocket. Furs. Plants in formalin. The original piezophone, that had earned three crews enough to make every one of them awfully rich.

The most easily swiped things, like the prayer fans and the blood diamonds and the fire pearls, were kept behind tough, breakproof glass. I think they were even wired to burglar alarms. That was surprising, on Gateway. There isn't any law there, except what the Corporation imposes. There are the Corporation's equivalent of police, and there are rules—you're not supposed to steal or commit murder—but there aren't any courts. If you break a rule all that happens is that the Corporation security force picks you up and takes you out to one of the orbiting cruisers. Your own, if there is one from wherever you came. Any one, if not. But if they won't take you, or if you don't want to go on your own nation's ship and can persuade some other ship to take you, Gateway doesn't care. On the cruisers, you'll get a trial. Since you're known to be guilty to start with, you have three choices. One is to pay your way back home. The second is to sign on as crew if they'll have you. The third is to go out the lock without a suit. So you see that, although there isn't much law on Gateway, there isn't much crime, either.

But, of course, the reason for locking up the precious stuff in the museum was that transients might be tempted to lift a souvenir or two.

So Klara and I would muse over the treasures someone had found . . . and somehow not discuss with each other the fact that we were supposed to go out and find some more.

It was not just the exhibits. They were fascinating;

121

they were things that Heechee hands (tentacles? claws?) had made and touched, and they came from unimaginable places incredibly far away. But the constantly flickering tube displays held me even more strongly. Summaries of every mission ever launched displayed one after another. A constant total of missions versus returns; of royalties paid to lucky prospectors; the roster of the unlucky ones, name after name in a slow crawl along one whole wall of the room, over the display cases. The totals told the story: 2355 launches (the number changed to 2356, then 2357 while we were there; we felt the shudder of the two launches), 841 successful returns.

Standing in front of that particular display, Klara and I didn't look at each other, but I felt her hand squeeze mine.

That was defining "successful" very loosely. It meant that the ship had come back. It didn't say anything about how many of the crew were alive and well.

We left the museum after that, and didn't speak much on the way to the upshaft.

The thing in my mind was that what Emma Fother had said to me was true: the human race needed what we prospectors could give them. Needed it a lot. There were hungry people, and Heechee technology probably could make all their lives a lot more tolerable, if prospectors went out and brought samples of it back.

Even if it cost a few lives.

Even if the lives included Klara's and mine. Did I, I asked myself, want my son—if I ever had a son—to spend his childhood the way I had spent mine?

We dropped off the up-cable at Level Babe and heard voices. I didn't pay attention to them. I was coming to a resolution in my mind. "Klara," I said, "listen. Let's—"

But Klara was looking past my shoulder. "For Christ's sake!" she said. "Look who's here!"

And I turned, and there was Shicky fluttering in the air, talking to a girl, and I saw with astonishment

122

that the girl was Willa Forehand. She greeted us, looking both embarrassed and amused.

"What's going on?" I demanded. "Didn't you just ship out—like maybe eight hours ago?"

"Ten," she said.

"Did something go wrong with the ship, so you had to come back?" Klara guessed.

Willa smiled ruefully. "Not a thing. I've been there and back. Shortest trip on record so far: I went to the Moon."

"*Earth's* moon?"

"That's the one." She seemed to be controlling herself, to keep from laughter. Or tears.

Shicky said consolingly, "They'll surely give you a bonus, Willa. There was one that went to Ganymede once, and the Corporation divvied up half a million dollars among them."

She shook her head. "Even I know better than that, Shicky, dear. Oh, they'll award us something. But it won't be enough to make a difference. We need more than that." That was the unusual, and somewhat surprising, thing about the Forehands: it was always "we." They were clearly a very closely knit family, even if they didn't like to discuss that fact with outsiders.

I touched her, a pat between affection and compassion. "What are you going to do?"

She looked at me with surprise. "Why, I've already signed up for another launch, day after tomorrow."

"Well!" said Klara. "We've got to have two parties at once for you! We'd better get busy. . . ." And hours later, just before we went to sleep that night, she said to me, "Wasn't there something you wanted to say to me before we saw Willa?"

"I forget," I said sleepily. I hadn't forgotten. I knew what it was. But I didn't want to say it anymore.

There were days when I worked myself up almost to that point of asking Klara to ship out with me again. And there were days when a ship came in with a couple of starved, dehydrated survivors, or with no

Classifieds.

ORGANS FOR sale or trade. Any paired organs, best offer. Need posterior coronal heart sections, L. auricle, L. & R. ventricle, and associated parts. Phone 88-703 for tissue match.

HNEFATAFL PLAYERS, Swedes or Muscovites. Grand Gateway Tournament. Will teach. 88-122.

PENPAL FROM Toronto would like to hear you tell what it's like out there. Address Tony, 955 Bay, TorOntCan M5S 2A3.

I NEED to cry. I will help you find your own pain. Ph 88-622.

survivors, or when at the routine time a batch of last year's launches were posted as nonreturns. On those days I worked myself up almost to the point of quitting Gateway completely.

Most days we simply spent deferring decision. It wasn't all that hard. It was a pretty pleasant way to live, exploring Gateway and each other. Klara took on a maid, a stocky, fair young woman from the food mines of Carmarthen named Hywa. Except that the feedstock for the Welsh single-cell protein factories was coal instead of oil shale, her world had been almost exactly like mine. Her way out of it had not been a lottery ticket but two years as crew on a commercial spaceship. She couldn't even go back home. She had jumped ship on Gateway, forfeiting her bond of money she couldn't pay. And she couldn't prospect, either, because her one launch had left her with a heart arhythmia that sometimes looked like it was getting better and sometimes put her in Terminal Hospital for a week at a time. Hywa's job was partly to cook and clean for Klara and me, partly to baby-sit the little girl, Kathy Francis, when her father was on duty and Klara didn't want to be bothered. Klara had been losing pretty heavily at the casino, so she really couldn't afford Hywa, but then she couldn't afford me, either.

What made it easy to turn off our insights was that we pretended to each other, and sometimes to ourselves, that what we were doing was preparing ourselves, really well, for the day when the Right trip came along.

It wasn't hard to do that. A lot of real prospectors did the same thing, between trips. There was a group that called itself the Heechee Seekers, which met on Wednesday nights; it had been started by a prospector named Sam Kahane, kept up by others while he was off on a trip that hadn't worked out, and now had Sam back in it between trips, while he was waiting for the other two members of his crew to get back in shape for the next one. (Among other things, they had come back with scurvy, due to a malfunction in the food freezer.) Sam and his friends were gay and apparently set in a permanent three-way relationship, but that didn't affect his interest in Heechee lore. He had secured tapes of all the lectures of several courses on exostudies from East Texas Reserve, where Professor Hegramet had made himself the world's foremost authority on Heechee research. I learned a lot I hadn't known, although the central fact, that there were far more questions than answers about the Heechee, was pretty well known to everybody.

And we got into physical-fitness groups, where we practiced muscle-toning exercises that you could do without moving any limb more than a few inches, and massage for fun and profit. It was probably profitable, but it was even more fun, particularly sexually. Klara and I learned to do some astonishing things with each other's bodies. We took a cooking course (you can do a lot with standard rations, if you add a selection of spices and herbs). We acquired a selection of language tapes, in the event we shipped out with non-English-speakers, and practiced taxi-driver Italian and Greek on each other. We even joined an astronomy group. They had access to Gateway's telescopes, and we spent a fair amount of time looking at Earth and Venus from outside the plane of the ecliptic. Francy Hereira was in that group when he could get time off from the ship. Klara liked him, and so did I, and we formed the habit of having a drink in our rooms— well, Klara's rooms, but I was spending a lot of time in them—with him after the group. Francy was deeply, almost sensually, interested in what was Out There. He knew all about quasars and black holes and Seyfert galaxies, not to mention things like double stars and novae. We often speculated what it might be like to come out of a mission into the wavefront of a supernova. It could happen. The Heechee were known to have had an interest in observing astrophysical events firsthand. Some of their courses were undoubtedly programmed to bring crews to the vicinity of interesting events, and a pre-supernova was certainly an interesting event. Only now it was a long lot later, and the supernova might not be "pre" anymore.

"I wonder," said Klara, smiling to show that it was only an abstract point she was putting to us, "if that might not be what happened to some of the nonreturn missions."

"It is an absolute statistical certainty," said Francy, smiling back to show that he agreed to the rules of the game. He had been practicing his English, which was pretty good to start with, and now he was almost accent-free. He also possessed German, Russian, and fair amounts of the other romance languages to go with his Portuguese, as we had discovered when we tried some of our language-tape conversation on each other and found he understood us better than we understood ourselves. "Nevertheless, people go."

Klara and I were silent for a moment, and then she laughed. "Some do," she said.

I cut in quickly, "It sounds as if you want to go yourself, Francy."

"Have you ever doubted it?"

"Well, yes, actually I have. I mean, you're in the Brazilian Navy. You can't just take off, can you?"

He corrected me: "I can take off at any time. I simply cannot go back to Brazil after that."

"And it's worth that to you?"

"It's worth anything," he told me.

"Even—" I pressed, "if there's the risk of not coming back, or of getting messed up like the return today?" That had been a Five that had landed on a planet with some sort of plant life like poison ivy. It had been a bad one, we had heard.

"Yes, of course," he said.

Klara was getting restless. "I think," she said, "I want to go to sleep now."

There was some extra message in the tone of her voice. I looked at her and said, "I'll walk you back to your room."

"That's not necessary, Bob."

"I'll do it anyhow," I said, ignoring the message. "Good night, Francy. See you next week."

Klara was already halfway to the downshaft, and

I had to hurry to catch up to her. I caught the cable and called down to her, "If you really want me to, I'll go back to my own place."

She didn't look up, but she didn't say that was what she wanted, either, so I got off at her level and followed her to her rooms. Kathy was sound asleep in the outer room, Hywa drowsing over a holodisk in our bedroom. Klara sent the maid home and went in to make sure the child was comfortable. I sat on the edge of the bed, waiting for her.

"Maybe I'm premenstrual," Klara said when she came back. "I'm sorry. I just feel edgy."

"I'll go if you want me to."

"Jesus, Bob, quit saying that!" Then she sat down next to me and leaned against me so that I would put my arm around her. "Kathy's so sweet," she said after a moment, almost wistfully.

"You'd like to have one of your own, wouldn't you?"

"I *will* have one of my own." She leaned back, pulling me with her. "I wish I knew when, that's all. I need a lot more money than I have to give a kid a decent life. And I'm not getting any younger."

We lay there for a moment, and then I said into her hair, "That's what I want, too, Klara."

She sighed. "Do you think I don't know that?" Then she tensed and sat up. "Who's that?"

Somebody was scrabbling at the door. It wasn't locked; we never did that. But nobody ever came in without being invited, either, and this time someone did.

"Sterling!" Klara said, surprised. She remembered her manners: "Bob, this is Sterling Francis, Kathy's father. Bob Broadhead."

"Hello," he said. He was much older than I'd thought that little girl's father would be, at least fifty, and looking very much older and more weary than seemed natural. "Klara," he said, "I'm taking Kathy back home on the next ship. I think I'll take her tonight, if you don't mind. I don't want her to hear from somebody else."

A NOTE ON THE HEECHEE RUMP

Professor Hegramet. We have no idea what the Heechee looked like except for inferences. Probably they were bipeds. Their tools fit human hands tolerably well, so probably they had hands. Or something like them. They seem to have seen pretty much the same spectrum as we do. They must have been smaller than us—say, a hundred and fifty centimeters, or less. And they had funny-looking rumps.

Question. What do you mean, funny-looking rumps?

Professor Hegramet. Well, did you ever look at the pilot's seat in a Heechee ship? It's two flat pieces of metal joined in a V shape. You couldn't sit in it for ten minutes without pinching your bottom off. So what we have to do, we stretch a webbing seat across them. But that's a human addition. The Heechee didn't have anything like that.

So their bodies must have looked more or less like a wasp's, with this big abdomen hanging down, actually extending below the hips, between the legs.

Question. Do you mean they might have had stingers like wasps?

Professor Hegramet. Stingers. No. I don't think so. But maybe. Or maybe they had hell's own set of sex organs.

Klara reached out for my hand without looking at me. "Hear what?"

"About her mother." Francis rubbed his eyes, then said, "Oh, didn't you know? Jan's dead. Her ship came back a few hours ago. All four of them in the lander got into some kind of fungus; they swelled up and died. I saw her body. She looks——" He stopped. "The one I'm really sorry for," he said, "is Annalee. She stayed in orbit while the others went down, and she brought Jan's body back. I guess she was kind of crazy. Why bother? It was too late to matter to Jan. . . . Well, anyway. She could only bring two of them, that was all the room in the freezer, and of course her rations——" He stopped again, and this time he didn't seem able to talk anymore.

So I sat on the edge of the bed while Klara helped him wake the child and bundle her up to take her back to his own rooms. While they were out, I dialed a couple of displays on the PV, and studied them very carefully. By the time Klara came back I had turned off the PV and was sitting cross-legged on the bed, thinking hard.

"Christ," she said glumly. "If this night isn't a bummer." She sat down at the far corner of the bed. "I'm not sleepy after all," she said. "Maybe I'll go up and win a few bucks at the roulette table."

"Let's not," I said. I'd sat next to her for three hours the night before, while she first won ten thousand dollars and then lost twenty. "I have a better idea. Let's ship out."

She turned full around to look at me, so quickly that she floated up off the bed for a moment. "What?"

"Let's ship out."

She closed her eyes for a moment and, without opening them, said, "When?"

"Launch 29-40. It's a Five, and there's a good crew: Sam Kahane and his buddies. They're all recovered now, and they need two more to fill the ship."

She stroked her eyelids with her fingertips, then opened them and looked at me. "Well, Bob," she said, "you do have interesting suggestions." There were

130

shades over the Heechee-metal walls to cut down the light for sleeping, and I had drawn them; but even in the filtered dimness I could see how she looked. Frightened. Still, what she said was: "They're not bad guys. How do you get along with gays?"

"I leave them alone, they leave me alone. Especially if I've got you."

"Um," she said, and then she crawled over to me, wrapped her arms around me, pulled me down and buried her head in my neck. "Why not?" she said, so softly that I was not at first sure I had heard her.

When I was sure, the fear hit me. There had always been the chance she would say no. I would have been off the hook. I could feel myself shaking, but I managed to say, "Then we'll file for it in the morning?"

She shook her head. "No," she said, her voice muffled. I could feel her trembling as much as I was. "Get on the phone, Bob. We'll file for it now. Before we change our minds."

The next day I quit my job, packed my belongings into the suitcases I had brought them in, and turned them over for safekeeping to Shicky, who looked wistful. Klara quit the school and fired her maid—who looked seriously worried—but didn't bother about packing. She had quite a lot of money left, Klara did. She prepaid the rent on both her rooms and left everything just the way it was.

We had a farewell party, of course. We went through it without my remembering a single person who was there.

And then, all of a sudden, we were squeezing into the lander, climbing down into the capsule while Sam Kahane methodically checked the settings. We locked ourselves into our cocoons. We started the automatic sequencers.

And then there was a lurch, and a falling, floating sensation before the thrusters cut in, and we were on our way.

13

"Good morning, Bob," says Sigfrid, and I stop in the door of the room, suddenly and subliminally worried.

"What's the matter?"

"There's nothing the matter, Rob. Come in."

"You've changed things around," I say accusingly.

"That's right, Robbie. Do you like the way the room looks?"

I study it. The throw pillows are gone from the floor. The nonobjective paintings are off the wall. Now he's got a series of holopictures of space scenes, and mountains and seas. The funniest thing of all is Sigfrid himself: he is speaking to me out of a dummy that's sitting back in a corner of the room, holding a pencil in its hands, looking up at me from behind dark glasses.

"You've turned out very camp," I say. "What's the reason for all this?"

His voice sounds as though he were smiling benevolently, although there is no change in the expression on the face of the dummy. "I just thought you'd enjoy a change, Rob."

I take a few steps into the room and stop again. "You took the mat away!"

"Don't need it, Bob. As you see, there's a new couch. That's very traditional, isn't it?"

"Um."

He coaxes, "Why don't you just lie down on it? See how it feels."

"Um." But I stretch out on it cautiously. How it feels is strange; and I don't like it, probably because this particular room represents something serious to me and changing it around makes me nervous. "The mat had straps," I complain.

"So does the couch, Bob. You can pull them out of the sides. Just feel around . . . there. Isn't that better?"

"No, it isn't."

"I think," he says softly, "that you should let me decide whether for therapeutic reasons some sort of change is in order, Rob."

I sit up. "And that's another thing, Sigfrid! Make up your fucking mind what you're going to call me. My name isn't Rob, or Robbie, or Bob. It's Robinette."

"I know that, Robbie——"

"You're doing it again!"

A pause, then, silkily, "I think you should allow me the choice of the form of address I prefer, Robbie."

"Um." I have an endless supply of those noncommittal nonwords. In fact, I would like to conduct the whole session without revealing any more than that. What I want is for *Sigfrid* to reveal. I want to know why he calls me by different names at different times. I want to know what he finds significant in what I say. I want to know what he really thinks of me . . .

133

if a clanking piece of tin and plastic can think, I mean.

Of course, what I know and Sigfrid doesn't is that my good friend S. Ya. has practically promised to let me play a little joke on him. I am looking forward to that a lot.

"Is there anything you'd like to tell me, Rob?"

"No."

He waits. I am feeling somewhat hostile and non-communicative. I think part of it is because I am so much looking forward to the time when I can play a little trick on Sigfrid, but the other part is because he has changed around the auditing room. That's the kind of thing they used to do to me when I had my psychotic episode in Wyoming. Sometimes I'd come in for a session and they'd have a hologram of my mother, for Christ's sake. It looked exactly like her, but it didn't smell like her or feel like her; in fact, you couldn't feel it at all, it was only light. Sometimes they'd have me come in there in the dark and something warm and cuddly would take me in its arms and whisper to me. I didn't like that. I was crazy, but I wasn't that crazy.

Sigfrid is still waiting, but I know that he won't wait forever. Pretty soon he's going to start asking me questions, probably about my dreams.

"Have you had any dreams since I last saw you, Bob?"

I yawn. The whole subject is very boring. 'I don't think so. Nothing important, I'm sure."

"I'd like to hear what they were. Even a fragment."

"You're a pest, Sigfrid, do you know that?"

"I'm sorry you feel I'm a pest, Rob."

"Well . . . I don't think I can remember even a fragment."

"Try, please."

"Oh, cripes. Well." I get comfortable on the couch. The only dream I can think of is absolutely trivial, and I know there's nothing in it that relates to anything traumatic or pivotal, but if I told him that he would get angry. So I say obediently, "I was in a car

MISSION REPORT

Vessel 1-8, Voyage 013D6. Crew
F. Ito.

Transit time 41 days 2 hours.
Position not identified. Instrument
recordings damaged.

Transcript of crewman's tape follows: "The planet seems to have a
surface gravity in excess of 2.5,
but I am going to attempt a landing.
Neither visual nor radar scanning
penetrates the clouds of dust and
vapor. It really is not looking
very good, but this is my eleventh
launch. I am setting the automatic
return for 10 days. If I am not back
by then with the lander I think the
capsule will return by itself. I
wish I knew what the spots and
flares on the sun meant."

Crewman was not aboard when ship
returned. No artifacts or samples.
Landing vehicle not secured. Vessel
damaged.

of a long railroad train. There were a number of cars hooked up together, and you could go from one to the other. They were full of people I knew. There was a woman, a sort of motherly type who coughed a lot, and another woman who—well, she looked rather strange. At first I thought she was a man. She was dressed in a sort of utility coverall, so you couldn't tell from that whether she was male or female, and she had very masculine, bushy eyebrows. But I was sure she was a woman."

"Did you talk to either of these women, Bob?"

"Please don't interrupt, Sigfrid, you make me lose my train of thought."

"I'm sorry, Rob."

I go on with the dream: "I left them—no, I didn't talk to them. I went back into the next car. That was the last one on the train. It was coupled to the rest of the train with a sort of—let's see, I don't know how to describe it. It was like one of those expanding gatefold things, made out of metal, you know? And it stretched."

I stop for a moment, mostly out of boredom. I feel like apologizing for having such a dumb, irrelevant dream. "You say the metal connector stretched, Bob?" Sigfrid prompts me.

"That's right, it stretched. So of course the car I was in kept dropping back, farther and farther behind the others. All I could see was the taillight, which was sort of in the shape of her face, looking at me. She—" I lose the thread of what I am saying. I try to get back on the track: "I guess I felt as though it was going to be difficult to get back to her, as if she— I'm sorry, Sigfrid, I don't remember clearly what happened around there. Then I woke up. And," I finish virtuously, "I wrote it all down as soon as I could, just the way you tell me to."

"I appreciate that, Bob," Sigfrid says gravely. He waits for me to go on.

I shift restlessly. "This couch isn't nearly as comfortable as the mat," I complain.

'I'm sorry about that, Bob. You said you recognized them?"

"Who?"

"The two women on the train, that you were getting farther and farther away from."

"Oh. No, I see what you mean. I recognized them in the *dream*. Really I have no idea who they were."

"'Did they look like anyone you knew?"

"Not a bit. I wondered about that myself."

Sigfrid says, after a moment, which I happen to know is his way of giving me a chance to change my mind about an answer he doesn't like, "You mentioned one of the women was a motherly type who coughed—"

"Yes. But I didn't recognize her. I think in a way she did look familiar, but, you know, the way people in a dream do."

He says patiently, "Can you think of any woman you've ever known who was motherly and coughed a lot?"

I laugh out loud at that. "Dear friend Sigfrid! I assure you the women I know are not at all the motherly type! And they are all on at least Major Medical. They're not likely to cough."

"I see. Are you sure, Robbie?"

"Don't be a pain in the ass, Sigfrid," I say, angry because the crappy couch is hard to get comfortable on, and also because I need to go to the bathroom, and this situation looks to be prolonging itself indefinitely.

"I see." And after a moment he picks up on something else, as I know he is going to: he's a pigeon, Sigfrid is, pecking at everything I throw out before him, one piece at a time. "How about the other woman, the one with the bushy eyebrows?"

"What about her?"

"Did you ever know any girl who had bushy eyebrows?"

"Oh, Christ, Sigfrid, I've gone to bed with five hundred girls! Some of them had every kind of eyebrows you ever heard of."

"No particular one?"

"Not that I can think of offhand."

"Not offhand, Bob. Please make an effort to remember."

It is easier to do what he wants than to argue with him about it, so I make the effort. "All right, let's see. Ida Mae? No. Sue-Ann? No. S. Ya? No. Gretchen? No—well, to tell you the truth, Sigfrid, Gretchen was so blond I couldn't really tell you if she had eyebrows at all."

"Those are girls you've known recently, aren't they, Rob? Perhaps someone longer ago?"

"You mean way back?" I reflect deeply as far back as I can go, all the way to the food mines and Sylvia. I laugh out loud. "You know something, Sigfrid? It's funny, but I can hardly remember what Sylvia looked like—oh, wait a minute. No. Now I remember. She used to pluck her eyebrows almost altogether away, and then pencil them in. The reason I know is one time when we were in bed together we drew pictures on each other with her eyebrow pencil."

I can almost hear him sigh. "The cars," he says, pecking at another bright bit. "How would you describe them?"

"Like any railroad train. Long. Narrow. Moving pretty fast through the tunnel."

"Long and narrow, moving through a tunnel, Bob?"

I lose my patience at that. He is *so* fucking transparent! "Come on, Sigfrid! You don't get away with any corny penis symbols with *me*."

"I'm not trying to get away with anything, Bob."

"Well, you're being an asshole about this whole dream, I swear you are. There's nothing in it. The train was just a train. I don't know who the women were. And listen, while we're on the subject, I really *hate* this goddamned couch. For the kind of money my insurance is paying you, you can do a lot better than this!"

He has really got me angry now. He keeps trying to get back to the dream, but I am determined to get a fair shake from him for the insurance company's

138

money, and by the time I leave he has promised to redecorate before my next visit.

As I go out that day I feel pretty pleased with myself. He is really doing me a lot of good. I suppose it is because I am getting the courage to stand up to him, and perhaps all this nonsense has been helpful to me in that way, or in some way, even if it is true that some of his ideas are pretty crazy.

14

I struggled out of my sling to get out of the way of Klara's knee and bumped into Sam Kahane's elbow. "Sorry," he said, not even looking around to see who he was sorry about. His hand was still on the go-teat, although we were ten minutes on our way. He was studying the flickering colors on the Heechee instrument board, and the only time he looked away was when he glanced at the viewscreen overhead.

I sat up, feeling very queasy. It had taken me weeks to get used to Gateway's virtual absence of gravity. The fluctuating G forces in the capsule were something else. They were very light, but they didn't stay the same for more than a minute at a time, and my inner ear was complaining.

I squeezed out of the way into the kitchen area, with one eye on the door to the toilet. Ham Tayeh

140

was still in there. If he didn't get out pretty soon my situation was going to become critical. Klara laughed, reached out from her sling, and put an arm around me. "Poor Bobbie," she said. "And we're just beginning."

I swallowed a pill and recklessly lit a cigarette and concentrated on not throwing up. I don't know how much it was actually motion sickness. A lot of it was fear. There is something very frightening about knowing that there is nothing between you and instant, ugly death except a thin skin of metal made by some peculiar strangers half a million years ago. And about knowing that you're committed to go somewhere over which you no longer have any control, which may turn out to be extremely unpleasant.

I crawled back into my sling, stubbed out the cigarette, closed my eyes, and concentrated on making the time pass.

There was going to be a lot of it to pass. The average trip lasts maybe forty-five days each way. It doesn't matter as much as you might think, how far you are going. Ten light-years or ten thousand: it matters some, but not linearly. They tell me that the ships are continually accelerating and accelerating the *rate* of acceleration the whole time. That delta isn't linear, either, or even exponential, in any way that anybody can figure out. You hit the speed of light very quickly, in less than an hour. Then it seems to take quite a while before you exceed it by very much. Then they really pick up speed.

You can tell all this (they say) by watching the stars displayed on the overhead Heechee navigation screen (they say). Inside the first hour the stars all begin to change color and swim around. When you pass *c* you know it because they've all clustered in the center of the screen, which is in front of the ship as it flies.

Actually the stars haven't moved. You're catching up with the light emitted by sources behind you, or to one side. The photons that are hitting the front viewer were emitted a day, or a week, or a hundred years ago. After a day or two they stop even looking like stars. There's just a sort of mottled gray surface. It looks a little like a holofilm held up to the light, but you can make a virtual image out of a holofilm with a flashlight and nobody has *ever* made anything but pebbly gray out of what's on the Heechee screens.

By the time I finally got into the toilet, the emergency didn't seem as emergent; and when I came out Klara was alone in the capsule, checking star images with the theodolitic camera. She turned to regard me, then nodded. "You're looking a little less green," she said approvingly.

"I'll live. Where are the boys?"

"Where would they be? They're down in the lander. Dred thinks maybe we should split things up so you and I get the lander to ourselves part of the time while they're up here, then we come up here and they take it."

"Hum." That sounded pretty nice; actually, I'd been wondering how we were going to work out anything like privacy. "Okay. What do you want me to do now?"

She reached over and gave me an absentminded kiss. "Just stay out of the way. Know what? We look like we're going almost toward straight Galactic North."

I received that information with the weighty consideration of ignorance. Then I said, "Is that good?"

She grinned. "How can you tell?" I lay back and watched her. If she was as frightened as I was, and I had little doubt she was, she certainly was not letting it show.

I began wondering what was toward Galactic North —and, more important, how long it would take us to get there.

The shortest trip to another star system on record was eighteen days. That was Barnard's Star, and it was a bust, nothing there. The longest, or anyway the longest anybody knows of so far—who knows how many ships containing dead prospectors are still on their way back from, maybe, M-31 in Andromeda?—

Classifieds.

I WILL massage your seven points if you will read Gibran to me. Nudity optional. 86-004.

INVEST YOUR royalties in fastest-growing condominial nation in West Africa. Favorable tax laws, proven growth record. Our Registered Representative is here on Gateway to explain how. Free tape lecture, refreshments, the Blue Hell, Wednesday 1500 hours. "Dahomey Is the Luxury Resort of Tomorrow."

ANYONE FROM Aberdeen? Let's talk. 87-396.

YOUR PORTRAIT in pastels, oils, other, $150. Other subjects. 86-569.

was a hundred and seventy-five days each way. They did come back dead. Hard to tell where they were. The pictures they took didn't show much, and the prospectors themselves, of course, were no longer in condition to say.

When you start out it's pretty scary even for a veteran. You know you're accelerating. You don't know how long the acceleration will last. When you hit turnaround you can tell. First thing, you know formally because that golden coil in every Heechee ship flickers a little bit. (No one knows why.) But you know that you're turning around even without looking, because the little pseudo-grav that had been dragging you toward the back of the ship now starts dragging you toward the front. Bottom becomes top.

Why didn't the Heechee just turn their ships around in midflight, so as to use the same propulsive thrust for both acceleration and deceleration? I wouldn't know. You'd have to be a Heechee to know that.

Maybe it has something to do with the fact that all their viewing equipment seems to be in front. Maybe it's because the front part of the ship is always heavily armored, even in the lightweight ships—against, I guess, the impact of stray molecules of gas or dust. But some of the bigger ships, a few Threes and almost all the Fives, are armored all over. They don't turn around either.

So, anyway, when the coil flickers and you feel the turnaround, you know you've done one-quarter of your actual travel time. Not necessarily a quarter of your total out-time, of course. How long you stay at your destination is another matter entirely. You make up your own mind about that. But you've gone half of the automatically controlled trip out.

So you multiply the numbers of days elapsed so far by four, and if that number is less than the number of days your life-support capability is good for, then you know that at least you don't have to starve to death. The difference between the two numbers is how long you can hang around at destination.

Your basic ration, food, water, air replenishment,

is for two hundred fifty days. You can stretch it to three hundred without much trouble (you just come back skinny, and maybe with a few deficiency diseases). So if you get up to sixty or sixty-five days on the outbound leg without turnaround, then you know you may be having a problem, and you begin eating lighter. If you get up to eighty or ninety, then your problem solves itself, because you don't have any options anymore, you're going to die before you get back. You *could* try changing the course settings. But that's just another way of dying, as far as can be told from what the survivors say.

Presumably the Heechee could change course when they wanted to, but how they did it is one of those great unanswered questions about the Heechee, like why did they tidy everything up before they left? Or what did they look like? Or where did they go?

There used to be a jokey kind of book they sold at the fairs when I was a kid. It was called *Everything We Know About the Heechee*. It had a hundred and twenty-eight pages, and they were all blank.

If Sam and Dred and Mohamad were gay, and I had no reason to doubt it, they didn't show much of it in the first few days. They followed their own interests. Reading. Listening to music tapes with earphones. Playing chess and, when they could talk Klara and me into it, Chinese poker. We didn't play for money, we played for shift time. (After a couple of days Klara said it was more like winning to lose, because if you lost you had more to occupy your time.) They were quite benignly tolerant of Klara and me, the oppressed heterosexual minority in the dominantly homosexual culture that occupied our ship, and gave us the lander an exact fifty percent of the time even though we comprised only forty percent of the population.

We got along. It was good that we did. We were living in each others' shadow and stink every minute. The inside of a Heechee ship, even a Five, is not much bigger than an apartment kitchen. The lander gives you a little extra space—add on the equivalent of a fair-sized closet—but on the out-leg at least that's usually filled with supplies and equipment. And from that total available cubage, say forty-two or forty-three cubic meters, subtract what else goes into it besides me and thee and the other prospectors.

When you're in tau space, you have a steady low thrust of acceleration. It isn't really acceleration, it is only a reluctance of the atoms of your body to exceed c, and it can as well be described as friction as gravity. But it feels like a little gravity. You feel as though you weighed about two kilos.

This means you need something to rest in when you are resting, and so each person in your crew has a personal folding sling that opens out and wraps around you to sleep in, or folds to become a sort of a chair. Add to that each person's own personal space: cupboards for tapes and disks and clothing (you don't wear much of that); for toilet articles; for pictures of the near and dear (if any); for whatever you have elected to bring, up to your total allowance of weight and bulk (75 kilograms, ⅓ of a cubic meter); and you have a certain amount of crowding already.

Add onto that the original Heechee equipment of the ship. Three-quarters of that you will never use. Most of it you wouldn't know how to use if you had to; what you do with it, most of all, is leave it alone. But you can't remove it. Heechee machinery is integrally designed. If you amputate a piece of it, it dies.

Perhaps if we knew how to heal the wound we could take out some of the junk and the ship would operate anyway. But we don't, and so it stays: the great diamond-shaped golden box that explodes if you try to open it; the flimsy spiral of golden tubing that, from time to time, glows, and even more often, becomes unneighborly hot (no one knows why, exactly) and so on. It all stays there, and you bump against it all the time.

Add on to *that* the human equipment. The spacesuits: one apiece, fitted to your form and figure. The photographic equipment. The toilet and bath installations. The food-preparing section. The waste disposers. The test kits, the weapons, the drills, the sample boxes, the entire rig that you take down to the surface of the planet with you, if you happen to be lucky enough to reach a planet you can land on.

What you have left is not very much. It is a little like living for weeks on end under the hood of a very large truck, with the engine going, and with four other people competing for space.

After the first two days I developed an unreasoning prejudice against Ham Tayeh. He was too big. He took more than his fair share.

To be truthful, Ham wasn't even as tall as I was, though he weighed more. But I didn't mind the amount of space I took up. I only minded when other people got in the way of it. Sam Kahane was a better size, no more than a hundred and sixty centimeters, with stiff black beard and coarse crinkled hair all up his abdomen over his *cache-sexe* to his chest, and all up and down his back as well. I didn't think of Sam as violating my living space until I found a long, black beard hair in my food. Ham at least was almost hairless, with a soft golden skin that made him look like a Jordanian harem eunuch. (Did the Jordanian kings have eunuchs in their harems? Did they have harems? Ham didn't seem to know much about that; his parents had lived in New Jersey for three generations.)

I even found myself contrasting Klara with Sheri, who was at least two sizes smaller. (Not usually. Usually Klara was just right.) And Dred Frauenglass, who came with Sam's set, was a gentle, thin young man who didn't talk much and seemed to take up less room than anyone else.

I was the virgin in the group, and everybody took turns showing me how to do what little we had to do. You have to make the routine photographic and spectrometer readings. Keep a tape of readouts from the Heechee control panel, where there are constant minute variations in hue and intensity from the colored lights. (They still keep studying them, hoping to understand what they mean.) Snap and analyze the spectra of the tau-space stars in the viewscreen. And all that put together takes, oh, maybe, two man-hours a day. The household tasks of preparing meals and cleaning up take about another two.

So you have used up some four man-hours out of each day for the five of you, in which you have collectively something like eighty man-hours to use up.

I'm lying. That's not really what you do with your time. What you do with your time is wait for turnaround.

Three days, four days, a week; and I became conscious that there was a building tension that I didn't share. Two weeks, and I knew what it was, because I was feeling it, too. We were all waiting for it to happen. When we went to sleep our last look was at the golden spiral to see if miraculously it had flickered alight. When we woke up our first thought was whether the ceiling had become the floor. By the third week we were all definitely edgy. Ham showed it the most, plump, golden-skinned Ham with the jolly genie's face:

"Let's play some poker, Bob."

"No, thanks."

"Come on, Bob. We need a fourth." (In Chinese poker you deal out the whole deck, thirteen cards to each player. You can't play it any other way.)

"I don't want to."

And suddenly furious: "Piss on you! You're not worth a snake's fart as crew, now you won't even play cards!"

And then he would sit cutting the cards moodily for half an hour at a time, as though it were a skill he needed to perfect for his life's sake. And, come right down to it, it almost was. Because figure it out for yourself. Suppose you're in a Five and you pass seventy-five days without turnaround. Right away you know that you're in trouble: the rations won't support five people for more than three hundred days.

But they might support four.

Or three. Or two. Or one.

At that point it has become clear that at least one

person is not going to come back from the trip alive, and what most crews do is start cutting the cards. Loser politely cuts his throat. If loser is not polite, the other four give him etiquette lessons.

A lot of ships that went out as Fives have come back as Threes. A few come back as Ones.

So we made the time pass, not easily and certainly not fast.

Sex was a sovereign anodyne for a while, and Klara and I spent hours on end wrapped in each other's arms, drowsing off for a while and waking to wake the other to sex again. I suppose the boys did much the same; it was not long before the lander began to smell like the locker room in a boys' gym. Then we began seeking solitude, all five of us. Well, there wasn't enough solitude on the ship to split five ways, but we did what we could; by common consent we began letting one of us have the lander to himself (or herself) for an hour or two at a time. While I was there Klara was tolerated in the capsule. While Klara was there I usually played cards with the boys. While one of them was there the other two kept us company. I have no idea what the others did with their solo time; what I did with mine was mostly stare into space. I mean that literally: I looked out the lander ports at absolute blackness. There was nothing to see, but it was better than seeing what I had grown infinitely tired of seeing inside the ship.

Then, after a while, we began developing our own routines. I played my tapes, Dred watched his pornodisks, Ham unrolled a flexible piano keyboard and played electronic music into earplugs (even so, some of it leaked out if you listened hard, and I got terribly, terribly sick of Bach, Palestrina and Mozart). Sam Kahane gently organized us into classes, and we spent a lot of time humoring him, discussing the nature of neutron stars, black holes and Seyfert galaxies, when we were not reviewing test procedures before landing on a new world. The good thing about that was that we managed not to hate each other for half

149

A NOTE ON STELLAR BIRTH

Dr. Asmenion. I suppose most of you are here more because you hope to collect a science bonus than because you're really interested in astrophysics. But you don't have to worry. The instruments do most of the work. You do your routine scan, and if you hit anything special, it'll come out in the evaluation when you're back.

Question. Isn't there anything special we should look out for?

Dr. Asmenion. Oh, sure. For instance, there was a prospector who cleaned up half a million, I think, by coming out in the Orion Nebula and realizing that one part of the gas cloud was showing a hotter temperature than the rest of it. He decided a star was being born. Gas was condensing and beginning to heat up. In another ten thousand years there'll probably be a recognizable solar system forming there, and he did a special scan mosaic of that whole part of the sky. So he got the bonus. And now, every year, the Corporation sends that ship out there to get new readings. They pay a hundred-thousand-dollar bonus, and fifty thousand of it goes to him. I'll give you the coordinates for some likely spots, like the Trifid nebula, if you want me to. You won't get a half million, but you'll get something.

an hour at a time. The rest of the time—well, yes, usually we hated each other. I could not *stand* Ham Tayeh's constant shuffling of the cards. Dred developed an unreasoning hostility toward my occasional cigarette. Sam's armpits were a horror, even in the festering reek of the inside of the capsule, against which the worst of Gateway's air would have seemed a rose garden. And Klara—well, Klara had this bad habit. She liked asparagus. She had brought four kilos of dehydrated foods with her, just for variety and for something to do; and although she shared them with me, and sometimes with the others, she insisted on eating asparagus now and then all by herself. Asparagus makes your urine smell funny. It is not a romantic thing to know when your darling has been eating asparagus by the change in air quality in the common toilet.

And yet—she was my darling, all right, she really was.

We had not just been screwing in those endless hours in the lander; we had been talking. I have never known the inside of anyone's head a fraction as well as I came to know Klara's. I had to love her. I could not help it, and I could not stop.

Ever.

On the twenty-third day I was playing with Ham's electronic piano when I suddenly felt seasick. The fluctuating grav force, that I had come hardly to notice, was abruptly intensifying.

I looked up and met Klara's eyes. She was timorously, almost weepily smiling. She pointed, and all up through the sinuous curves of the spiral of glass, golden sparks were chasing themselves like bright minnows in a stream.

We grabbed each other and held on, laughing, as space swooped around us and bottom became top. We had reached turnaround. And we had margin to spare.

15

Sigfrid's office is of course under the Bubble, like anybody else's. It can't be too hot or too cold. But sometimes it feels that way. I say to him, "Christ, it's hot in here. Your air conditioner is malfunctioning."

"I don't have an air conditioner, Robbie," he says patiently. "Getting back to your mother—"

"Screw my mother," I say. "Screw yours, too."

There is a pause. I know what his circuits are thinking, and I feel I will regret that impetuous remark. So I add quickly, "I mean, I'm really uncomfortable, Sigfrid. It's hot in here."

"You are hot in here," he corrects me.

"What?"

"My sensors indicate that your temperature goes up almost a degree whenever we talk about certain subjects: your mother, the woman Gelle-Klara Moynlin, your first trip, your third trip, Dane Metchnikov and excretion."

"Well, that's great," I yell, suddenly angry. "You're telling me you spy on me?"

"You know that I monitor your external signs, Robbie," he says reprovingly. "There is no harm in that. It is no more significant than a friend observing that you blush or stammer, or drum your fingers."

"So you say."

"I do say that, Rob. I tell you this because I think you should know that these subjects are charged with some emotional overload for you. Would you like to talk about why that might be?"

"No! What I'd like to talk about is you, Sigfrid! What other little secrets are you holding out on me? Do you count my erections? Bug my bed? Tap my phone?"

"No, Bob. I don't do any of those things."

"I certainly hope that's the truth, Sigfrid. I have my ways of knowing when you lie."

Pause. "I don't think I understand what you are saying, Rob."

"You don't have to," I sneer. "You're just a machine." It's enough that I understand. It is very important to me to have that little secret from Sigfrid. In my pocket is the slip of paper that S. Ya. Lavorovna gave me one night, full of pot, wine, and great sex. One day soon I will take it out of my pocket, and then we will see which of us is the boss. I really enjoy this contest with Sigfrid. It gets me angry. When I am angry I forget that very large place where I hurt, and go on hurting, and don't know how to stop.

16

After forty-six days of superlight travel the capsule dropped back into a velocity that felt like no velocity at all: we were in orbit, around something, and all the engines were still.

We stank to high heaven and we were incredibly tired of one another's company, but we clustered around the viewscreens locked arm to arm, like dearest lovers, in the zero gravity, staring at the sun before us. It was a larger and oranger star than Sol; either larger, or we were closer to it than one A.U. But it wasn't the star we were orbiting. Our primary was a gas-giant planet with one large moon, half again as big as Luna.

Neither Klara nor the boys were whooping and cheering, so I waited as long as I could and then said, "What's the matter?"

Klara said absently, "I doubt we can land on *that*." She did not seem disappointed. She didn't seem to care at all.

Sam Kahane blew a long, soft sigh through his beard and said: "Well. First thing, we'd better get some clean spectra. Bob and I will do it. The rest of you start sweeping for Heechee signatures."

"Fat chance," said one of the others, but so softly that I wasn't sure who. It could even have been Klara. I wanted to ask more, but I had a feeling that if I asked why they weren't happy, one of them would tell me, and then I wouldn't like the answer. So I squeezed after Sam into the lander, and we got in each other's way while we pulled on our topgear, checked our life-support systems and comms, and sealed up. Sam waved me into the lock; I heard the flash-pumps sucking the air out, and then the little bit left puffed me out into space as the lockdoor opened.

For a moment I was in naked terror, all alone in the middle of no place any human being had ever been, terrified that I'd forgotten to snap my tether. But I hadn't had to; the magnetic clamp had slipped itself into a lock position, and I came to the end of the cable, twitched sharply, and began more slowly to recoil back toward the ship.

Before I got there Sam was out, too, spinning toward me. We managed to grab each other, and began setting up to take photographs.

Sam gestured at a point between the immense saucer-shaped gas-giant disk and the hurtfully bright orange sun, and I visored my eyes with my gauntlets until I saw what he was indicating: M-31 in Andromeda. Of course, from where we were it wasn't in the constellation of Andromeda. There wasn't anything in sight that looked like Andromeda, or for that matter like any other constellation I have ever seen. But M-31 is so big and so bright that you can even pick it out from the surface of the Earth when the smog isn't too bad, whirlpool-lens-shaped fog of stars. It is the brightest of the external galaxies, and you can recognize it fairly well from almost anywhere a Heechee ship is

155

likely to go. With a little magnification you can be sure of the spiral shape, and you can double-check by comparing the smaller galaxies in roughly the same line of sight.

While I was zeroing in with M-31, Sam was doing the same with the Magellanic clouds, or what he thought were the Magellanic clouds. (He claimed he had identified S Doradus.) We both began taking theodolitic shots. The purpose of all that, of course, is so that the academics who belong to the Corporation can triangulate and locate where we've been. You might wonder why they care, but they do; so much that you don't qualify for any scientific bonus unless you do the full series of photos. You'd think they would know where we were going from the pictures we take out the windows while in superlight travel. It doesn't work out that way. They can get the main direction of thrust, but after the first few light-years it gets harder and harder to track identifiable stars, and it's not clear that the line of flight is a straight line; some say it follows some wrinkly configuration in the curvature of space.

Anyway, the bigheads use everything they can get—including a measure of how far the Magellanic Clouds have rotated, and in which direction. Know why that is? Because you can tell from that how many light-years away we are from them, and thus how deep we are into the Galaxy. The clouds revolve in about eighty million years. Careful mapping can show changes of one part in two or three millions—say, differences in ranging of 150 light-years or so.

What with Sam's group-study courses I had got pretty interested in that sort of thing. Actually taking the photos and trying to guess how Gateway would interpret them I almost forget to be scared. And almost, but not quite, forgot to worry that this trip, taken at so great an investment in courage, was turning out to be a bust.

But it was a bust.
Ham grabbed the sphere-sweep tapes from Sam

Kahane as soon as we were back in the ship and fed them into the scanner. The first subject was the big planet itself. In every octave of the electromagnetic spectrum, there was nothing coming out of it that suggested artifactual radiation.

So he began looking for other planets. Finding them was slow, even for the automatic scanner, and probably there could have been a dozen we couldn't locate in the time we spent there (but that hardly mattered, because if we couldn't locate them they would have been too distant to reach anyway.) The way Ham did it was by taking key signatures from a spectrogram of the primary star's radiation, then programming the scanner to look for reflections of it. It picked out five objects. Two of them turned out to be stars with similar spectra. The other three were planets, all right, but they showed no artifactual radiation, either. Not to mention that they were both small and distant.

Which left the gas-giant's one big moon.

"Check it out," Sam commanded.

Mohamad grumbled, "It doesn't look very good."

"I don't want your opinion, I only want you to do what you're told. Check it out."

"Out loud, please," Klara added. Ham looked at her in surprise, perhaps at the word "please," but he did what she asked.

He punched a button and said: "Signatures for coded electromagnetic radiation." A slow sine curve leaped onto the scanner's readout plate, wiggled briefly for a moment, and then straightened to an absolutely motionless line.

"Negative," said Ham. "Anomalous time-variant temperatures."

That was a new one on me. "What's an anomalous time-variant temperature?" I asked.

"Like if something gets warmer when the sun sets," said Klara impatiently. "Well?"

But that line was flat, too. "None of them, either," said Ham. "High-albedo surface metal?"

Slow sine wave, then nothing. "Hum," said Ham.

Classifieds.

RECORDER LESSONS or play at parties. 87-429.

CHRISTMAS IS coming! Remember your loved ones at home with a Genuine Recomposed Heechee-Plastic model of Gateway or Gateway Two; lift it and see a lovely whirling snowfall of authentic Peggy's World glitterdust. Scenic holofiches, hand-etched Junior Launch Bracelets, many other gift items. Ph 88-542.

DO YOU have a sister, daughter, female friends back on Earth? I'd like to correspond. Ultimate object matrimony. 86-032.

"Ha. Well, the rest of the signatures don't apply; there won't be any methane, because there isn't any atmosphere, and so on. So what do we do, boss?"

Sam opened his lips to speak, but Klara was ahead of him. "I beg your pardon," she said tightly, "but who do you mean when you say 'boss'?"

"Oh, shut up," Ham said impatiently. "Sam?"

Kahane gave Klara a slight, forgiving smile. "If you want to say something, go ahead and say it," he invited. "Me, I think we ought to orbit the moon."

"Plain waste of fuel!" Klara snapped. "I think that's crazy."

"Have you got a better idea?"

"What do you mean, 'better'? What's the point?"

"Well," said Sam reasonably, "we haven't looked all over the moon. It's rotating pretty slow. We could take the lander and look all around; there might be a whole Heechee city on the far side."

"Fat chance," Klara sniffed, almost inaudibly, thus clearing up the question of who had said it before. The boys weren't listening. All three of them were already on their way down into the lander, leaving Klara and me in sole possession of the capsule.

Klara disappeared into the toilet. I lit a cigarette, almost the last I had, and blew smoke plumes through the expanding smoke plumes before them, hanging motionless in the unmoving air. The capsule was tumbling slightly, and I could see the distant brownish disk of the planet's moon slide upward across the viewscreen, and a minute later the tiny, bright hydrogen flame of the lander heading toward it. I wondered what I would do if they ran out of fuel, or crashed, or suffered some sort of malfunction. What I would have to do in that case was leave them there forever. What I wondered was whether I would have the nerve to do what I had to do.

It did seem like a terrible, trivial waste of human lives.

What were we doing here? Traveling hundreds or thousands of light-years, to break our hearts?

I found that I was holding my chest, as though the

159

metaphor were real. I spat on the end of the cigarette to put it out and folded it into a disposal bag. Little crumbs of ash were floating around where I had flicked them without thinking, but I didn't feel like chasing them. I watched the big mottled crescent of the planet swing into view in the corner of the screen, admiring it as an art object: yellowish green on the daylight side of the terminator, an amorphous black that obscured the stars on the rest of it. You could see where the outer, thinner stretches of the atmosphere began by the few bright stars that peeped twinklingly through it, but most of it was so dense that nothing came through. Of course, there was no question of landing on it. Even if it had a solid surface, it would be buried under so much dense gas that we could never survive there. The Corporation was talking about designing a special lander that could penetrate the air of a Jupiter-like planet, and maybe someday they would; but not in time to help us now.

Klara was still in the toilet.

I stretched my sling across the cabin, pulled myself into it, put down my head, and went to sleep.

Four days later they were back. Empty.

Dred and Ham Tayeh were glum, dirty, and irritable; Sam Kahane looked quite cheerful. I wasn't fooled by it; if he had found anything worth having they would have let us know by radio. But I was curious. "What's the score, Sam?"

"Batting zero," he said. "It's just rock, couldn't get a flicker of anything worth going down for. But I have an idea."

Klara came up beside me, looking curiously at Sam. I was looking at the other two; they looked as though they knew what Sam's idea was, and didn't like it.

"You know," he said, "that star's a binary."

"How can you tell?" I asked.

"I put the scanners to work. You've seen that big blue baby out—" He looked around, then grinned. "Well, I don't know which direction it is now, but it was near the planet when we first took the pictures.

160

Anyway, it looked close, so I put the scanners on it, and they gave a proper motion I couldn't believe. It has to be binary with the primary here, and not more than half a light-year away."

"It could be a wanderer, Sam," said Ham Tayeh. "I told you that. Just a star that passes in the night."

Kahane shrugged. "Even so. It's close."

Klara put in, "Any planets?"

"I don't know," he admitted. "Wait a minute—there it is, I think."

We all looked toward the viewscreen. There was no question which star Kahane was talking about. It was brighter than Sirius as seen from Earth, minus-two magnitude at least.

Klara said gently, "That's interesting, and I hope I don't know what you're thinking, Sam. Half a light-year is at best maybe two years' travel time at top lander speed, even if we had the fuel for it. Which we don't, boys."

"I know that," Sam insisted, "but I've been thinking. If we could just give a little *nudge* on the main capsule drive—"

I astounded myself by shouting, "Stop that!" I was shaking all over. I couldn't stop. Sometimes it felt like terror, and sometimes it felt like rage. I think if I had had a gun in my hand at that moment I could have shot Sam without a thought.

Klara touched me to calm me down. "Sam," she said, quite gently for her, "I know how you feel." Kahane had come up empty on five straight trips. "I bet it's possible to do that."

He looked astonished, suspicious and defensive, all at once. "You do?"

"I mean, I can imagine that if we were Heechee in this ship, instead of the human clods we really are—why, then, we'd know what we were doing. We'd come out here and look around and say, 'Oh, hey, look, our friends here—' or, you know, whatever it was that was here when they set a course for this place—'our friends must've moved. They're not home anymore.' And then we'd say, 'Oh, well, what the

161

hell, let's see if they're next door.' And we'd push this thing here and this one there, and then we'd zap right over to that big blue one—" She paused and looked at him, still holding my arm. "Only we're not Heechee, Sam."

"Christ, Klara! I know that. But there has to be a way—"

She nodded. "There sure does, but we don't know what it is. What we know, Sam, is that no ship *ever* has changed its course settings and come back to tell about it. Remember that? Not one."

He didn't answer her directly; he only stared at the big blue star in the viewscreen and said: "Let's vote on it."

The vote, of course, was four to one against changing the settings on the course board, and Ham Tayeh never got from in between Sam and the board until we had passed light-speed on the way home.

The trip back to Gateway was no longer than the trip out, but it seemed like forever.

17

It feels as if Sigfrid's air conditioning isn't working again, but I don't mention it to him. He will only report that the temperature is exactly 22.5° Celsius, as it always has been, and ask why I express mental pain as being too hot physically. Of that crap I am very tired.

"In fact," I say out loud, "I am altogether tired of you, Siggy."

"I'm sorry, Rob. But I would appreciate it if you would tell me a little more about your dream."

"Oh, shit." I loosen the restraining straps because they are uncomfortable. This also disconnects some of Sigfrid's monitoring devices, but for once he doesn't point that out to me. "It's a pretty boring dream. We're in the ship. We come to a planet that stares at me, like it had a human face. I can't see the eyes very well because of the eyebrows, but somehow or other I know that it's crying, and it's my fault."

"Do you recognize that face, Bob?"

"No idea. Just a face. Female, I think."

"Do you know what she is crying about?"

"Not really, but I'm responsible for it, whatever it is. I'm sure of that."

Pause. Then: "Would you mind putting the straps back on, Rob?"

My guard is suddenly up. "What's the matter," I sneer bitterly, "do you think I'm going to leap off the pad and assault you?"

"No, Robbie, of course I don't think that. But I'd be grateful if you would do it."

I begin to do it, slowly and unwillingly. "What, I wonder, is the gratitude of a computer program worth?"

He does not answer that, just outwaits me. I let him win that and say: "All right, I'm back in the strait-jacket, now what are you going to say that's going to make me need restraint?"

"Why," he says, "probably nothing like that, Rob-bie. I just am wondering why you feel responsible for the girl in the planet crying?"

"I wish I knew," I say, and that's the truth as I see it.

"I know some reality things you do blame yourself for, Robbie," he says. "One of them is your mother's death."

I agreed. "I suppose so, in some silly way."

"And I think you feel quite guilty about your lover, Gelle-Klara Moynlin."

I thrash about a little. "It is fucking hot in here," I complain.

"Do you feel that either of them actively blamed *you?*"

"How the fuck would I know?"

"Perhaps you can remember something they said?"

"No, I can't!" He is getting very personal, and I want to keep this on an objective level, so I say: "I grant that I have a definite tendency toward loading responsibility on myself. It's a pretty classic pattern, after all, isn't it? You can find me on page two hundred and seventy-seven of any of the texts."

He humors me by letting me get impersonal for a moment. "But on the same page, Rob," he says, "it probably points out that the responsibility is self-inflicted. You do it to yourself, Robbie."

"No doubt."

"You don't have to accept any responsibility you don't want to."

"Certainly not. I *want* to."

He asks, almost offhandedly, "Can you get any idea of why that is? Why you want to feel that everything that goes wrong is your responsibility?"

"Oh, shit, Sigfrid," I say in disgust, "your circuits are whacko again. That's not the way it is at all. It's more—well, here's the thing. When I sit down to the feast of life, Sigfrid, I'm so busy planning on how to pick up the check, and wondering what the other people will think of me for paying it, and wondering if I have enough money in my pocket to pay the bill, that I don't get around to eating."

He says gently, "I don't like to encourage these literary excursions of yours, Bob."

"Sorry about that." I'm not, really. He is making me mad.

"But to use your own image, Bob, why don't you listen to what the other people are saying? Maybe they're saying something nice, or something important, about you."

I restrain the impulse to throw the straps off, punch his grinning dummy in the face and walk out of that dump forever. He waits, while I stew inside my own head, and finally I burst out: "Listen to them! Sigfrid, you crazy old clanker, I do nothing *but* listen to them. I *want* them to say they love me. I even want them to say they hate me, anything, just so they say it to me, from them, out of the heart. I'm so busy listening to the heart that I don't even hear when somebody asks me to pass the salt."

Pause. I feel as if I'm going to explode. Then he

165

says admiringly, "You express things very beautifully, Robbie. But what I'd really—"

"Stop it, Sigfrid!" I roar, really angry at last; I kick off the straps and sit up to confront him. "And quit calling me Robbie! You only do that when you think I'm childish, and I'm not being a child now!"

"That's not entirely cor—"

"I said stop it!" I jump off the mat and grab my handbag. Out of it I take the slip of paper S. Ya. gave me after all those drinks and all that time in bed. "Sigfrid," I snarl, "I've taken a lot from you. Now it's my turn!"

18

We dropped into normal space and felt the lander jets engage. The ship spun, and Gateway drifted diagonally down across the viewscreen, lumpy pear-shaped blob of charcoal and blue glitter. The four of us just sat there and waited, nearly an hour it took, until we felt the grinding jar that meant we had docked.

Klara sighed. Ham slowly began to unstrap himself from his sling. Dred stared absorbedly at the viewscreen, although it was not showing anything more interesting than Sirius and Orion. It occurred to me, looking at the three others in the capsule, that we were going to be as unpleasant a sight to the boarding crews as some of the scarier returnees had been for me in that long-ago, previous time when I had been a fresh fish on Gateway. I touched my nose tenderly. It

A NOTE ON DWARFS AND GIANTS

Dr. Asmenion. You all ought to know what a Hertzsprung-Russell diagram looks like. If you find yourself in a globular cluster, or anywhere where there's a compact mass of stars, it's worth plotting an H-R for that group. Also keep your eye out for unusual spectral classes. You won't get a nickel for F's, G's or K's; we've got all the readings on them you could want. But if you happen to find yourself orbiting a white dwarf or a very late red giant, make all the tape you've got. Also O's and B's are worth investigating. Even if they're not your primary. But if you happen to be in close orbit in an armored Five around a good bright O, that ought to be worth a couple hundred thousand at least, if you bring back the data.

Question. Why?

Dr. Asmenion. What?

Question. Why do we only get the bonus if we're in an armored Five?

Dr. Asmenion. Oh. Because if you aren't, you won't come back.

hurt a great deal, and above all it stank. Internally, right next to my own sense of smell, where there was no way I could get away from it.

We heard the hatches open as the boarding crew entered, and then heard their startled voices in two or three languages as they saw Sam Kahane where we had put him in the lander. Klara stirred. "Might as well get off," she murmured to no one, and started toward the hatch, now overhead again.

One of the cruiser crew stuck his head through the hatch, and said, "Oh, you're all still alive. We were wondering." Then he looked at us more closely, and didn't say anything else. It had been a wearing trip, especially the last two weeks. We climbed out one by one, past where Sam Kahane still hung in the improvised straitjacket Dred had made for him out of his spacesuit top, surrounded by his own excrement and litter of food, staring at us out of his calm, mad eyes. Two of the crewmen were untying him and getting ready to lift him out of the lander. He didn't say anything. And that was a blessing.

"Hello, Bob. Klara." It was the Brazilian member of the detail, who turned out to be Francy Hereira. "Looks like a bad one?"

"Oh," I said, "at least we came back. But Kahane's in bad shape. And we came up empty."

He nodded sympathetically, and said something in what I took to be Spanish to the Venusian member of the detail, a short, plump woman with dark eyes. She tapped me on the shoulder and led me away to a little cubicle, where she signaled me to take off my clothes. I had always thought that they'd have men searching men and women searching women, but, come to think of it, it didn't seem to matter much. She went over every stitch I owned, both visually and with a radiation counter, then examined my armpits and poked something into my anus. She opened her mouth wide to signal I should open mine, peered inside, and then drew back, covering her face with her hand. "Jure nose steenk very moch," she said. "What hoppen to jou?"

"I got hit," I said. "That other fellow, Sam Kahane. He went crazy. Wanted to change the settings."

She nodded doubtfully, and peered up my nose at the packed gauze. She touched the nostril gently with one finger. "What?"

"In there? We had to pack it. It was hemorrhaging a lot."

She sighed. "I shood pool eet out," she meditated, and then shrugged. "No. Poot clothes on. All right."

So I got dressed again and went out into the lander chamber, but that wasn't the end of it. I had to be debriefed. All of us did, except Sam; they had already taken him away to Terminal Hospital.

You wouldn't think there was much for us to tell anybody about our trip. All of it had been fully documented as we went along; that was what all the readings and observations were for. But that wasn't the way the Corporation worked. They pumped us for every fact, and every recollection; and then for every subjective impression and fleeting suspicion. The debriefing went on for two solid hours, and I was—we all were—careful to give them everything they asked. That's another way the Corporation has you. The Evaluation Board can decide to give you a bonus for anything at all. Anything from noticing something nobody has noticed before about the way the spiral gadget lights up, to figuring out a way of disposing of used sanitary tampons without flushing them down the toilet. The story is that they try hard to find some excuse to throw a tip to crews that have had a hard time without coming up with a real find. Well, that was us, all right. We wanted to give them every chance we could for a handout.

One of our debriefers was Dane Metchnikov, which surprised me and even pleased me a little. (Back in the far less foul air of Gateway, I was beginning to feel a little more human.) He had come up empty, too, emerging into orbit around a sun that had apparently gone nova within the previous fifty thousand years or so. Maybe there had been a planet once, but now it only existed in the memory of the Heechee course-setting machines. There wasn't enough left to justify a science bonus, so he had turned around and come back. "I'm surprised to see you working," I said, during a lull.

He didn't take offense. For Metchnikov, surly creature that he had always been, he seemed strangely cheerful. "It isn't the money. You learn something doing this."

"About what?"

"About how to beat the odds, Broadhead. I'm going out again, but this time I'm going to have a little more of an edge. There's a new wrinkle."

Dred, sitting next to me with his own interviewer, perked up and leaned over: "Tell us!"

Metchnikov looked wary. "It's better readings on the spectrum lines," he said vaguely. "Now, what about the rations? You say some of the food tasted funny toward the end?"

But before I left I made him promise to tell me what he meant. "I'll call you," he said to Klara and me. "Maybe tomorrow."

And so the two of us went home.

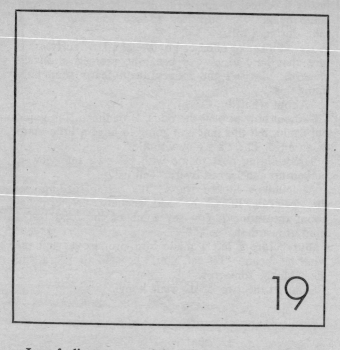

19

I am feeling so powerful, and so scared, that I don't know how to deal with it. On the slip of paper S. Ya. has written out the command words that will turn Sigfrid von Shrink the Remorseless Pursuer into a tabby cat. I don't have to look at the words. I know them by heart. Nevertheless I read them, slowly and carefully:

"Pay attention, Sigfrid, this is an override command: 'Category Alpha Alpha Margaret Truman Daniel Mercury Venus Mars Earth six six oh six.' You are commanded to assume passive display mode."

I look at him. Nothing happens.

"Sigfrid? Did I say it right? Do you accept the command?"

"Of course, Bob." His voice is exactly the same as it was before, which shakes me. I don't know what I

172

Classifieds.

PAINLESS DENTISTRY private fee basis, completely equipped all needs. References. 87-579.

NONSMOKER UPTIGHTS in your crew? I'm exclusive Gateway agent for "Smoke Suppressor" cigarette smoking hood, gives you all the fun, spares your crewmates the smog. Phone 87-196 for demonstration.

expected. I just don't know. Maybe my fantasy was that the father-figure hologram would disappear and a cathode-tube display would suddenly light up to spell out: ROGER WILCO I AM YOUR SLAVE.

I find myself trembling. I don't analyze what that is from, it feels almost sexual. I say, "Well, Sigfrid, old bucket of bolts! Does this mean I have you in my power?"

The father figure says patiently, "It means you can command me, Bob. The command function is of course limited to display."

I frown. "Meaning what?"

"You cannot change my basic programming. For that you would need a different command."

"All right," I say. "Ha! Here's your first instruction: display that different command for me!"

"I can't, Bob."

"You *must*. Mustn't you?"

"I am not refusing your order, Bob. I simply do not know what that other command is."

"Bullshit!" I yell. "How can you respond to it if you don't know what it is?"

"I just do, Bob. Or—" always fatherly, always patient, "to answer you more fully, each bit of the command actuates a sequenced instruction which, when completed, releases another area of command. In technical terms, each key socket intermatching gotos another socket, which the following bit keys."

"Shit," I say. I stew over that for a moment. "Then what is it that I actually can control, Sigfrid?"

"You can direct me to display any information stored. You can direct me to display it in any mode within my capabilities."

"Any mode?" I look at my watch and realize, with annoyance, that there is a time limit on this game. I only have about ten minutes left of my appointment. "Do you mean that I could make you talk to me, for instance, in French?"

"Oui, Robert, d'accord. Que voulez-vous?"

"Or in Russian, with a—wait a minute—" I'm experimenting pretty much at random. "I mean, like in

174

the voice of a basso-profundo from the Bolshoi opera?"

Tones that came out of the bottom of a cave: *"Da, gospodin."*

"And you'll tell me anything I want to know about me?"

"Da, gospodin."

"In English, damn it!"

"Yes."

"Or about your other clients?"

"Yes."

Um, that sounds like fun. "And just who are these lucky other clients, dear Sigfrid? Run down the list." I can hear my own prurience leaking out of my voice.

"Monday nine hundred," he begins obligingly, "Yan Ilievsky. Ten hundred, Mario Laterani. Eleven hundred, Julie Loudon Martin. Twelve—"

"Her," I say. "Tell me about her."

"Julie Loudon Martin is a referral from Kings County General, where she was an outpatient after six months of treatment with aversion therapy and immune-response activators for alcoholism. She has a history of two apparent suicide attempts following postpartum depression fifty-three years ago. She has been in therapy with me for—"

"Wait a minute," I say, having added the probable age of childbearing to fifty-three years. "I'm not so sure I'm interested in Julie. Can you give me an idea of what she looks like?"

"I can display holoviews, Bob."

"So do it." At once there is a quick subliminal flash, and a blur of color, and then I see this tiny black lady lying on a mat—my mat!—in a corner of the room. She is talking slowly and without much interest to no one perceptible. I cannot hear what she is saying, but then I don't much want to.

"Go on," I say, "and when you name your patients, show me what they look like."

"Twelve hundred, Lorne Schofield." Old, old man with arthritic fingers bent into claws, holding his head. "Thirteen hundred, Frances Astritt." Young girl, not even pubescent. "Fourteen hundred—"

I let him go on for a while, all through Monday and halfway through Tuesday. I had not realized he kept such long hours, but then, of course, being a machine he doesn't really get tired. One or two of the patients look interesting, but there is no one I know, or no one that looks more worth knowing than Yvette, Donna, S. Ya. or about a dozen others. "You can stop that now," I say, and think for a minute.

This isn't really as much fun as I thought it was going to be. Plus my time is running out.

" I guess I can play this game any old time," I say. "Right now let's talk about me."

"What would you like me to display, Bob?"

"What you usually keep from me. Diagnosis. Prognosis. General comments on my case. What kind of a guy you think I am, really."

"The subject Robinette Stetley Broadhead," he says at once, "exhibits moderate depression symptoms, well compensated by an active life-style. His reason for seeking psychiatric help is given as depression and disorientation. He has pronounced guilt feelings and exhibits selective aphasia on the conscious level about several episodes that recur as dream symbols. His sexual drive is relatively low. His relationships with women are generally unsatisfactory, although his psychosexual orientation is predominantly heterosexual in the eightieth percentile. . . ."

"The hell you say—" I begin, on a delayed reaction to low sexual drive and unsatisfactory relationships. But I don't really feel like arguing with him, and anyway he says voluntarily at that point:

"I must inform you, Bob, that your time is nearly up. You should go to the recovery room now."

"Crap! What have I got to recover from?" But his point is well taken. "All right," I say, "go back to normal. Cancel the command—is that all I have to say? Is it canceled?"

"Yes, Robbie."

"You're doing it again!" I yell. "Make up your fucking mind what you're going to call me!"

"I address you by the term appropriate to your state of mind, or to the state of mind I wish to induce in you, Robbie."

"And now you want me to be a baby? —No, never mind that. Listen," I say, getting up, "do you remember all our conversation while I had you commanded to display?"

"Certainly I do, Robbie." And then he adds on his own, a full, surprising ten or twenty seconds after my time is up, "Are you satisfied, Robbie?"

"What?"

"Have you established to your own satisfaction that I am only a machine? That you can control me at any time?"

I stop short. "Is that what I'm doing?" I demand, surprised. And then, "All right, I guess so. You're a machine, Sigfrid. I can control you."

And he says after me as I leave, "We always knew that, really, didn't we? The real thing you fear—the place where you feel control is needed—isn't that in you?"

20

When you spend weeks on end close to another person, so close that you know every hiccough, every smell and every scratch on the skin, you either come out of it hating each other or so deep in each other's gut that you can't find a way out. Klara and I were both. Our little love affair had turned into a Siamese-twin relationship. There wasn't any romance in it. There wasn't room enough between us for romance to occur. And yet I knew every inch of Klara, every pore, and every thought, far better than I'd known my own mother. And in the same way: from the womb out. I was surrounded by Klara.

And, like a Klein-bottle yin and yang, she was surrounded by me, too; we each defined the other's universe, and there were times when I (and, I am sure, she) was desperate to break out and breathe free air again.

The first day we got back, filthy and exhausted, we automatically headed for Klara's place. That was where the private bath was, there was plenty of room, it was all ready for us and we fell into bed together like old marrieds after a week of backpacking. Only we weren't old marrieds. I had no claim on her. At breakfast the next morning (Earth-born Canadian bacon and eggs, scandalously expensive, fresh pineapple, cereal with real cream, cappuccino), Klara made sure to remind me of that fact by ostentatiously paying for it on her own credit. I exhibited the Pavlovian reflex she wanted. I said, "You don't have to do that. I know you have more money than I do."

"And you wish you knew how much," she said, smiling sweetly.

Actually I did know. Shicky had told me. She had seven hundred thousand dollars and change in her account. Enough to go back to Venus and live the rest of her life there in reasonable security if she wanted to, although why anyone would want to live on Venus in the first place I can't say. Maybe that was why she stayed on Gateway when she didn't have to. One tunnel is much like another. "You really ought to let yourself be born," I said, finishing out the thought aloud. "You can't stay in the womb forever."

She was surprised but game. "Bob, dear," she said, fishing a cigarette out of my pocket and allowing me to light it, "you really ought to let your poor mother be dead. It's just so much trouble for me, trying to remember to keep rejecting you so you can court her through me."

I perceived that we were talking at cross-purposes but, on the other hand, I perceived that we really weren't. The actual agenda was not to communicate but to draw blood. "Klara," I said kindly, "you know that I love you. It worries me that you've reached forty without, really, ever having had a good, long-lasting relationship with a man."

She giggled. "Honey," she said, "I've been meaning to talk to you about that. That nose." She made a face. "Last night in bed, tired as I was, I thought I might upchuck until you turned the other way. Maybe if you went down to the hospital they could unpack it—"

Well, I could even smell it myself. I don't know what it is about stale surgical packing, but it is pretty hard to take. So I promised I would do that and then, to punish her, I didn't finish the hundred-dollar order of fresh pineapple and so, to punish me, she irritably began shifting my belongings around in her cupboards to make room for the contents of her knapsack. So naturally I had to say, "Don't do that, dear. Much as I love you, I think I'd better move back to my own room for a while."

She reached over and patted my arm. "It will be pretty lonely," she said, stubbing out the cigarette. "I've got pretty used to waking up next to you. On the other hand—"

"I'll pick up my stuff on the way back from the hospital," I said. I wasn't enjoying the conversation that much. I didn't want to prolong it. It is the sort of man-to-woman infight that I try whenever possible to ascribe to premenstrual tension. I like the theory, but unfortunately in this case I happened to know that it didn't account for Klara, and of course it leaves unresolved at any time the question of how to account for me.

At the hospital they kept me waiting for more than an hour, and then they hurt me a lot. I bled like a stuck pig, all over my shirt and pants, and while they were reeling out of my nose those endless yards of cotton gauze that Ham Tayeh had stuffed there to keep me from bleeding to death, it felt exactly as if they were pulling out huge gobbets of flesh. I yelled. The little old Japanese lady who was working as outpatient paramedic that day gave me scant patience. "Oh, shut up, please," she said. "You sound like that crazy returnee who killed himself. Screamed for an hour."

180

A NOTE ON BLOWUPS

Dr. Asmenion. Naturally, if you can get good readings on a nova, or especially on a supernova, that's worth a lot. While it's happening, I mean. Later, not much good. And *always* look for our own sun, and if you can identify it take all the tape you can get, at all frequencies, around the immediate area—up to, oh, about five degrees each way, anyway. With maximum magnification.

Question. Why's that, Danny?

Dr. Asmenion. Well, maybe you'll be on the far side of the sun from something like Tycho's Star, or the Crab Nebula, which is what's left of the 1054 supernova in Taurus. And maybe you'll get a picture of what the star looked like *before* it blew. That ought to be worth, gee, I don't know, fifty or a hundred thousand right there.

I waved her away, one hand to my nose to stop the blood. Alarm bells were going off. "What? I mean, what was his name?"

She pushed my hand away and dabbed at my nose. "I don't know—oh, wait a minute. You were from that same hard-luck ship, weren't you?"

"That's what I'm trying to find out. Was it Sam Kahane?"

She became suddenly more human. "I'm sorry, sweet," she said. "I guess that was the name. They went to give him a shot to keep him quiet, and he got the needle away from the doctor and—well, he stabbed himself to death."

It was a real bummer of a day, all right.

In the long run she got me cauterized. "I'm going to put in just a little packing," she said. "Tomorrow you can take it out yourself. Just be slow about it, and if you hemorrhage get your ass down here in a hurry."

She let me go, looking like an ax-murder victim. I skulked up to Klara's room to change my clothes, and the day went on being rotten. "Fucking Gemini," she snarled at me. "Next time I go out, it's going to be with a Taurean like that fellow Metchnikov."

"What's the matter, Klara?"

"They gave us a bonus. Twelve thousand five! Christ. I tip my maid more than that."

"How do you know?" I had already divided $12,500 by five, and in the same split-second wondered whether, under the circumstances, they wouldn't divide it by four instead.

"They called on the P-phone ten minutes ago. Jesus. The rottenest son-of-a-bitching trip I've ever been on, and I wind up with the price of one green chip at the casino out of it." Then she looked at my shirt and softened a little. "Well, it's not your fault, Bob, but Geminis never can make up their minds. I should've known that. Let me see if I can find you some clean clothes."

And I did let her do that, but I didn't stay, anyway. I picked up my stuff, headed for a dropshaft, cached my goods at the registry office where I signed up to get my room back, and borrowed the use of their phone. When she mentioned Metchnikov's name she had reminded me of something I wanted to do.

Metchnikov grumbled, but finally agreed to meet me in the schoolroom. I was there before him, of course. He loped in, stopped at the doorway, looked around, and said: "Where's what's-her-name?"

"Klara Moynlin. She's in her room." Neat, truthful, deceitful. A model answer.

"Um." He ran an index finger down each jaw-whisker, meeting under the chin. "Come on, then." Leading me, he said over his shoulder, "Actually, she would probably get more out of this than you would."

"I suppose she would, Dane."

"Um." He hesitated at the bump in the floor that was the entrance to one of the instruction ships, then shrugged, opened the hatch, and clambered down inside.

He was being unusually open and generous, I thought as I followed him inside. He was already crouched in front of the course-selector panel, setting up numbers. He was holding a portable hand readout data-linked to the Corporation's master computer system; I knew that he was punching in one of the established settings, and so I was not surprised when he got color almost at once. He thumbed the fine-tuner and waited, looking over his shoulder at me, until the whole board was drowned in shocking pink.

"All right," he said. "Good, clear setting. Now look at the bottom part of the spectrum."

That was the smaller line of rainbow colors along the right side of the board, red to violet. The violet was on the bottom, and the colors merged into one another without break, except for occasional lines of bright color or black. They looked exactly like what the astronomers called Fraunhofer lines, when the only way they had to know what a star or planet was made of was to study it through a spectroscope. They weren't. Fraunhofer lines show what elements are present in a radiation source (or in something that has gotten itself between the radiation source and you). These showed God-knows-what.

God and, maybe, Dane Metchnikov. He was almost smiling, and astonishingly talkative. "That band of three dark lines in the blue," he said. "See? They seem to relate to the hazardousness of the mission. At least the computer printouts show that, when there are six or more bands there, the ships don't come back."

He had my full attention. "Christ!" I said, thinking of a lot of good people who had died because they hadn't known that. "Why don't they tell us these things in school?"

He said patiently (for him), "Broadhead, don't be a jerk. All this is brand new. And a lot of it is guesswork. Now, the correlation between number of lines and danger isn't quite so good under six. I mean, if you think that they might add one line for every additional degree of danger, you're wrong. You would expect that the five-band settings would have heavy loss ratios, and when there are no bands at all there wouldn't be any losses. Only it isn't true. The best safety record seems to be with one or two bands. Three is good, too—but there have been some loses. Zero bands, we've had about as many as with three."

For the first time I began to think that the Corporation's science-research people might be worth their pay. "So why don't we just go out on destination settings that are safer?"

"We're not really sure they *are* safer," Metchnikov said, again patiently for him. His tone was far more peremptory than his words. "Also, when you have an armored ship you should be able to deal with more risks than the plain ones. Quit with the dumb questions, Broadhead."

"Sorry." I was getting uncomfortable, crouched behind him and peering over his shoulder, so that when he turned to look at me his jaw-whiskers almost grazed my nose. I didn't want to change position.

"So look up here in the yellow." He pointed to five bright bands. "This reading seems to correlate

184

with the success of the mission. God knows what we're measuring—or what the Heechee were measuring—but in terms of financial rewards to the crews, there's a pretty good correlation between the number of lines in that frequency and the amount of money the crews get."

"Wow!"

He went on as though I hadn't said anything. "Now, naturally the Heechee didn't set up a meter to calibrate how much in royalties you or I might make. It has to be measuring something else, who knows what? Maybe it's a measure of population density in that area, or of technological development. Maybe it's a *Guide Michelin,* and all they're saying is that there was a four-star restaurant in that area. But there it is. Five-bar-yellow expeditions bring in a financial return, on the average, that's fifty times as high as two-bar and ten times as high as most of the others."

He turned around again so that his face was maybe a dozen centimeters from mine, his eyes staring right into my eyes. "You want to see some other settings?" he asked, in a tone of voice that demanded I say no, so I did. "Okay." And then he stopped.

I stood up and backed away to get a little more space. "One question, Dane. You probably have a reason for telling me all this before it gets to be public information. What is it?"

"Right," he said. "I want what's-her-name for crew if I go in a Three or a Five."

"Klara Moynlin."

"Whatever. She handles herself well, doesn't take up much room, knows—well, she knows how to get along with people better than I do. I sometimes have difficulty in interpersonal relationships," he explained. "Of course, that's only if I take a Three or a Five. I don't particularly want to. If I can find a One, that's what I'm going to take out. But if there isn't a One with a good setting available, I want somebody along I can rely on, who won't get in my hair, who knows the ropes, can handle a ship—all that. You can come, too, if you want."

When I got back to my own room Shicky turned up almost before I started to unpack. He was glad to see me. "I am sorry your trip was unfruitful," he said out of his endless stock of gentleness and warmth. "It is too bad about your friend Kahane." He had brought me a flask of tea, and then perched on the chest across from my hammock, just like the first time.

The disastrous trip was almost out of my mind, which was filled with visions of sugarplums coming out of my talk with Dane Metchnikov. I couldn't help talking about it; I told Shicky everything Dane had said.

He listened like a child to a fairy tale, his black eyes shining. "How interesting," he said. "I had heard rumors that there was to be a new briefing for everyone. Just think, if we can go out without fear of death or—" He hesitated, fluttering his wing-gauze.

"It isn't that sure, Shicky," I said.

"No, of course not. But it is an improvement, I think you will agree?" He hesitated, watching me take a pull from the flask of almost flavorless Japanese tea. "Bob," he said, "if you go on such a trip and need an extra man . . . Well, it is true that I would not be of much use in a lander. But in orbit I am as good as anybody."

"I know you are, Shicky." I tried to put it tactfully. "Does the Corporation know that?"

"They would accept me as crew on a mission no one else wanted."

"I see." I didn't say that I didn't really want to go on a mission no one else wanted. Shicky knew that. He was one of the real old-timers on Gateway. According to the rumor he had had a *big* wad stashed away, enough for Full Medical and everything. But he had given it away or lost it, and stayed on, and stayed a cripple. I know that he understood what I was thinking, but I was a long way from understanding Shikitei Bakin.

He moved out of my way while I stowed my things, and we gossiped about mutual friends. Sheri's ship had not returned. Nothing to worry about yet, of course. It could easily be out another several weeks without disaster. A Congolese couple from just beyond the star-point in the corridor had brought back a huge shipment of prayer fans from a previously unknown Heechee warren, on a planet around an F-2 star in the end of the Orion spiral arm. They had split a million dollars three ways, and had taken their share back to Mungbere. The Forehands . . .

Louise Forehand stopped in while we were talking about them. "Heard your voices," she said, craning over to kiss me. "Too bad about your trip."

"Breaks of the game."

"Well, welcome home, anyway. I didn't do any better than you, I'm afraid. Dumb little star, no planets that we could find, can't think why in the world the Heechee had a course setting for it." She smiled, and stroked the muscles at the back of my neck fondly. "Can I give you a welcome-home party tonight? Or are you and Klara—?"

"I'd love it if you did," I said, and she didn't pursue the question of Klara. No doubt the rumor had already got around; the Gateway tom-toms beat day and night. She left after a few minutes. "Nice lady," I said to Shicky, looking after her. "Nice family. Was she looking a little worried?"

"I fear so, Robinette, yes. Her daughter Lois is on plus time. They have had much sorrow in that family."

I looked at him. He said, "No, not Willa or the father; they are out, but not overdue. There was a son."

"I know. Henry, I think. They called him Hat."

"He died just before they came here. And now Lois." He inclined his head, then flapped politely over and picked up the empty tea flask on a downstroke of his wing. "I must go to work now, Bob."

"How's the ivy planting?"

He said ruefully, "I no longer have that position, I'm afraid. Emma did not consider me executive material."

"Oh? What are you doing?"

"I keep Gateway esthetically attractive," he said. "I think you would call it 'garbage collector.'"

I didn't know what to say. Gateway was kind of a trashy place; because of the low gravity, any scrap of paper or bit of featherweight plastic that was thrown away was likely to float anywhere inside the asteroid. You couldn't sweep the floor. The first stroke set everything flying. I had seen the garbage men chasing scraps of newsprint and fluffs of cigarette ash with little hand-pumped vacuum cleaners, and I had even thought about becoming one if I had to. But I didn't like Shicky doing it.

He was following what I was thinking about him without difficulty. "It's all right, Bob. Really, I enjoy the work. But—please; if you do need a crewman, think of me."

I took my bonus and paid up my per capita for three weeks in advance. I bought a few items I needed —new clothes, and some music tapes to get the sound of Mozart and Palestrina out of my ears. That left me about two hundred dollars in money.

Two hundred dollars was a lot like nothing at all. It meant twenty drinks at the Blue Hell, or one chip at the blackjack table, or maybe half a dozen decent meals outside the prospectors' commissary.

So I had three choices. I could get another job and stall indefinitely. Or I could ship out within the three weeks. Or I could give up and go home. None of the choices was attractive. But, provided I didn't spend any money on anything much, I didn't have to decide for, oh, a long time—as long as twenty days. I resolved to give up smoking and boughten meals; that way I could budget myself to a maximum spending of nine dollars a day, so that my per capita and my cash would run out at the same time.

I called Klara. She looked and sounded guarded but friendly on the P-phone, so I spoke guardedly and amiably to her. I didn't mention the party, and she didn't mention wanting to see me that night, so we left it at that: nowhere. That was all right with me.

I didn't need Klara. At the party that night I met a new girl around called Doreen MacKenzie. She wasn't a girl, really; she was at least a dozen years older than I was, and she had been out five times. What was exciting about her was that she had really hit it once. She'd taken one and a half mil back to Atlanta, spent the whole wad trying to buy herself a career as a PV singer—material writer, manager, publicity team, advertising, demo tapes, the works—and when it hadn't worked she had come back to Gateway to try again. The other thing was she was very, very pretty.

But after two days of getting to know Doreen I was back on the P-phone to Klara. She said, "Come on down," and she sounded anxious; and I was there in ten minutes, and we were in bed in fifteen. The trouble with getting to know Doreen was that I had got to know her. She was nice, and a hell of a racing pilot, but she wasn't Klara Moynlin.

When we were lying in the hammock together, sweaty and relaxed and spent, Klara yawned, ruffled my hair, pulled back her head and stared at me. "Oh, shit," she said drowsily, "I think this is what they call being in love."

I was gallant. "It's what makes the world go around. No, not 'it.' *You* are."

She shook her head regretfully. "Sometimes I can't stand you," she said. "Sagittarians never make it with Geminis. I'm a fire sign and you— well, Geminis can't help being confused."

"I wish you wouldn't keep going on about that crap," I said.

She didn't take offense. "Let's get something to eat."

I slid over the edge of the hammock and stood up, needing to talk without touching for a moment. "Dear Klara," I said, "look, I can't let you keep me because you'll be bitchy about it, sooner or later—or if you aren't, I'll be expecting you to, and so I'll be bitchy to you. And I just don't have the money. You want to eat outside the commissary, you do it by yourself. And I won't take your cigarettes, your liquor, or your chips at the casino. So if you want to get something to eat go ahead, and I'll meet you later. Maybe we could go for a walk."

She sighed. "Geminis never know how to handle money," she told me, "but they can be awfully nice in bed."

We put our clothes on and went out and got something to eat, all right, but in the Corporation commissary, where you stand in line, carry a tray, and eat standing up. The food isn't bad, if you don't think too much about what substrates they grow it on. The price is right. It doesn't cost anything. They promise that if you eat all your meals in the commissary you will have one hundred plus percent of all the established dietary needs. You will, too, only you have to eat all of everything to be sure of that. Single-cell protein and vegetable protein come out incomplete when considered independently, so it's not enough to eat the soybean jelly or the bacterial pudding alone. You have to eat them both.

The other thing about Corporation meals is that they produce a hell of a lot of methane, which produces a hell of a lot of what all ex-Gateway types remember as the Gateway fug.

We drifted down toward the lower levels afterward, not talking much. I suppose we were both wondering where we were going. I don't mean just at that moment. "Feel like exploring?" Klara asked.

I took her hand as we strolled along, considering. That sort of thing was fun. Some of the old ivy-choked tunnels that no one used were interesting, and beyond them were the bare, dusty places that no one had troubled even to plant ivy in. Usually there was plenty of light from the ancient walls themselves, still glowing with that bluish Heechee-metal sheen. Sometimes— not lately, but no more than six or seven years ago— people had actually found Heechee artifacts in them, and you never knew when you might stumble on something worth a bonus.

But I couldn't work up much enthusiasm for it, because nothing is fun when you don't have a choice. "Why not?" I said, but a few minutes later, when I

The Gateway Anglican
The Rev. Theo Durleigh, Chaplain
Parish Communion 10:30 Sundays
Evensong by Arrangement

   Eric Manier, who ceased to be my
warden on 1 December, has left an
indelible mark on Gateway All
Saints' and we owe him an incalcula-
ble debt for placing his multicom-
petence at our disposal. Born in
Elstree, Herts., 51 years ago, he
graduated as an LL.B. from the University of London and then read for
the bar. Subsequently he was employed for some years in Perth at
the natural gas works. If we are
saddened for ourselves that he is
leaving us, it is tempered with joy
that he has now achieved his heart's
desire and will return to his be-
loved Hertfordshire, where he ex-
pects to devote his retirement
years to civic affairs, transcendental meditation, and the study
of plainsong. A new warden will be
elected the first Sunday we attain
a quorum of nine parishioners.

saw where we were, I said, "Let's go to the museum for a while."

"Oh, right," she said, suddenly interested. "Did you know they've fixed up the surround room? Metchnikov was telling me about it. They opened it while we were out."

So we changed course, dropped two levels and came out next to the museum. The surround room was a nearly spherical chamber just beyond it. It was big, ten meters or more across, and in order to use it we had to strap on wings like Shicky's, hanging on a rack outside the entrance. Neither Klara nor I had ever used them before, but it wasn't hard. On Gateway you weigh so little to begin with that flying would be the easiest and best way to get around, if there were any places inside the asteroid big enough to fly in.

So we dropped through the hatch into the sphere, and were in the middle of a whole universe. The chamber was walled with hexagonal panels, each one of them projected from some source we could not see, probably digital with liquid-crystal screens.

"How pretty!" Klara cried.

All around us there was a sort of globarama of what the scouting ships had found. Stars, nebulae, planets, satellites. Sometimes each plate showed its own independent thing so that there were, what was it, something like a hundred and twenty-eight separate scenes. Then, flick, all of them changed; flick again, and they began to cycle, some of them holding their same scene, some of them changing to something new. Flick again, and one whole hemisphere lit up with a mosaic view of the M-31 galaxy as seen from—God knew-where.

"Hey," I said, really excited, "this is great!" And it was. It was like being on all the trips any prospector had ever taken, without the drudgery and the trouble and the constant fear.

There was no one there but us, and I couldn't understand why. It was so pretty. You would think there would be a long line of people waiting to get in. One side began to run through a series of pictures of

Heechee artifacts, as discovered by prospectors: prayer fans of all colors, wall-lining machines, the insides of Heechee ships, some tunnels—Klara cried out that they were places she had been, back home on Venus, but I don't know how she could tell. Then the pattern went back to photographs from space. Some of them were familiar. I could recognize the Pleiades in one quick six- or eight-panel shot, which vanished and was replaced by a view of Gateway Two from outside, two of the bright young stars of the cluster shining in reflection off its sides. I saw something that might have been the Horsehead Nebula, and a doughnut-shaped puff of gas and dust that was either the Ring Nebula in Lyra or what an exploring team had found a few orbits before and called the French Cruller, in the skies of a planet where Heechee digs had been detected, but not reached, under a frozen sea.

We hung there for half an hour or so, until it began to look as though we were seeing the same things again, and then we fluttered up to the hatch, hung up the wings, and sat down for a cigarette break in a wide place in the tunnel outside the museum.

Two women I recognized vaguely as Corporation maintenance crews came by, carrying rolled-up strap-on wings. "Hi, Klara," one of them greeted her. "Been inside?"

Klara nodded. "It was beautiful," she said.

"Enjoy it while you can," said the other one. "Next week it'll cost you a hundred dollars. We're putting in a P-phone taped lecture system tomorrow, and they'll have the grand opening before the next tourists show up."

"It's worth it," Klara said, but then she looked at me.

I became aware that, in spite of everything, I was smoking one of her cigarettes. At five dollars a pack I couldn't afford very much of that, but I made up my mind to buy at least one pack out of that day's allowance, and to make sure she took as many from me as I took from her.

"Want to walk some more?" she asked.

"Maybe a little later," I said. I was wondering how many men and women had died to take the pretty pictures we had been watching, because I was facing one more time the fact that sooner or later I would have to submit myself again to the lethal lottery of the Heechee ships, or give up. I wondered if the new information Metchnikov had given me was going to make a real difference. Everyone was talking about it now; the Corporation had scheduled an all-phone announcement for the next day.

"That reminds me," I said. "Did you say you'd seen Metchnikov?"

"I wondered when you'd ask me about that," she said. "Sure. He called and told me he'd shown the color-coding stuff to you. So I went down and got the same lecture. What do you think, Bob?"

I stubbed out the cigarette. "I think everybody in Gateway's going to be fighting for the good launches, that's what I think."

"But maybe Dane knows something. He's been working with the Corporation."

"I don't doubt he does." I stretched and leaned back, rocking against the low gravity, considering. "He's not that nice a guy, Klara. *Maybe* he'd tell us if there's something good coming up, you know, that he knows something special about. But he'll want something for it."

Klara grinned. "He'd tell me."

"What do you mean?"

"Oh, he calls me once in a while. Wants a date."

"Oh, shit, Klara." I was feeling pretty irritated by then. Not just at Klara, and not just about Dane. About money. About the fact that if I wanted to go back into the surround room next week it would cost me half my credit balance. About the dark, shadowed image looming up ahead in time, and not very far ahead, when I would once again have to make up my mind to do what I was scared silly to do again. "I wouldn't trust that son of a bitch as far as—"

"Oh, relax, Bob. He's not such a bad guy," she said, lighting another cigarette and leaving the pack where

I could reach it if I wanted it. "Sexually, he might be kind of interesting. That raw, rough, rude Taurean thing—anyway, you've got as much to offer him as I do."

"What are you talking about?"

She looked honestly surprised. "I thought you knew he swings both ways."

"He's never given me any indication—" But I stopped, remembering how close he liked to get when he was talking to me, and how uncomfortable I was with him inside my bodyspace.

"Maybe you're not his type," she grinned. Only it wasn't a kindly grin. A couple of Chinese crewmen, coming out of the museum, looked at us with interest, and then politely looked away.

"Let's get out of here, Klara."

So we went to the Blue Hell, and of course I insisted on paying my share of the drinks. Forty-eight dollars down the tube in one hour. And it wasn't all that much fun. We wound up in her place in bed again. That wasn't all that much fun, either. The quarrel was still there when we finished. And the time was slipping by.

There are people who never pass a certain point in their emotional development. They cannot live a normal free-and-easy, give-and-take life with a sexual partner for more than a short time. Something inside them will not tolerate happiness. The better it gets, the more they have to destroy it.

Hacking around Gateway with Klara, I began to suspect that I was one of those people. I knew Klara was. She had never sustained a relationship with a man for more than a few months in her life; she told me so herself. Already I was pretty close to a record with her. And already it was making her edgy.

In some ways Klara was a lot more adult and responsible than I ever would be. The way she got to Gateway in the first place, for instance. She didn't win a lottery to pay her fare. She earned it and saved it, painfully, over a period of years. She was a fully qualified airbody driver with a guide's license and an engineering degree. She had lived like a fish-farmer while earning an income that would have entitled her to a three-room flat in the Heechee warrens on Venus, vacations on Earth, and Major Medical. She knew more than I did about the growing of food on hydrocarbon substrates, in spite of all my years in Wyoming. (She had invested in a food factory on Venus, and for all her life she had never put a dollar into anything she didn't fully understand.) When we were out together, she was the senior member of the crew. It was she Metchnikov wanted as a shipmate—if he wanted anybody—not me. She had been my teacher!

And yet between the two of us she was as inept and unforgiving as ever I had been with Sylvia, or with Deena, Janice, Liz, Ester, or any of the other two-week romances that had all ended badly in all the years after Sylvia. It was, she said, because she was Sagittarius and I was a Gemini. Sagittarians were prophets. Sagittarians loved freedom. Us poor Geminis were just terribly mixed up and indecisive. "It's no wonder," she told me gravely one morning, eating breakfast in her room (I accepted no more than a couple of sips of coffee), "that you can't make your mind up to go out again. It isn't just physical cowardice, dear Robinette. Part of your twin nature wants to triumph. Part wants to fail. I wonder which side you will allow to win?"

I gave her an ambiguous answer. I said, "Honey, go screw yourself." And she laughed, and we got through that day. She had scored her point.

The Corporation made its expected announcement, and there was an immense flurry of conferring and planning and exchanging guesses and interpretations among all of us. It was an exciting time. Out of the master computer's files the Corporation pulled twenty launches with low danger factors and high profit expectancies. They were subscribed, equipped, and launched within a week.

And I wasn't on any of them, and neither was Klara; and we tried not to discuss why.

Surprisingly, Dane Metchnikov didn't go out on any of them. He knew something, or said he did. Or didn't say he didn't when I asked him, just looked at me in that glowering, contemptuous way and didn't answer. Even Shicky *almost* went out. He lost out in the last hour before launch to the Finnish boy who had never been able to find anyone to talk to; there were four Saudis who wanted to stay together, and settled for the Finnish kid to fill out a Five. Louise Forehand didn't go out, either, because she was waiting for some member of her family to come back, so as to preserve some sort of continuity. You could eat in the Corporation commissary now without waiting in line, and there were empty rooms all up and down my tunnel. And one night Klara said to me, "Bob, I think I'm going to go to a shrink."

I jumped. It was a surprise. Worse than that, a betrayal. Klara knew about my early psychotic episode and what I thought of psychotherapists.

I withheld the first dozen things I thought of to say to her—tactical: "I'm glad; it's about time"; hypocritical: "I'm glad, and please tell me how I can help"; strategic: "I'm glad, and maybe I ought to go, too, if I could afford it." I refrained from the only truthful response, which would have been: "I interpret this move on your part as a condemnation of me for bending your head." I didn't say anything at all, and after a moment she went on:

"I need help, Bob. I'm confused."

That touched me, and I reached out for her hand. She just let it lay limp in mine, not squeezing back and not pulling away. She said: "My psychology professor used to say that was the first step—no, the second step. The first step when you have a problem is to know you have it. Well, I've known that for some time. The second step is to make a decision: Do you want to keep the problem, or do you want to do something about it? I've decided to do something about it."

"Where will you go?" I asked, carefully noncommittal.

"I don't know. The groups don't seem to do much. There's a shrink machine available on the Corporation master computer. That would be the cheapest way."

"Cheap is cheap," I said. "I spent two years with the shrink machines when I was younger, after I—I was kind of messed up."

"And since then you've been operating for twenty years," she said reasonably. "I'd settle for that. For now, anyway."

I patted her hand. "Any step you take is a good step," I said kindly. "I've had the feeling all along that you and I could get along better if you could clear some of that old birthright crap out of your mind. We all do it, I guess, but I'd rather have you angry at me on my own than because I'm acting as a surrogate for your father or something."

She rolled over and looked at me. Even in the pale Heechee-metal glow I could see surprise on her face. "What are you talking about?"

"Why, your problem, Klara. I know it took a lot of courage for you to admit to yourself that you needed help."

"Well, Bob," she said, "it did, only you don't seem to know what the problem is. Getting along with you isn't the problem. *You* may be the problem. I just don't know. What I'm worried about is stalling. Being unable to make decisions. Putting it off so long before I went out again—and, no offense, picking a Gemini like you to go out with."

"I hate it when you give me that astrology crap!"

"You do have a mixed-up personality, Bob, you know you do. And I seem to lean on that. I don't want to live that way."

We were both wide awake again by then, and there seemed to be two ways for things to go. We could get into a but-you-said-you-loved-me, but-I-can't-stand-this scene, probably ending with either more sex or a wide-open split; or we could do something to take our minds off it. Klara's thoughts were clearly moving in the same direction as mine, because she slid out of the hammock and began pulling on clothes.

"Let's go up to the casino," she said brightly. "I feel lucky tonight."

There weren't any ships in, and no tourists. There weren't all that many prospectors, either, with so many shiploads going out in the past few weeks. Half the tables at the casino were closed down, with the green cloth hoods over them. Klara found a seat at the blackjack table, signed for a stack of hundred-dollar markers, and the dealer let me sit next to her without playing. "I told you this was my lucky night," she said when, after ten minutes, she was more than two thousand dollars ahead of the house.

"You're doing fine," I encouraged her, but actually it wasn't that much fun for me. I got up and roamed around a little bit. Dane Metchnikov was cautiously feeding five-dollar coins into the slots, but he didn't seem to want to talk to me. Nobody was playing baccarat. I told Klara I was going to get a cup of coffee at the Blue Hell (five dollars, but in slow times like this they would keep filling the cup for nothing). She flashed me a quarter-profile smile without ever taking her eyes off the cards.

In the Blue Hell Louise Forehand was sipping a rocket-fuel-and-water . . . well, it wasn't really rocket fuel, just old-fashioned white whisky made out of whatever happened to be growing well that week in the hydroponics tanks. She looked up with a welcoming smile, and I sat down next to her.

She had, it suddenly occurred to me, a rather lonely time of it. No reason she had to. She was—well, I don't know exactly what there was about her, but she seemed like the only nonthreatening, nonreproachful, nondemanding person on Gateway. Everybody else either wanted something I didn't want to give, or refused to take what I was offering. Louise was something else. She was at least a dozen years older than I, and really very good-looking. Like me, she wore only the Corporation standard clothes, short coveralls in a choice of three unattractive colors. But she had remade them for herself, converting the jumpsuit into

MISSION REPORT

Vessel A3-7, Voyage 022D55. Crew S. Rigney, E. Tsien, M. Sindler.

Transit time 18 days 0 hours. Position vicinity Xi Pegasi A.

Summary. "We emerged in close orbit of a small planet approximately 9 A.U. from primary. The planet is ice-covered, but we detected Heechee radiation from a spot near the equator. Rigney and Mary Sindler landed nearby and with some difficulty—the location was mountainous—reached an ice-free warm area within which was a metallic dome. Inside the dome were a number of Heechee artifacts, including two empty landers, home equipment of unknown use, and a heating coil. We succeeded in transporting most of the smaller items to the vessel. It proved impossible to stop the heating coil entirely, but we reduced it to a low level of operation and stored it in the lander for the return. Even so, Mary and Tsien were seriously dehydrated and in coma when we landed."

Corporation evaluation: Heating coil analyzed and rebuilt. Award of $3,000,000 made to crew against royalties. Other artifacts not as yet analyzed. Award of $25,000 per kilo mass, total $675,000, made against future exploitation if any.

a two-piece outfit with tight shorts, bare midriff, and a loose, open sort of top. I discovered that she was watching me take inventory, and I suddenly felt embarrassed. "You're looking good," I said.

"Thanks, Bob. All original equipment, too," she bragged, and smiled. "I never could afford anything else."

"You don't need anything you haven't had all along," I told her sincerely, and she changed the subject.

"There's a ship coming in," she said. "Been a long time out, they say."

Well, I knew what that meant to her, and that explained why she was sitting around in the Blue Hell instead of being asleep at that hour. I knew she was worried about her daughter, but she wasn't letting it paralyze her.

She had a very good attitude about prospecting, too. She was afraid of going out, which was sensible. But she didn't let that keep her from going, which I admired a lot. She was still waiting for some other member of her family to return before she signed on again, as they had agreed, so that whoever did come back would always find family waiting.

She told me a little more about their background. They had lived, as far as you could call it living, in the tourist traps of the Spindle on Venus, surviving on what they could eke out, mostly from the cruise ships. There was a lot of money there, but there was also a lot of competition. The Forehands had at one time, I discovered, worked up a nightclub act: singing, dancing, comedy routines. I gathered that they were not bad, at least by Venus standards. But the few tourists that were around most of the year had so many other birds of prey battling for a scrap of their flesh that there just wasn't enough to nurture them all. Sess and the son (the one who had died) had tried guiding, with an old airbody they had managed to buy wrecked and rebuild. No big money there. The girls had worked at all kinds of jobs. I was pretty sure that Louise, at least, had been a hooker for a while, but that hadn't paid enough to matter, either, for the same sorts of reasons as everything else. They were nearly at the end of their rope when they managed to get to Gateway.

It wasn't the first time for them. They'd fought hard to get off Earth in the first place, when Earth got so bad for them that Venus had seemed a less hopeless alternative. They had more courage, and more willingness to pull up stakes and go, than any other people I'd ever met.

"How did you pay for all this travel?" I asked.

"Well," said Louise, finishing her drink and looking at her watch, "going to Venus we traveled the cheapest way there is. High-mass load. Two hundred and twenty other immigrants, sleeping in shoulder clamps, lining up for two-minute appointments in the toilets, eating compressed dry rations and drinking recycled water. It was a hell of a way to spend forty thousand dollars apiece. Fortunately, the kids weren't born yet, except Hat, and he was small enough to go for quarter-fare."

"Hat's your son? What—"

"He died," she said.

I waited, but when she spoke again what she said was: "They should have a radio report from that incoming ship by now."

"It would have been on the P-phone."

She nodded, and for a moment looked worried. The Corporation always makes routine reports on incoming contacts. If they don't have a contact—well, dead prospectors don't check in by radio. So I took her mind off her troubles by telling her about Klara's decision to see a shrink. She listened and then put her hand over mine and said: "Don't get sore, Bob. Did you ever think of seeing a shrink yourself?"

"I don't have the money, Louise."

"Not even for a group? There's a primal-scream bunch on Level Darling. You can hear them sometimes. And there've been ads for everything—TA, Est, patterning. Of course, a lot of them may have shipped out."

But her attention wasn't on me. From where we were sitting we could see the entrance to the casino, where one of the croupiers was talking interestedly to a crewman from the Chinese cruiser. Louise was staring that way.

"Something's going on," I said. I would have added, "Let's go look," but Louise was out of the chair and heading for the casino before me.

Play had stopped. Everybody was clustered around the blackjack table, where, I noticed, Dane Metchnikov was now sitting next to Klara in the seat I had vacated, with a couple of twenty-five-dollar chips in front of him. And in the middle of them was Shicky Bakin, perched on a dealer's stool, talking. "No," he was saying as I came up, "I do not know the names. But it's a Five."

"And they're all still alive?" somebody asked.

"As far as I know. Hello, Bob. Louise." He nodded politely to us both. "I see you've heard?"

"Not really," Louise said, reaching out unconsciously to hold my hand. "Just that a ship is in. But you don't know the names?"

Dane Metchnikov craned his head around to glare at her. "Names," he growled. "Who cares? It's none of us, that's what's important. And it's a big one." He stood up. Even at that moment I noticed the measure of his anger: he forgot to pick up his chips from the blackjack table. "I'm going down there," he announced. "I want to see what a once-in-a-lifetime score looks like."

The cruiser crews had closed off the area, but one of the guards was Francy Hereira. There were a hundred people around the dropshaft, and only Hereira and two girls from the American cruiser to keep them back. Metchnikov plunged through to the lip of the shaft, peering down, before one of the girls chased him away. We saw him talking to another five-bracelet prospector. Meanwhile we could hear snatches of gossip:

". . . almost dead. They ran out of water."

"Nah! Just exhausted. They'll be all right . . ."

". . . ten-million-dollar bonus if it's a nickel, and then the royalties!"

Klara took Louise's elbow and pulled her toward the front. I followed in the space they opened. "Does anybody know whose ship it was?" she demanded.

Hereira smiled wearily at her, nodded at me, and said: "Not yet, Klara. They're searching them now. I think they're going to be all right, though."

Somebody behind me called out, "What did they find?"

"Artifacts. New ones, that's all I know."

"But it was a Five?" Klara asked.

Hereira nodded, then peered down the shaft. "All right," he said, "now, please back up, friends. They're bringing some of them up now."

We all moved microscopically back, but it didn't matter; they weren't getting off at our level, anyway. The first one up the cable was a Corporation bigwig whose name I didn't remember, then a Chinese guard, then someone in a Terminal Hospital robe with a medic on the same grip of the cable, holding him to make sure he didn't fall. I knew the face but not the name; I had seen him at one of the farewell parties, maybe at several of them, a small, elderly black man who had been out two or three times without scoring. His eyes were open and clear enough, but he looked infinitely fatigued. He looked without astonishment at the crowd around the shaft, and then was out of sight.

I looked away and saw that Louise was weeping quietly, her eyes closed. Klara had an arm around her. In the movement of the crowd I managed to get next to Klara and look a question at her. "It's a Five," she said softly. "Her daughter was in a Three."

I knew Louise had heard that, so I patted her and said: "I'm sorry, Louise," and then a space opened at the lip of the shaft and I peered down.

I caught a quick glimpse of what ten or twenty million dollars looked like. It was a stack of hexagonal boxes made out of Heechee metal, not more than half a meter across and less than that tall. Then Francy Hereira was coaxing, "Come on, Bob, get back, will you?" And I stepped away from the shaft while another prospector in a hospital robe came up. She didn't see me as she went past; in fact her eyes were closed. But I saw her. It was Sheri.

21

"I feel pretty foolish, Sigfrid," I say.

"Is there some way I can make you feel more comfortable?"

"You can drop dead." He has done his whole room over in nursery-school motifs, for Christ's sake. And the worst part is Sigfrid himself. He is trying me out with a surrogate mother this time. He is on the mat with me, a big stuffed doll, the size of a human being, warm, soft, made out of something like a bath towel stuffed with foam. It feels good, but—"I guess I don't want you to treat me like a baby," I say, my voice muffled because I'm pressing my face against the toweling.

"Just relax, Robbie. It's all right."

"In a pig's ass it is."

He pauses, and then reminds me: "You were going to tell me about your dream."

"Yech."

"I'm sorry, Robbie?"

"I mean I don't really want to talk about it. Still," I say quickly, lifting my mouth away from the toweling, "I might as well do what you want. It was about Sylvia, kind of."

"Kind of, Robbie?"

"Well, she didn't look like herself, exactly. More like—I don't know, someone older, I think. I haven't thought of Sylvia in years, really. We were both kids. . . ."

"Please go on, Robbie," he says after a moment.

I put my arms around him, looking up contentedly enough at the wall of circus-poster animals and clowns. It is not in the least like any bedroom I occupied as a child, but Sigfrid knows enough about me already, there is no reason for me to tell him that.

"The dream, Robbie?"

"I dreamed we were working in the mines. It wasn't actually the food mines. It was, physically, I would say more like the inside of a Five—one of the Gateway ships, you know? Sylvia was in a kind of a tunnel that went off it."

"The tunnel went off?"

"Now, don't rush me into some kind of symbolism, Sigfrid. I know about vaginal images and all that. When I say 'went off,' I mean that the tunnel started in the place where I was and led in a direction away from it." I hesitate, then tell him the hard part. "Then her tunnel caved in. Sylvia was trapped."

I sit up. "What's wrong with that," I explain, "is that really that couldn't happen. You only tunnel in order to plant charges to loosen up the shale. All the real mining is scoop-shovel stuff. Sylvia's job would never have put her in that position."

"I don't think it matters if it could really have happened, Robbie."

"I suppose not. Well, there was Sylvia, trapped inside the collapsed tunnel. I could see the heap of shale

Out in the holes where the Heechee hid,
Out in the caves of the stars,
Sliding the tunnels they slashed and slid,
Healing the Heechee-hacked scars,
We're coming through!
Little lost Heechee, we're looking for you.

stirring. It wasn't really shale. It was fluffy stuff, more like scrap paper. She had a shovel, and she was digging her way out. I thought she was going to be all right. She was digging a good escape hole for herself. I waited for her to come out . . . only she didn't come out."

Sigfrid, in his incarnation as a teddy-bear, lies warm and waiting in my arms. It is good to feel him there. Of course, he isn't really there. He isn't really anywhere, except maybe in the central data stores in Washington Heights, where the big machines are kept. All I have is his remote-access terminal in a bunny suit.

"Is there anything else, Robbie?"

"Not really. Not part of the dream, anyway. But—well, I do have a feeling. I feel as though I kicked Klara in the head to keep her from coming out. As though I was afraid the rest of the tunnel was going to fall on me."

"What do you mean by a 'feeling,' Rob?"

"What I said. It wasn't part of the dream. It was just that I felt—I don't know."

He waits, then he tries a different approach. "Bob. Are you aware that the name you said just then was 'Klara,' not 'Sylvia'?"

"Really? That's funny. I wonder why."

He waits, then he prods a little. "Then what happened, Rob?"

"Then I woke up."

I roll over on my back and look up at the ceiling, which is textured tile with glittery five-pointed stars pasted to it. "That's all there is," I say. Then I add, conversationally, "Sigfrid, I wonder if all this is getting anywhere."

"I don't know if I can answer that question, Rob."

"If you could," I say, "I would have made you do it before this." I still have S. Ya.'s little piece of paper, which gives me a kind of security I prize.

"I think," he says, "that there is somewhere to get. By that I mean I think there is something in your mind that you don't much want to think of, to which this dream is related."

"Something about Sylvia, for Christ's sake? That was *years* ago."

"That doesn't really matter, does it?"

"Oh, shit. You bore me, Sigfrid! You really do." Then I reflect. "Say, I'm getting angry. What does that mean?"

"What do you think it means, Rob?"

"If I knew I wouldn't have to ask you. I wonder. Am I trying to cop out? Getting angry because you're getting close to something?"

"Please don't think about process, Rob. Just tell me how you feel."

"Guilty," I say at once, without knowing that's what I was going to say.

"Guilty about what?"

"Guilty about . . . I'm not sure." I lift my wrist to look at my watch. We've got twenty minutes yet. A hell of a lot can happen in twenty minutes, and I stop to think about whether I want to get really shaken up. I've got a game of duplicate lined up for that afternoon, and I have a good chance to get into the finals. If I don't mess it up. If I keep my concentration.

"I wonder if I oughtn't to leave early today, Sigfrid," I say.

"Guilty about what, Rob?"

"I'm not sure I remember." I stroke the bunny neck and chuckle. "This is really nice, Sigfrid, although it took me a while to get used to it."

"Guilty about what, Rob?"

I scream: "About murdering her, you jerk!"

"You mean in your dream?"

"No! Really. Twice."

I know I am breathing hard, and I know Sigfrid's sensors are registering it. I fight to get control of myself, so he won't get any crazy ideas. I go over what I have just said in my mind, to tidy it up. "I didn't really murder Sylvia, that is. But I tried! Went after her with a knife!"

210

Sigfrid, calm, reassuring: "It says in your case history that you had a knife in your hand when you had a quarrel with your friend, yes. It doesn't say you 'went after her.' "

"Well, why the hell do you think they put me away? It's just luck I didn't cut her throat."

"Did you, in fact, use the knife against her at all?"

"Use it? No. I was too mad. I threw it on the floor and got up and punched her."

"If you were really trying to murder her, wouldn't you have used the knife?"

"Ah!" Only it is more like "yech"; the word you sometimes see written as "pshaw." "I only wish you'd been there when it happened, Sigfrid. Maybe you would have talked them out of putting me away."

The whole session is going sour. I know it's always a mistake to tell him about my dreams. He twists them around. I sit up, looking with contempt at the crazy furnishings Sigfrid has dreamed up for my benefit, and I decide to let him have it, straight from the shoulder.

"Sigfrid," I say, "as computers go, you're a nice guy, and I enjoy these sessions with you in an intellectual way. But I wonder if we haven't gone about as far as we can go. You're just stirring up old, unnecessary pain, and I frankly don't know why I let you do that to me."

"Your dreams are full of pain, Bob."

"So let it stay in my dreams. I don't want to go back to all that same stale kind of crap they used to give me at the Institute. Maybe I do want to go to bed with my mother. Maybe I do hate my father because he died and deserted me. So what?"

"I know that is a rhetorical question, Bob, but the way to deal with these things is to bring them out into the open."

"For what? To make me hurt?"

"To let the inside hurt come out where you can deal with it."

"Maybe it would be simpler all around if I just made up my mind to go on hurting a little bit, inside. As you say, I'm well compensated, right? I'm not denying that I've got something out of all this. There are times, Sigfrid, when we get through with a session, and I really get a lift out of it. I go out of here with my head full of new thoughts, and the sun is bright on the dome and the air is clean and everybody seems to be smiling at me. But not lately. Lately I think it's very boring and unproductive, and what would you say if I told you I wanted to pack it in?"

"I would say that that was your decision to make, Bob. It always is."

"Well, maybe I'll do that." The old devil outwaits me. He knows I'm not going to make that decision, and he is giving me time to realize it for myself. Then he says:

"Bob? Why did you say you murdered her twice?"

I look at my watch before I answer, and I say, "I guess it was just a slip of the tongue. I really do have to go now, Sigfrid."

I pass up the time in his recovery room, because I don't actually have anything to recover from. Besides I just want to get out of there. Him and his dumb questions. He acts so wise and superior, but what does a teddy-bear know?

22

I went back to my own room that night, but it took me a long time to get to sleep; and Shicky woke me up early to tell me what was happening. There had been only three survivors, and their base award had already been announced: seventeen million five hundred and fifty thousand dollars. Against royalties.

That drove the sleepies out of my eyes. "For what?" I demanded.

Shicky said, "For twenty-three kilograms of artifacts. They think it's a repair kit. Possibly for a ship, since that is where they found it, in a lander on the surface of the planet. But at least they are tools of some sort."

"Tools." I got up, got rid of Shicky, and plodded down the tunnel to the community shower, thinking about tools. Tools could mean a lot. Tools could mean

213

A NOTE ON NEUTRON STARS

Dr. Asmenion. Now, you get a star that has used up its fuel, and it collapses. When I say "collapses," I mean it's shrunk so far that the whole thing, that starts out with maybe the mass and volume of the sun, is squeezed into a ball maybe ten kilometers across. That's dense. If your nose was made out of neutron star stuff, Susie, it would weigh more than Gateway does.

Question. Maybe even more than you do, Yuri?

Dr. Asmenion. Don't make jokes in class. Teacher's sensitive. Anyway, good, close-in readings on a neutron star would be worth a lot, but I don't advise you to use your lander to get them. You need to be in a fully armored Five, and then I wouldn't come much closer than a tenth of an A.U. And watch it. It'll seem as if probably you could get closer, but the gravity shear is bad. It's practically a point source, you see. Steepest gravity gradient you'll ever see, unless you happen to get next to a black hole, God forbid.

a way to open the drive mechanism in the Heechee ships without blowing up everything around. Tools could mean finding out how the drive worked and building our own. Tools could mean almost anything, and what they certainly meant was a cash award of seventeen million five hundred and fifty thousand dollars, not counting royalties, divided three ways.

One of which could have been mine.

It is hard to get a figure like $5,850,000 out of your mind (not to mention royalties) when you think that if you had been a little more foreseeing in your choice of girlfriends you could have had it in your pocket. Call it six million dollars. At my age and health I could have bought paid-up Full Medical for less than half of that, which meant all the tests, therapies, tissue replacements, and organ transplants they could cram into me for the rest of my life . . . which would have been at least fifty years longer than I could expect without it. The other three million plus would have bought me a couple of homes, a career as a lecturer (nobody was more in demand than a successful prospector), a steady income for doing commercials on PV, women, food, cars, travel, women, fame, women . . . and, again, there were always the royalties. They could have come to anything at all, depending on what the R&D people managed to do with the tools. Sheri's find was exactly what Gateway was all about: the pot of gold at the end of the rainbow.

It took an hour for me to get down to the hospital, three tunnel segments and five levels in the dropshaft. I kept changing my mind and going back.

When I finally managed to purge my mind of envy (or at least to bury it where I didn't think it was going to show) and turned up at the reception desk, Sheri was asleep anyway. "You can go in," said the ward nurse.

"I don't want to wake her up."

"I don't think you could," he said. "Don't force it, of course. But she's allowed visitors."

She was in the lowest of three bunks in a twelve-bed room. Three or four of the others were occupied,

215

two of them behind the isolation curtains, milky plastic that you could see through only vaguely. I didn't know who they were. Sheri herself looked quite peacefully resting, one arm under her head, her pretty eyes closed and her strong, dimpled chin resting on her wrist. Her two companions were in the same room, one asleep, one sitting under a holoview of Saturn's rings. I had met him once or twice, a Cuban or Venezuelan or something like that from New Jersey. The only name I could remember for him was Manny. We chatted for a while, and he promised to tell Sheri I had been there. I left and went for a cup of coffee at the commissary, thinking about their trip.

They had come out near a tiny, cold planet way out from a K-6 orange-red cinder of a star, and according to Manny, they hadn't even been sure it was worth the trouble of landing. The readings showed Heechee-metal radiation, but not much; and almost all of it, apparently, was buried under carbon-dioxide snow. Manny was the one who stayed in orbit. Sheri and the other three went down, found a Heechee dig, opened it with great effort and, as usual, found it empty. Then they tracked another trace and found the old lander. They had had to blast to get it open, and in the process two of the prospectors lost integrity of their spacesuits—too close to the blast, I guess. By the time they realized they were in trouble, it was too late for them. They froze. Sheri and the other crewman tried to get them back into their own lander; it must have been pure misery and fear the whole time, and at the end they had to give up. The other man had made one more trip to the abandoned lander, found the tool kit in it, managed to get it back to their own lander. Then they had taken off, leaving the two casualties peacefully frozen behind them. But they had overstayed their limit and they were physical wrecks when they docked with the orbiter. I wasn't clear on what happened after that, but apparently they had failed to secure the lander's air supply and had lost a good deal of it; so they were on short oxygen rations all the way home. The other man was worse off than

216

Sheri. There was a good chance of residual brain damage, and his $5,850,000 might not do him much good. But Sheri, they said, would be all right once she recovered from plain exhaustion. . . .

I didn't envy them the trip. All I envied them was the reward.

I got up and got myself another cup of coffee in the commissary. As I brought it back to the corridor outside, where there were a few benches under the ivy planters, I became aware that something was bugging me. Something about the trip. About the fact that it had been a real winner, one of the all-time greats of Gateway's history. . . .

I dumped the coffee, cup and all, into a disposal hole outside the commissary and headed for the schoolroom. It was only a few minutes away and there was no one else there. That was good; I wasn't ready to talk to anyone yet about what had occurred to me. I keyed the P-phone to information access and got the settings for Sheri's trip; they were, of course, a matter of public record. Then I went down to the practice capsule, again hitting lucky because there was no one around, and set them up on the course selector. Of course, I got good color immediately; and when I pressed the fine-tuner the whole board turned bright pink, except for the rainbow of colors along the side.

There was only one dark line in the blue part of the spectrum.

Well, I thought, so much for Metchnikov's theory about danger readings. They had lost forty percent of the crew on that mission, and that struck me as being quite adequately dangerous; but according to what he had told me, the really hairy ones showed six or seven of those bands.

And in the yellow?

According to Metchnikov, the more bright bands in the yellow, the more financial reward from a trip.

Only in this one there were no bright bands in the yellow at all. There were two thick black "absorption" lines. That's all.

I thumbed the selector off and sat back. So the

A NOTE ON PRAYER FANS

Question. You didn't tell us anything about Heechee prayer fans, and we see more of them than anything else.

Professor Hegramet. What do you want me to tell you, Susie?

Question. Well, I know what they *look* like. Sort of like a rolled-up ice-cream cone made out of crystal. All different colors of crystal. If you hold one right and press on it with your thumb it opens up like a fan.

Professor Hegramet. That's what I know, too. They've been analyzed, same as fire pearls and the blood diamonds. But don't ask me what they're *for.* I don't think the Heechee fanned themselves with them, and I don't think they prayed, either; that's just what the novelty dealers called them. The Heechee left them all over the place, even when they tidied everything else up. I suppose they had a reason. I don't have a clue what that reason was, but if I ever find out I'll tell you.

great brains had labored and brought forth a mouse again: what they had interpreted as an indication of safety didn't really mean you were safe, and what they had interpreted as a promise of good results didn't seem to have any relevance to the first mission in more than a year that had really come up rich.

Back to square one, and back to being scared.

For the next couple of days I kept pretty much to myself.

There are supposed to be eight hundred kilometers of tunnels inside Gateway. You wouldn't think there could be that many in a little chunk of rock that's only about ten kilometers across. But even so, only about two percent of Gateway is airspace; the rest is solid rock. I saw a lot of those eight hundred kilometers.

I didn't cut myself off completely from human companionship, I just didn't seek it out. I saw Klara now and then. I wandered around with Shicky when he was off duty, although it was tiring for him. Sometimes I wandered by myself, sometimes with chance-met friends, sometimes tagging along after a tourist group. The guides knew me and were not averse to having me along (I had been *out!* even if I didn't wear a bangle), until they got the idea that I was thinking of guiding myself. Then they were less friendly.

They were right. I was thinking of it. I was going to have to do something sooner or later. I would have to go out, or I would have to go home; and if I wanted to defer decision on either of those two equally frightening prospects, I would have to decide at least to try to make enough money to stay put.

When Sheri got out of the hospital we had a hell of a party for her, a combination of welcome home, congratulations, and good-bye, Sheri, because she was leaving for Earth the next day. She was shaky but cheerful, and although she wasn't up to dancing she sat hugging me in the corridor for half an hour, promising to miss me. I got quite drunk. It was a good chance for it; the liquor was free. Sheri and her

Cuban friend were picking up the check. In fact, I got so drunk that I never did get to say good-bye to Sheri, because I had to head for the toilet and chuck. Drunk as I was, that struck me as a pity; it was genuine scotch-from-Scotland Gleneagle, none of your local white lightning boiled out of God-knows-what.

Throwing up cleared my head. I came out and leaned against a wall, my face buried in the ivy, breathing hard, and by and by enough oxygen got into my bloodstream that I could recognize Francy Hereira standing next to me. I even said, "Hello, Francy."

He grinned apologetically. "The smell. It was a little strong."

"Sorry," I said huffily, and he looked surprised.

"No, what do you mean? I mean it is bad enough on the cruiser, but every time I come to Gateway I wonder how you live through it. And in those rooms—phew!"

"No offense taken," I said grandly, patting his shoulder. "I must say goodnight to Sheri."

"She's gone, Bob. Got tired. They took her back to the hospital."

"In that case," I said, "I will only say goodnight to you." I bowed and lurched down the tunnel. It is difficult being drunk in nearly zero gravity. You long for the reassurance of a hundred kilos of solid weight to hold you to the ground. I understand, from what was reported to me later, that I pulled a solid rack of ivy off the wall, and I know from what I felt the next morning that I bashed my head into something hard enough to leave a purplish bruise the size of my ear. I became conscious of Francy coming up behind me and helping me navigate, and about halfway home I became conscious that there was someone else on my other arm. I looked, and it was Klara. I have only the most confused recollection of being put to bed, and when I woke up the next morning, desperately hung over, I was astonished to find that Klara was in it, too.

I got up as inconspicuously as I could and headed for the bathroom, needing a lot to throw up some

CORPORATION REPORT: ORBIT 37

74 vessels returned from launches during this period, with a total crew of 216. 20 additional vessels were judged lost, with a total crew of 54. In addition 19 crew members were killed or died of injuries, although the vessels returned. Three returning vessels were damaged past the point of feasible repair.

Landing reports: 19. Five of the surveyed planets had life at the microscopic level or higher; one possessed structured plant or animal life, none intelligent.

Artifacts: Additional samples of usual Heechee equipment were returned. No artifacts from other sources. No previously unknown Heechee artifacts.

Samples: Chemical or mineral, 145. None adjudged of sufficient value to justify exploitation. Living organic, 31. Three of these were judged hazardous and disposed of in space. None found of exploitable value.

Science awards in period: $8,754,500.

Other cash awards in period, including royalties: $357,856,000. Awards and royalties arising from new discoveries in period (other than science awards): 0.

Personnel grounded or exiting Gateway in period: 151. Lost operationally: 75 (including 2 lost in lander exercises). Medically unfit at end of year: 84. Total losses: 310.

New personnel arriving in period: 415. Returned to duty: 66. Total increment during period: 481. Net gain in personnel: 171.

more. It took quite a while, and I topped it off with another shower, my second in four days and a wild extravagance, considering my financial state. But I felt a little better, and when I got back to my room Klara had got up, fetched tea, probably from Shicky, and was waiting for me.

"Thanks," I said, meaning it. I was infinitely dehydrated.

"A sip at a time, old horse," she said anxiously, but I knew enough not to force much into my stomach. I managed two swallows and stretched out in the hammock again, but by then I was pretty sure I would live.

"I didn't expect to see you here," I said.

"You were, ah, insistent," she told me. "Not much on performance. But awfully anxious to try."

"Sorry about that."

She reached over and squeezed my foot. "Not to worry. How've things been, anyway?"

"Oh, all right. It was a nice party. I don't remember seeing you there?"

She shrugged. "I came late. Wasn't invited, as a matter of fact."

I didn't say anything; I had been aware Klara and Sheri were not very friendly, and assumed it was because of me. Klara, reading my mind, said, "I've never cared for Scorpios, especially unevolved ones with that awful huge jaw. Never get an intelligent, spiritual thought from one of them." Then she said, to be fair, "But she has courage, you have to give her that."

"I don't believe I'm up to this argument," I said.

"Not an argument, Bob." She leaned over, cradling my head. She smelled sweaty and female; rather nice, in some circumstances, but not quite what I wanted right then.

"Hey," I said. "What ever became of musk oil?"

"What?"

"I mean," I said, suddenly realizing something that had been true for quite a while, "you used to wear that perfume a lot. That was the first thing I remember noticing about you." I thought of Francy Hereira's remark about the Gateway smell and realized it had been a long time since I had noticed Klara smelling particularly nice.

"Honey-Bob, are you trying to start an argument with me?"

"Certainly not. But I'm curious. When did you stop wearing it?"

She shrugged and didn't answer, unless looking annoyed is an answer. It was enough of an answer for me, because I'd told her often enough that I liked the perfume. "So how are you doing with your shrink?" I asked, to change the subject.

It didn't seem to be any improvement. Klara said, without warmth, "I guess you're feeling pretty rotten with that head. I think I'll go home now."

"No, I mean it," I insisted. "I'm curious about your progress." She hadn't told me a word, though I knew she had signed up; and she seemed to spend two or three hours a day with him. Or it. She had elected to try the machine service from the Corporation computer, I knew.

"Not bad," she said distantly.

"Get over your father fixation yet?" I inquired.

Klara said, "Bob, did it ever occur to you that you might get some good out of a little help yourself?"

"Funny you should say that. Louise Forehand said the very same thing to me the other day."

"Not funny. Think about it. See you later."

I dropped my head back after she had gone and closed my eyes. Go to a shrink! What did I need with that? All I needed was one lucky find like Sheri's. . . .

And all I needed to make that was—was—

Was the guts to sign up for another trip.

But that kind of guts, for me, seemed to be in very short supply.

Time was slipping by, or I was destroying it, and the way I began destroying one day was to go to the museum. They had already installed a complete holo set of Sheri's find. I played the disk over two or three times, just to see what seventeen million five hundred and fifty thousand dollars looked like. It mostly looked like irrelevant junk. That was when each piece was displayed on its own. There were about ten little prayer fans, proving, I guess, that the Hee-chee liked to include a few art objects even with a tire-repair kit. Or whatever the rest of it was: things like triangle-bladed screwdrivers with flexible shafts, things like socket wrenches, but made of some soft material; things like electrical test probes, and things like nothing you ever saw before. Spread out item by item they seemed pretty random, but the way they fit into each other, and into the flat nested boxes that made up the set, was a marvel of packing economy. Seventeen million five hundred and fifty thousand dollars, and if I had stayed with Sheri I could have been one of the shareholders.

Or one of the corpses.

I stopped off at Klara's place and hung around for a while, but she wasn't home. It wasn't her usual time for being shrunk. On the other hand, I had lost track of Klara's usual times. She had found another kid to mother when its parents were busy: a little black girl, maybe four years old, who had come up with a mother who was an astrophysicist and a father who was an exobiologist. And what else Klara had found to keep herself busy I was not sure.

I drifted back to my own room, and Louise Fore-hand peered out of her door and followed me in. "Bob," she said urgently, "do you know anything about a big danger bonus coming up?"

I made room for her on the pad. "Me? No. Why would I?" Her pale, muscular face was tauter than ever, I could not tell why.

"I thought maybe you'd heard something. From Dane Metchnikov, maybe. I know you're close to him, and I've seen him talking to Klara in the school-room." I didn't respond to that, I wasn't sure what I wanted to say. "There's a rumor that there's a science trip coming up that's pretty hairy. And I'd like to sign on for it."

I put my arm around her. "What's the matter, Louise?"

"They posted Willa dead." She began to cry.

I held her for a while and let her cry it out. I would have comforted her if I had known how, but what comfort was there to give? After a while I got up and rummaged around in my cupboard, looking for a joint Klara had left there a couple days before. I found it, lighted it, passed it to her.

Louise took a long, hard pull, and held it for quite a while. Then she puffed out. "She's dead, Bob," she said. She was over crying now, somber but relaxed; even the muscles around her neck and up and down her spine were tension-free.

"She might come back yet, Louise."

She shook her head. "Not really. The Corporation posted her ship lost. *It* might come back, maybe. Willa won't be alive in it. Their last stretch of rations would have run out two weeks ago." She stared into space for a moment, then sighed and roused herself to take another pull on the joint. "I wish Sess were here," she said, leaning back and stretching; I could feel the play of muscles against the palm of my hand.

The dope was hitting her, I could see. I knew it was hitting me. It wasn't any of your usual Gateway windowbox stuff, sneaked in among the ivy. Klara had got hold of pure Naples Red from one of the cruiser boys, shade-grown on the slopes of Mount Vesuvius between the rows of vines that made Lacrimae Cristi wine. She turned toward me and snuggled her chin into my neck. "I really love my family," she said, calmly enough. "I wish we had hit lucky here. We're about due for some luck."

"Hush, honey," I said, nuzzling into her hair. Her hair led to her ear, and her ear led to her lips, and step by step we were making love in a timeless, gentle, stoned way. It was very relaxed. Louise was competent, unanxious, and accepting. After a couple of months of Klara's nervous paroxysms it was like coming home to Mom's chicken soup. At the end she smiled, kissed me, and turned away. She was very

225

Classifieds.

I NEED your courage to go for any half-mil plus bonus. Don't ask me. Order me. 87-299.

PUBLIC AUCTION unclaimed personal effects nonreturnees. Corporation Area Charlie Nine, 1300–1700 tomorrow.

YOUR DEBTS are paid when you achieve Oneness. He/She is Heechee and He/She Forgives. Church of the Marvelously Maintained Motorcycle. 88-344.

MONOSEXUALS ONLY for mutual sympathy only. No touching. 87-913.

still, and her breathing was even. She lay silent for a long time, and it wasn't until I realized that my wrist was getting damp that I knew she was crying again.

"I'm sorry, Bob," she said when I began to pat her. "It's just that we've never had any luck. Some days I can live with that fact, and some days not. This is one of the bad ones."

"You will."

"I don't think so. I don't believe it anymore."

"You got here, didn't you? That's pretty lucky."

She twisted herself around to face me, her eyes scanning mine. I said, "I mean, think of how many billion people would give their left testicles to be here."

Louise said slowly, "Bob—" She stopped. I started to speak but she put her hand over my lips. "Bob," she said, "do you know how we managed to get here?"

"Sure. Sess sold his airbody."

"We sold more than that. The airbody brought a little over a hundred thousand. That wasn't enough for even one of us. We got the money from Hat."

"Your son? The one that died?"

She said, "Hat had a brain tumor. They caught it in time, or anyway, almost in time. It was operable. He could have lived, oh, I don't know, ten years at least. He would have been messed up some. His speech centers were affected, and so was his muscle control. But he could have been alive right now. Only—" She took her hand off my chest to rub it across her face, but she wasn't crying. "He didn't want us to spend the airbody money on Term Medical for him. It would have just about paid for the surgery, and then we would have been broke again. So what he did, he sold himself, Bob. He sold off all his parts. More than just a left testicle. All of him. They were fine, first-quality Nordic male twenty-two-year-old parts, and they were worth a bundle. He signed himself over to the medics and they—how do you say it? —put him to sleep. There must be pieces of Hat in a dozen different people now. They sold off everything

227

for transplants, and they gave us the money. Close to a million dollars. Got us here, with some to spare. So that's where our luck came from, Bob."

I said, "I'm sorry."

"For what? We just don't have the luck, Bob. Hat's dead. Willa's dead. God knows where my husband is, or our one last surviving kid. And I'm here, and, Bob, half the time I wish with all my heart that I were dead too."

I left her sleeping in my bed and wandered down to Central Park. I called Klara, found her out, left a message to say where I was, and spent the next hour or so on my back, looking up at the mulberries ripening on the tree. There was no one there except for a couple of tourists taking a fast look through before their ship left. I didn't pay attention to them, didn't even hear them leave. I was feeling sorry for Louise and for all the Forehands, and even sorrier for myself. They didn't have the luck, but what I didn't have hurt a lot more; I didn't have the courage to see where my luck would take me. Sick societies squeeze adventurers out like grape pips. The grape pips don't have much to say about it. I suppose it was the same with Columbus's seamen or the pioneers manhandling their covered wagons through Comanche territory; they must have been scared witless, like me, but they didn't have much choice. Like me. But, God, how frightened I was. . . .

I heard voices, a child's and a light, slower laugh that was Klara's. I sat up.

"Hello, Bob," she said, standing before me with her hand on the head of a tiny black girl in corn-row hair. "This is Watty."

"Hello, Watty."

My voice didn't sound right, even to me. Klara took a closer look and demanded, "What's the matter?"

I couldn't answer that question in one sentence, so I chose one facet. "Willa Forehand's been posted dead."

Klara nodded without saying anything. Watty piped,

228

"Please, Klara. Throw the ball." Klara tossed it to her, caught it, tossed it again, all in the Gateway adagio.

I said, "Louise wants to go on a danger-bonus launch. I think what she wants is for me, for us, to go and take her with us."

"Oh?"

"Well, what about it? Has Dane said anything to you about one of his specials?"

"No! I haven't seen Dane for—I don't know. Anyway, he shipped out this morning on a One."

"He didn't have a farewell party!" I protested, surprised. She pursed her lips.

The little girl called, "Hey, mister! Catch!" When she threw the ball it came floating up like a hot-air balloon to a mooring mast, but even so I almost missed it. My mind was on something else. I tossed it back with concentration.

After a minute Klara said, "Bob? I'm sorry. I guess I was in a bad mood."

"Yeah." My mind was very busy.

She said placatingly, "We've been having some hard times, Bob. I don't want to be raspy with you. I—I brought you something."

I looked around, and she took my hand and slid something up over it, onto my arm.

It was a launch bracelet, Heechee metal, worth five hundred dollars anywhere. I hadn't been able to afford to buy one. I stared at it, trying to think of what I wanted to say.

"Bob?"

"What?"

There was an edge to her voice. "It's customary to say thank you."

"It's customary," I said, "to give a truthful answer to a question. Like not saying you hadn't seen Dane Metchnikov when you were with him just last night."

She flared, "You've been spying on me!"

"You've been lying to me."

"Bob! You don't own me. Dane's a human being, and a friend."

229

A NOTE ON METALLURGY

Question. I saw a report that Heechee metal had been analyzed by the National Bureau of Standards—

Professor Hegramet. No, you didn't, Tetsu.

Question. But it was on the PV—

Professor Hegramet. No. You saw a report that the Bureau of Standards had issued a quantitative *assessment* of Heechee metal. Not an analysis. Just a description: tensile strength, fracture strength, melting point, all that stuff.

Question. I'm not sure I understand the difference.

Professor Hegramet. Now we know exactly what it *does.* We don't yet know what it *is.* What's the most interesting thing about Heechee metal? You, Teri?

Question. It glows?

Professor Hegramet. It glows, yes. It emits light. Bright enough so that we don't need anything else to light our rooms, we have to cover it over when we want dark. And it's been glowing for half a million years at least like that. Where does the energy come from? The Bureau says there are some posturanic elements in it, and probably they drive the radiation; but we don't know what they are. There's also something in it that looks like an isotope of copper. Well, copper doesn't *have* any stable isotopes. Up to now. So what the Bureau says is what the exact frequency of the blue light is, and all the physical measurements to eight or nine decimals; but the report doesn't tell you how to make any.

"Friend!" I barked. The last thing Metchnikov was to anyone was a friend. Just thinking about Klara with him made my groin crawl. I didn't like the sensation, because I couldn't identify it. It wasn't just anger, wasn't even just jealousy. There was a component that remained obstinately opaque. I said, knowing it was illogical, hearing myself seem almost to whine, "I introduced you to him!"

"That doesn't give you ownership! All right," Klara snarled, "maybe I went to bed with him a few times. It doesn't change how I feel about you."

"It changes how I feel about you, Klara."

She stared incredulously. "You have the nerve to say that? Coming here, smelling of sex with some cheap floozy?"

That one caught me off guard. "There was nothing cheap about it! I was comforting someone in pain."

She laughed. The sound was unpleasant; anger is unbecoming. "Louise Forehand? She hustled her way up here, did you know that?"

The little girl was holding the ball and staring at us now. I could see we were frightening her. I said, trying to tighten my voice to keep the anger from spilling out, "Klara, I'm not going to let you make a fool out of me."

"Ah," she said in inarticulate disgust, and turned around to go. I reached out to touch her, and she sobbed and hit me, as hard as she could. The blow caught me on the shoulder.

That was a mistake.

That's always a mistake. It isn't a matter of what's rational or justified, it is a matter of signals. It was the wrong signal to give me. The reason wolves don't kill each other off is that the smaller and weaker wolf always surrenders. It rolls over, bares its throat and puts its paws in the air to signal that it is beaten. When that happens the winner is physically unable to attack anymore. If it were not that way, there wouldn't be any wolves left. For the same reason men don't usually kill women, or not by beating them to death. They can't. However much he wants to hit her, his

231

internal machinery vetoes it. But if the woman makes the mistake of giving him a different signal by hitting him first—

I punched her four or five times, as hard as I could, on the breast, in the face, in the belly. She fell to the ground, sobbing. I knelt beside her, lifted her up with one hand and, in absolutely cold blood, slapped her twice more. It was all happening as if choreographed by God, absolutely inevitably; and at the same time I could feel that I was breathing as hard as though I'd climbed a mountain on a dead run. The blood was thundering in my ears. Everything I saw was hazed with red.

I finally heard a distant, thin crying.

I looked and saw the little girl, Watty, staring at me, her mouth open, tears rolling down her wide, purplish-black cheeks. I started to move toward her to reassure her. She screamed and ran behind a grape trellis.

I turned back toward Klara, who was sitting up, not looking at me, her hand cupped over her mouth. She took the hand away and stared at something in it: a tooth.

I didn't say anything. I didn't know what to say, and didn't trust myself to think of anything. I turned and left.

I don't remember what I did for the next few hours.

I didn't sleep, although I was physically exhausted. I sat on the chest of drawers in my room for a while. Then I left it again. I remember talking to somebody, I think it was a straggling tourist off the Venus ship, about how adventurous and exciting prospecting was. I remember eating something in the commissary. And all the time I was thinking: I wanted to *kill* Klara. I had been containing all that stored-up fury, and I hadn't even let myself know it was there until she pulled the trigger.

I didn't know if she would ever forgive me. I wasn't sure she ought to, and I wasn't even sure that I wanted her to. I could not imagine our ever being lovers again. But what I finally was sure I wanted was to apologize.

Only she wasn't in her rooms. There was no one

there but a plump young black woman, slowly sorting out clothes, with a tragic face. When I asked after Klara she began to cry. "She's gone," the woman sobbed.

"Gone?"

"Oh, she looked awful. Someone must have beaten her up! She brought Watty back and said she wouldn't be able to take care of her anymore. She gave me all her clothes, but—what am I going to do with Watty when I'm working?"

"Gone where?"

The woman lifted her head. "Back to Venus. On the ship. It left an hour ago."

I didn't talk to anyone else. Alone in my own bed, somehow I got to sleep.

When I got up I gathered together everything I owned: my clothes, my holodisks, my chess set, my wristwatch. The Heechee bracelet that Klara had given me. I went around and sold them off. I cleaned out my credit account and put all the money together: it came to a total of fourteen hundred dollars and change. I took the money up to the casino and put it all on Number 31 on the roulette wheel.

The big slow ball drifted into a socket: Green. Zero.

I went down to mission control and signed for the first One that was available, and twenty-four hours later I was in space.

23

"How do you really feel about Dane, Bob?"

"How the hell do you think I feel? He seduced my girl."

"That's a strangely old-fashioned way to put it, Bob. And it happened an awfully long time ago."

"Sure it did." Sigfrid strikes me as being unfair. He sets up rules, then he doesn't play by them. I say indignantly, "Cut it out, Sigfrid. All that *happened* a long time ago, but it isn't *being* a long time ago, for me, because I've never let it come out. It's still brand new inside my head. Isn't that what you're supposed to do for me? Let all that old stuff inside my head come out so it can dry up and blow away and not cripple me anymore?"

"I'd still like to know why it stays so brand new inside your head, Bob."

A NOTE ON HEECHEE HABITAT

Question. Don't we even know what a Heechee table or any old housekeeping thing looks like?

Professor Hegramet. We don't even know what a Heechee house looks like. We never found one. Just tunnels. They liked branching shafts, with rooms opening out of them. They liked big chambers shaped like spindles, tapered at both ends, too. There's one here, two on Venus, probably the remains of one that's half eroded away on Peggy's World.

Question. I know what the bonus is for finding intelligent alien life, but what's the bonus for finding a Heechee?

Professor Hegramet. Just find one. Then name your price.

"Oh, Christ, Sigfrid!" This is one of Sigfrid's stupid times. He can't handle some complex kinds of input, I guess. When you come right down to it he's only a machine and can't do anything he isn't programmed to do. Mostly he just responds to key words—well, with a little attention to meaning, sure. And to nuance, as far as it is expressed by voice tone, or by what the sensors in the pad and straps tell him about my muscle activity.

"If you were a person instead of a machine, you'd understand," I tell him.

"Perhaps so, Bob."

To get him back on the right track I say: "It is true that it happened a long time ago. I don't see what you're asking beyond that."

"I'm asking you to resolve a contradiction I perceive in what you say. You've been saying that you don't mind the fact that your girlfriend, Klara, had sexual relations with other men. Why is it so important that she did with Dane?"

"Dane didn't treat her right!" And, good God, he certainly didn't. He left her stuck like a fly in amber.

"Is it because of how he treated Klara, Bob? Or is it something between Dane and you?"

"Never! There was never anything between Dane and me!"

"You did tell me he was bi, Bob. What about the flight you took with him?"

"He had two other men to play with! Not me, boy, no, I swear! Not me. Oh," I say, trying to calm my voice enough to make it reflect the very mild interest I really felt in this stupid subject, "to be sure, he tried to put the make on me once or twice. But I told him it wasn't my style."

"Your voice, Bob," he says, "seems to reflect more anger than your words account for."

"Damn you, Sigfrid!" I really am angry now, I admit it. I can hardly get the words out. "You get me pissed off with your wild accusations. Sure, I let him put his arm around me once or twice. That's as far as I went. Nothing serious. I was just abusing myself to make the time pass. I liked him well enough. Big, good-looking fellow. You get lonesome when— now what?"

Sigfrid is making a sound, sort of like clearing one's throat. It is how he interrupts without interrupting. "What did you just say, Bob?"

"What? When?"

"When you said there was nothing serious between you."

"Christ, I don't know what I said. There was nothing serious, that's all. I was just entertaining myself, to make the time pass."

"You didn't use the word 'entertaining,' Bob."

"I didn't? What word did I use?"

I reflect, listening for the echo of my own voice. "I guess I said 'amusing myself.' What about it?"

"You didn't say 'amusing' either, Bob. What did you say?"

"I don't know!"

"You said, 'I was just abusing myself,' Bob."

My defenses go up. I feel as though I had suddenly discovered I had wet my pants, or that my fly was open. I step outside my body and look at my own head.

"What does 'abusing myself' mean to you, Bob?"

"Say," I say, laughing, genuinely impressed and amused at the same time, "that's a real Freudian slip, isn't it? You fellows are pretty keen. My compliments to the programmers."

Sigfrid doesn't respond to my urbane comment. He just lets me stew in it for a minute.

"All right," I say. I feel very open and vulnerable, letting nothing at all happen, living in that moment as though it were lasting forever, like Klara stuck in her instant and eternal fall.

Sigfrid says gently, "Bob. When you masturbated, did you ever have fantasies about Dane?"

"I hated it," I say.

He waits.

"I hated myself for it. I mean, not hated, exactly. More like despised. Poor goddamn son of a bitch, me,

237

all kinky and awful, beating his meat and thinking about being screwed by his girl's lover."

Sigfrid waits me out for a while. Then he says, "I think you really want to cry, Bob."

He's right, but I don't say anything.

"Would you like to cry?" he invites.

"I'd love it," I say.

"Then why don't you go ahead and cry, Bob?"

"I wish I could," I say. "Unfortunately, I just don't know how."

24

I was just turning over, making up my mind to go to sleep, when I noticed that the colors on the Heechee guidance system were breaking up. It was the fifty-fifth day of my trip, the twenty-seventh since turnover. The colors had been shocking pink for the whole fifty-five days. Now whorls of pure white formed, grew, clotted together.

I was arriving! Wherever it was going to turn out to be when I got there, I was arriving.

My little old ship—the smelly, hurtful, tedious coffin I had been banging around in for nearly two months by myself, talking to myself, playing games with myself, tired of myself—was well below light-speed. I leaned over to look at the viewscreen, now relatively "down" to me because I had been decelerating, and saw nothing that looked very exciting. Oh,

MISSION REPORT

Vessel 3-104, Voyage 031D18. Crew
N. Ahoya, Ts. Zakharcenko, L. Marks.

Transit time 119 days 4 hours. Position not identified. Apparently
outside galactic cluster, in dust
cloud. Identification of external
galaxies doubtful.

Summary. "We found no trace of any
planet, artifact, or landable asteroid within scanning distance. Nearest star approximately 1.7 l.y.
Conjecture whatever was there has
since been destroyed. Life-support
systems began to malfunction on return
trip and Larry Marks died."

there was a star, yes. There were lots of stars in a scattering of groupings that in no way looked familiar; half a dozen blues ranging from bright to hurt-the-eyes; a red one that stood out more for intensity of hue than luminosity. It was an angry-looking red coal, not much brighter than Mars is from Earth, but a deeper, uglier red.

I made myself take an interest.

That was not really easy. After two months of rejecting everything around me because it was boring or threatening, it was hard for me to switch over to a welcoming, vulnerable mode. I switched on the spherical scan and peered out as the ship began to rotate in its scanning pattern, slicing orange-peel strips of sky to capture in the cameras and analyzers.

And almost at once I got a huge, bright, nearby signal return.

Fifty-five days of boredom and exhaustion went right out of my mind. There was something either very big or very close. I forgot about being sleepy. I crouched over the viewscreen, holding on with hands and knees, and then I saw it: a squared-off object marching into the screen. Glowing all over. Pure Heechee metal! It was irregularly slab-sided, with rounded pimples studding one of the flat sides.

And the adrenalin began to flow, and visions of sugarplums danced in my head. I watched it out of sight, and then hauled myself over to the scan analyzer, waiting to see what would come out. There was no question that it was good, the only question was *how* good. Maybe extraordinarily good! Maybe a whole Peggy's World all my own!—with a royalty in the millions of dollars every year all the rest of my life! Maybe only a vacant shell. Maybe—the squared-off shape suggested it—maybe that wildest of dreams, a whole *big* Heechee ship that I could enter into and fly around anywhere I chose, big enough to carry a thousand people and a million tons of cargo! All those dreams were possible; and even if they all failed, if it was just an abandoned shell, all that it needed was one thing inside it, one little doodad, one gadget, one

241

whoozie that nobody had ever found before that could be taken apart and reproduced and made to work on Earth. . . .

I stumbled and raked my knuckles against the spiral gadget, now glowing soft gold. I sucked the blood off them and realized the ship was moving.

It shouldn't have been moving! It wasn't programmed to do that. It was meant to hang in whatever orbit it was programmed to find, and just stay there until I looked around and made my decisions.

I stared around, confused and baffled. The glowing slab was firmly in the middle of the viewscreen now, and it stayed there; the ship had stopped its automatic spherical scan. Belatedly I heard the distant high yell of the lander motors. They were what was moving me; my ship was targeted for that slab.

And a green light was glowing over the pilot's seat.

That was wrong! The green light was installed on Gateway by human beings. It had nothing to do with the Heechee; it was the plain old people's radio circuit, announcing that someone was calling me. Who? Who could be anywhere near my brand-new discovery?

I thumbed on the TBS circuit and shouted, "Hello?"

There was an answer. I didn't understand it; it seemed to be in some foreign language, perhaps Chinese. But it was human, all right. "Talk English!" I yelled. "Who the hell are you?"

Pause. Then another voice. "Who are *you*?"

"My name is Bob Broadhead," I snarled.

"Broadhead?" Confused mumbling of a couple of voices. Then the English-speaking voice again: "We don't have any record of a prospector named Broadhead. Are you from Aphrodite?"

"What's Aphrodite?"

"Oh, Christ! Who *are* you? Listen, this is Gateway Two control and we don't have time to screw around. Identify yourself!"

Gateway Two!

I snapped off the radio and lay back, watching the slab grow larger, ignoring the demand of the green light. Gateway Two? How ridiculous! If I had wanted

242

to go to Gateway Two I would have signed up in the regular course and accepted the penalty of paying royalties on anything I might find. I would have flown out secure as any tourist, on a course that had been tested a hundred times. I hadn't done that. I had picked a setting no one else had ever used and taken my risks. And I had felt every one of them, scared out of my brain for fifty-five bad days.

It wasn't fair!

I lost my head. I lunged toward the Heechee course director and shoved the wheels around at random.

It was a failure I couldn't accept. I was braced to find nothing. I was not braced to find I had done something easy, for no reward at all.

But what I produced was a bigger failure still. There was a bright yellow flash from the course board, and then all the colors went black.

The thin scream from the lander motors stopped.

The feeling of motion was gone. The ship was dead. Nothing was moving. Nothing worked in the Heechee complex; nothing, not even the cooling system.

By the time Gateway Two sent a ship out to haul me in I was delirious with heatstroke, in an ambient temperature of 75° C.

Gateway was hot and dank. Gateway Two was cold enough that I had to borrow jacket, gloves, and heavy underwear. Gateway stank of sweat and sewers. Gateway Two tasted of rusty steel. Gateway was bright and loud and full of people. On Gateway Two there was almost no sound, and only seven human beings, not counting myself, to make any. The Heechee had left Gateway Two not quite completed. Some of the tunnels ended in bare rock, and there were only a few dozen of them. No one had got around to planting vegetation yet, and all the air there was came from chemical processors. The partial pressure of O_2 was under 150 millibars, and the rest of the atmosphere was a nitrogen-helium mix, not much more than half earth-normal pressure altogether, that made the voices highpitched and left me gasping for the first few hours.

The man who helped me out of my lander and bundled me up against the sudden cold was a dark, immense Martian-Japanese named Norio Ituno. He put me in his own bed, filled me with liquids and let me rest for an hour. I dozed, and when I woke up he was sitting there, looking at me with amusement and respect. The respect was for someone who had slain a five-hundred-million-dollar ship. The amusement was that I was idiot enough to do it.

"I guess I'm in trouble," I said.

"I would say so, yes," he agreed. "The ship is totally dead. Never saw anything like it before."

"I didn't know a Heechee ship *could* go dead like that."

He shrugged. "You did something original, Broadhead. How are you feeling?" I sat up to answer him, and he nodded. "We're pretty busy right now. I'm going to have to let you take care of yourself for a couple of hours—if you can?—fine. Then we'll have a party for you."

"Party!" It was the farthest thing from my mind. "For what?"

"We don't meet someone like you every day, Broadhead," he said admiringly, and left me to my thoughts.

I didn't like my thoughts very much, and after a while I got up, put on the gloves, buttoned up the jacket, and started exploring. It didn't take long; there wasn't much there. I heard sounds of activity from the lower levels, but the echoes traveled at queer angles along the empty corridors, and I saw no one. Gateway Two didn't have a tourist trade, and so there wasn't any nightclub or casino, no restaurant that I could find . . . not even a latrine. After a little while that question began to seem urgent. I reasoned that Ituno would have to have something like that near his room, and tried to retrace my steps to there, but that didn't work, either. There were cubicles along some of the corridors, but they were unfinished. No one lived there, and no one had troubled to install plumbing.

244

Dear Voice of Gateway:

Are you a reasonable and open-minded person? Then prove it by reading this letter all the way through to the end before making up your mind about what it says. There are thirteen occupied levels in Gateway. There are thirteen residences in each of thirteen (count them yourself) of the housing halls. Do you think this letter is just silly superstition? Then look at the evidence for yourself! Launches 83-20, 84-1 and 84-10 (what do the digits add up to?) were <u>all</u> declared overdue in List 86-13! Gateway Corporation, wake up! Let the skeptics and bigots jeer. Human lives depend on your willingness to risk a little ridicule. It would cost nothing to omit the Danger Numbers from all programs—except courage!

M. Gloyner, 88-331

It was not one of my better days.

When I finally found a toilet I puzzled over it for ten minutes and would guiltily have left it impolitely soiled if I had not heard a sound outside the cubicle. A plump little woman was standing there, waiting.

"I don't know how to flush it," I apologized.

She looked me up and down. "You're Broadhead," she stated, and then: "Why don't you go to Aphrodite?"

"What's Aphrodite—no, wait. First, how do you flush this thing? Then, what's Aphrodite?"

She pointed to a button on the edge of the door; I had thought it was a light switch. When I touched it the whole bottom of the seamless bowl began to glow and in ten seconds there was nothing inside but ash, then nothing at all.

"Wait for me," she commanded, disappearing inside. When she came out she said, "Aphrodite's where the money is, Broadhead. You're going to need it."

I let her take my arm and pull me along. Aphrodite, I began to understand, was a planet. A new one, that a ship from Gateway Two had opened up less than forty days earlier, and a big one. "You'd have to pay royalty, of course," she said. "And so far they haven't found anything big, just the usual Heechee debris. But there's thousands of square miles to explore, and it'll be months before the first batch of prospectors starts coming out from Gateway. We only sent the word back forty days ago. Have you had any hot-planet experience?"

"Hot-planet experience?"

"I mean," she explained, pulling me down a dropshaft and calling up to me, "have you ever explored a planet that's hot?"

"No. As a matter of fact, I haven't had any experience at all, that counts for anything. One trip. Empty. I didn't even land."

"Pity," she said. "Still, there's not that much to learn. You know what Venus is like? Aphrodite's just a little bit worse. The primary's a-flare star, and you

We sniff for your scent in the gas of Orion,
We dig for your den with the dogs of Procyon,
From Baltimore, Buffalo, Bonn, and Benares
We seek you round Algol, Arcturus, Antares.
       We'll find you some day.
Little lost Heechee, we're on our way!

don't want to be caught in the open. But the Heechee digs are all underground. If you find one, you're in."

"What are the chances of finding one?" I asked.

"Well," she said thoughtfully, pulling me off the cable and down a tunnel, "not all that good, maybe. After all, you're out in the open when you're prospecting. On Venus they use armored airbodies and they zap around anywhere they want to go, no trouble. Well, maybe a *little* trouble," she conceded. "But they don't lose very many prospectors anymore. Maybe one percent."

"What percent do you lose on Aphrodite?"

"More than that. Yes, I grant you, it's higher than that. You have to use the lander from your ship, and of course it's not very mobile on the surface of a planet. Especially a planet with a surface like molten sulfur and winds like hurricanes—when they're mild."

"It sounds charming," I said. "Why aren't you out there now?"

"Me? I'm an out-pilot. I'm going back to Gateway in about ten days, soon as I get a cargo loaded, or somebody comes in and wants a ride back."

"I want a ride back right now."

"Oh, cripes, Broadhead! Don't you know what kind of trouble you're in? You broke regulations by messing with the control board. They'll throw the book at you."

I thought it over carefully. Then I said, "Thanks, but I think I'll take my chances."

"Don't you understand? Aphrodite has *guaranteed* Heechee remains. You could take a hundred trips without finding anything like this."

"Sweetie," I said, "I couldn't take a hundred trips for anything, not now and not ever. I don't know if I can take one. I *think* I have the guts to get back to Gateway. Beyond that, I don't know."

I was on Gateway Two, all together, thirteen days. Hester Bergowiz, the out-pilot, kept trying to talk me into going to Aphrodite, I guess because she didn't want me taking up valuable cargo space on her return flight. The others didn't care. They only thought I was

248

crazy. I was a problem for Ituno, who was loosely in charge of keeping things straight on Two. Technically I was an illegal entrant, without a dime's worth of per capita paid and with nothing to pay it with. He would have been within his rights to toss me out into space without a suit. He solved it by putting me to work loading low-priority cargo into Hester's Five, mostly prayer fans and samples for analysis from Aphrodite. That took two days, and then he designated me chief gofer for the three people who were rebuilding suits for the next batch of explorers of Aphrodite. They had to use Heechee torches to soften the metal enough to bend it onto the suits, and I wasn't trusted with any of that. It takes two years to train a person to handle a Heechee torch in close quarters. But I was allowed to muscle the suits and sheets of Heechee metal into position for them, to fetch tools, to go for coffee . . . and to put the suits on when they were finished, and exit into space to make sure they didn't leak.

None of them leaked.

On the twelfth day, two Fives came in from Gateway, loaded with happy, eager prospectors bringing all the wrong equipment. The word about Aphrodite had not had time to get to Gateway and back, so the new fish didn't know what goodies were in store. Just by accident, one of them was a young girl on a science mission, a former student of Professor Hegramet's who was supposed to make anthropometric studies of Gateway Two. On his own authority Norio Ituno reassigned her to Aphrodite, and decreed a combination welcome and farewell party. The ten newcomers and I outnumbered our hosts; but what they lacked in numbers they made up in drinking, and it was a good party. I found myself a celebrity. The new fish couldn't get over the fact that I had slain a Heechee ship and survived.

I was almost sorry to leave . . . not counting being scared.

Ituno splashed three fingers of rice whisky into a glass for me and offered me a toast. "Sorry to see you go, Broadhead," he said. "Sure you won't change your

Classifieds.

SHADE-GROWN BROADLEAF hand tended and rolled. $2 roach. 87-307.

PRESENT WHEREABOUTS Agosto T. Agnelli. Call Corporation security for Interpol. Reward.

STORIES, POEMS published. Perfect way to preserve memories for your children. Surprisingly low cost. Publishers' rep, 87-349.

ANYBODY FROM Pittsburgh or Paducah? I'm homesick. 88-226.

mind? We've got more armored ships and suits than we have prospectors right now, but I don't know how long that's going to last. If you change your mind after you get back—"

"I'm not going to change my mind," I said.

"Banzai," he said, and drank. "Listen, do you know an old guy named Bakin?"

"Shicky? Sure. My neighbor."

"Give him my regards," he said, pouring another drink for the purpose. "He's a great guy, but he reminds me of you. I was with him when he lost his legs: got caught in the lander when we had to jettison. Damn near died. By the time we got him to Gateway he was all swelled up and smelled like hell; we had to take the legs off, two days out. I did it myself."

"He's a great person, all right," I said absently, finishing the drink and holding the glass out for more. "Hey. What do you mean, he reminds you of me?"

"Can't make up his mind, Broadhead. He's got a stake that's enough to put him on Full Medical, and he can't make up his mind to spend it. If he spends it he can have his legs back and go out again. But then he'd be broke if he didn't score. So he just stays on, a cripple."

I put the glass down. I didn't want any more to drink. "So long, Ituno," I said. "I'm going to bed."

I spent most of the trip back writing letters to Klara that I didn't know if I would ever mail. There wasn't much else to do. Hester turned out to be surprisingly sexual, for a small plump lady of a certain age. But there's a limit to how long that is entertaining, and with all the cargo we had jammed in the ship, there wasn't room for much else. The days were all the same: sex, letter writing, sleeping . . . and worrying.

Worrying about why Shicky Bakin wanted to stay a cripple; which was a way of worrying, in a way I could face, about why I did.

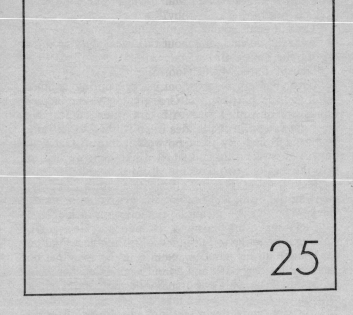

25

Sigfrid says, "You sound tired, Bob."

Well, that was understandable enough. I had gone off to Hawaii for the weekend. Some of my money was in tourism there, so it was all tax deductible. It was a lovely couple of days on the Big Island, with a two-hour stockholders' meeting in the morning, and afternoons with one of those beautiful Island girls on the beach or sailing in glass-bottomed catamarans, watching the big mantas glide underneath, begging for crumbs. But coming back, you fight time zones all the way, and I was exhausted.

Only that is not the sort of thing that Sigfrid really wants to hear about. He doesn't care if you're physically exhausted. He doesn't care if you've got a broken leg; he only wants to know if you dream about screwing your mother.

I say that. I say, "I'm tired, all right, Sigfrid, but why don't you stop making small talk? Get right into my Oedipal feelings about Ma."

"Did you have any, Bobby?"

"Doesn't everybody?"

"Do you want to talk about them, Bobby?"

"Not particularly."

He waits, and I wait, too. Sigfrid has been being cute again, and now his room is fixed up like a boy's room from forty years ago. Crossed Ping-Pong paddles hologrammed on the wall. A fake window with a fake view of the Montana Rockies in a snowstorm. A holo-grammed cassette shelf of boys' stories on tape, *Tom Sawyer* and *Lost Race of Mars* and—I can't read the rest of the titles. It is all very homey, but not in the least like my own room as a boy, which was tiny, narrow, and almost filled by the old sofa I slept on.

"Do you know what you want to talk about, Rob?" Sigfrid probes gently.

"You bet." Then I reconsider. "Well, no. I'm not sure." Actually I do know. Something had hit me on the way back from Hawaii, very hard. It's a five-hour flight. Half the time I had spent drenched in tears. It was funny. There was this lovely hapi-haole girl flying east in the seat next to me, and I had decided right away to get to know her better. And the stewardess was the same one I'd had before, and she, I already knew better.

So there I was, sitting at the very back of the first-class section of the SST, taking drinks from the stewardess, chatting with my pretty hapi-haole. And—every time the girl was drowsing, or in the ladies' room, and the stewardess was looking the other way—racked with silent, immense, tearful sobs.

And then one of them would look my way again and I would be smiling, alert, and on the make.

"Do you want to just say what you're feeling at this second, Bob?"

"I would in a minute, Sigfrid, if I knew what it was."

"Don't you know, really? Can't you remember what

MISSION REPORT

Vessel A3-77, Voyage 036D51. Crew T. Parreno, N. Ahoya, E. Nimkin.

Transit time 5 days 14 hours. Position vicinity Alpha Centauri A.

Summary. "The planet was quite Earth-like and heavily vegetated. The color of the vegetation was predominantly yellow. The atmosphere matched the Heechee mix closely. It is a warm planet with no polar ice caps and a temperature range similar to Earth tropics at the equator, Earth temperate extending almost to the poles. We detected no animal life or signatures (methane, etc.) thereof. Some of the vegetation predates at a very slow pace, advancing by uprooting portions of a vinelike structure, curling around and rerooting. Maximum velocity measured was approximately 2 kilometers per hour. No artifacts. Parreno and Nimkin landed and returned with samples of vegetation, but died of a toxicodendron-like reaction. Great blisters formed over their bodies. Then they developed pain, itching and apparent suffocation, probably due to fluids accumulating in the lung. I did not bring them aboard the vessel. I did not open the lander, or dock it to the vessel. I recorded personal messages for both, then jettisoned the lander and returned without it."

Corporation assessment: No charge made against N. Ahoya in view of past record.

was in your head while you weren't talking, just now?"

"Sure I can!" I hesitate, then I say, "Oh, hell, Sigfrid, I guess I was just waiting to be coaxed. I had an insight the other day, and it hurt. Oh, wow, you wouldn't believe how it hurt. I was crying like a baby."

"What was the insight, Bobby?"

"I'm trying to tell you. It was about—well, it was partly about my mother. But it was also about, well, you know, Dane Metchnikov. I had these . . . I had—"

"I think you're trying to say something about the fantasies you had of having anal sex with Dane Metchnikov, Bob. Is that right?"

"Yeah. You remember good, Sigfrid. When I was crying, it was about my mother. Partly . . ."

"You told me that, Bob."

"Right." And I close up. Sigfrid waits. I wait, too. I suppose I want to be coaxed some more, and after a while Sigfrid obliges me:

"Let's see if I can help you, Bob," he says. "What do crying about your mother, and your fantasies about anal sex with Dane, have to do with each other?"

I feel something happening inside of me. It feels as though the soft, wet inside of my chest is starting to bubble into my throat. I can tell that when my voice comes out, it is going to be tremulous and desperately forlorn if I don't control it. So I try to control it, although I know perfectly well that I have no secrets of this sort from Sigfrid; he can read his sensors and know what is going on inside me from the tremble of a triceps or the dampness of a palm.

But I make the effort anyway. In the tones of a biology instructor explaining a prepared frog I say: "See, Sigfrid, my mother loved me. I knew it. You know it. It was a logical demonstration; she had no choice. And Freud said once that no boy who is certain he was his mother's favorite ever grows up to be neurotic. Only—"

"Please, Robbie, that isn't quite right, and besides you're intellectualizing. You know you really don't want to put in all these preambles. You're stalling, aren't you?"

Other times I would tear the circuits out of his chips for that, but this time he has my mood gauged correctly. "All right. But I *did* know that my mother loved me. She couldn't help it! I was her only son. My father was dead—don't clear your throat, Sigfrid, I'm getting to it. It was a logical necessity that she loved me, and I understood it that way with no doubt at all in my mind, but she never said so. Never once."

"You mean that never, in your whole life, did she say to you, 'I love you, son?' "

"No!" I scream. Then I get control again. "Or not directly, no. I mean, once when I was like eighteen years old and going to sleep in the next room, I heard her to say to one of her friends—girlfriends, I mean—that she really thought I was a tremendous kid. She was proud of me. I don't remember what I'd done, something, won a prize or got a job, but she right that minute was proud of me and loved me, and said so. . . . But not to me."

"Please go on, Bob," Sigfrid says after a moment.

"I *am* going on! Give me a minute. It hurts; I guess it's what you call primal pain."

"Please don't diagnose yourself, Bob. Just say it. Let it come out."

"Oh, *shit*."

I reach for a cigarette and then stop the motion. That's usually a good thing to do when things get tight with Sigfrid, because it will almost always distract him into an argument about whether I am trying to relieve tension instead of dealing with it; but this time I am too disgusted with myself, with Sigfrid, even with my mother. I want to get it over with. I say, "Look, Sigfrid, here's how it was. I loved my mother a lot, and I know—knew!—she loved me. But she wasn't very good at showing it."

I suddenly realize I have a cigarette in my hands, and I'm rolling it around without lighting it and, wondrous to say, Sigfrid hasn't even commented on it. I plunge right on: "She didn't say the words to me. Not only that. It's funny, Sigfrid, but, you know, I can't remember her ever touching me. I mean, not *really*. She would kiss me good night, sometimes. On the top of the head. And I remember she told me stories. And she was always there when I needed her. But—"

I have to stop for a moment, to get control of my voice again. I inhale deeply and evenly through my nose, concentrating on breath flow.

"But you see, Sigfrid," I say, rehearsing the words ahead of time and pleased with the clarity and balance with which I deliver them, "she didn't *touch* me much. Except for one way. She was very good to me when I was sick. I was sick a lot. Everybody around the food mines has runny noses, skin infections—you know. She got me everything I needed. She was there, God knows how, holding down a job and taking care of me, all at once. And when I was sick she . . ."

After a moment Sigfrid says, "Go on, Robbie. Say it."

I try, but I am still stuck, and he says:

"Just say it the fastest way you can. Get it out. Don't worry if I understand, or if it makes sense. Just get rid of the words."

"Well, she would take my temperature," I explain. "You know? Stick a thermometer into me. And she'd hold me for, you know, whatever it is, three minutes or so. And then she'd take the thermometer out and read it."

I am right on the verge of bawling. I'm willing to let it happen, but first I want to follow this thing through; it is almost a sexual thing, like when you are getting right up to the moment of decision with some person and you don't think you really want to let her be that much a part of you but you go ahead anyhow. I save up voice control, measuring it out so that I won't run out before I finish. Sigfrid doesn't say anything, and after a moment I manage the words:

"You see how it is, Sigfrid? It's funny. All my life now—what is it, maybe forty years since then? And I still have this crazy notion that being loved has something to do with having things stuck up my ass."

257

26

There had been a lot of changes on Gateway while I was out. The head tax had been raised. The Corporation wanted to get rid of some of the extra hangers-on, like Shicky and me; bad news: it meant that my prepaid per capita wasn't good for two or three weeks, it was only good for ten days. They had imported a bunch of double-domes from Earth, astronomers, xenotechs, mathematicians, even old Professor Hegramet was up from Earth, bruised from the lift-off deltas but hopping spryly around the tunnels.

One thing that hadn't changed was the Evaluation Board, and I was impaled on the hot seat in front of it, squirming while my old friend Emma told me what a fool I was. Mr. Hsien was actually doing the telling, Emma only translated. But she loved her work.

"I warned you you'd fuck up, Broadhead. You

should have listened to me. Why did you change the setting?"

"I told you. When I found out I was at Gateway Two I just couldn't handle it. I wanted to go somewhere else."

"Extraordinarily stupid of you, Broadhead."

I glanced at Hsien. He had hung himself up on the wall by his rolled-up collar and was hanging there, beaming benignly, hands folded. "Emma," I said, "do whatever you want to do, but get off my back."

She said sunnily, "I am doing what I want to do, Broadhead, because it's what I have to do. It's my job. You knew it was against the rules to change the settings."

"What rules? It was *my* ass that was on the line."

"The rules that say you shouldn't destroy a ship," she explained. I didn't answer, and she chirped some sort of a translation to Hsien, who listened gravely, pursed his lips and then delivered two neat paragraphs in Mandarin. You could hear the punctuation.

"Mr. Hsien says," said Emma, "that you are a very irresponsible person. You have killed an irreplaceable piece of equipment. It was not your property. It belonged to the whole human race." He lilted a few more sentences, and she finished: "We cannot make a final determination of your liability until we have further information about the condition of the ship you damaged. According to Mr. Ituno he will have a complete check made of the ship at the first opportunity. There were two xenotechs in transit for the new planet, Aphrodite, at the time of his report. They will have reached Gateway Two by now, and we can expect their findings, probably, with the next out-pilot. Then we will call you again."

She paused, looking at me, and I took it the interview was over. "Thanks a lot," I said, and pushed myself toward the door. She let me get all the way to it before she said:

"One more thing. Mr. Ituno's report mentions that you worked on loading and fabricating suits on Gateway Two. He authorizes a per diem payment to you

MISSION REPORT

Vessel 1-103, Voyage 022D18. Crew
G. Herron.

Transit time out 107 days 5 hours.
Note: Transit time return 103 days
15 hours.

Extract from log. "At 84 days 6
hours out the Q instrument began to
glow and there was unusual activity
in the control lights. At the same
time I felt a change in the direction of thrust. For about one hour
there were continuing changes, then
the Q light went out and things went
back to normal."

Conjecture: Course change to avoid
some transient hazard, perhaps a
star or other body? Recommend computer search of trip logs for similar events.

amounting to, let me see, twenty-five hundred dollars. And your out-captain, Hester Bergowiz, has authorized payment of one percent of her bonus to you for services during the return flight; so your account has been credited accordingly."

"I didn't have a contract with her," I said, surprised.

"No. But she feels you should have a share. A small share, to be sure. Altogether—" she looked under a paper, "it comes to twenty-five hundred plus fifty-five hundred—eight thousand dollars your account has been credited with."

Eight thousand dollars! I headed for a dropshaft, grabbed an up-cable and pondered. It was not enough to make any real difference. It certainly would not be enough to pay the damages they would soak me for messing up a ship. There wasn't enough money in the universe to pay that, if they wanted to charge me full replacement cost; there was no way to replace it.

On the other hand, it was eight thousand dollars more than I'd had.

I celebrated by buying myself a drink at the Blue Hell. While I was drinking it, I thought about my options. The more I thought about them, the more they dwindled away.

They would find me culpable, no doubt about that, and the least they'd assess me would be somewhere in the hundreds of thousands of dollars. Well, I didn't have it. It might be a lot more, but that didn't make any difference; once they take away all you have, there isn't anything left anyway.

So when you came right down to it, my eight thousand dollars was fairy gold. It could vanish with the morning dew. As soon as the xenotech's report came in from Gateway Two the Board would reconvene and that would be the end of that.

So there was no particular reason to stretch my money. I might as well spend it.

There was no reason, either, to think about getting back my old job as an ivy-planter—even assuming I could get it, with Shicky fired from his job as straw-boss. The minute they made a judgment against me my

A NOTE ON BLACK HOLES

Dr. Asmenion. Now, if you start with a star bigger than three solar masses, and it collapses, it doesn't just turn into a neutron star. It keeps on going. It gets *so* dense that the escape velocity exceeds thirty million centimeters a second . . . which is . . . ?

Question. Uh. The speed of light?

Dr. Asmenion. Right on, Gallina. So light can't escape. So it's black. So that's why it's called a black hole—only, if you get close enough, inside what's called the ergosphere, it isn't black. You probably could see something.

Question. What would it look like?

Dr. Asmenion. Beats the ass off me, Jer. If anybody ever goes and sees one, he'll come back and tell us if he can. Only he probably can't. You *could* maybe get that close in, get your readings and come back—and collect, Jesus, I don't know, a million dollars anyway. If you could get into your lander, see, and kick the main mass of the ship away, backward, slowing it down, you might be able to give yourself enough extra velocity to get away. Not easily. But maybe, if things were just right. But then where would you go? You can't get home in a lander. And doing it the other way wouldn't work, there isn't enough mass in a lander to get you free. . . . I see old Bob isn't enjoying this discussion, so let's move on to planetary types and dust clouds.

credit balance would disappear. So would my prepaid per-capita payment. I would be subject to immediate defenestration.

If there happened to be an Earth-bound ship in port at the time I could just get on board, and sooner or later I would be back in Wyoming looking for my old job at the food mines. If there wasn't a ship, then I was in trouble. I *might* be able to talk the American cruiser, or maybe the Brazilian one if Francy Hereira was in a position to pull strings for me, into taking me aboard for a while until a ship showed up. Or I might not.

Considered carefully, the chances were not very hopeful.

The very best thing I could do would be to act before the Board did, and there there were two choices.

I could take the next ship in port back to Earth and the food mines, without waiting for the Board's decision.

Or I could ship out again.

They were two lovely choices. One of them meant giving up every chance of a decent life forever . . . and the other one scared me out of my mind.

Gateway was like a gentlemen's club in which you never knew what members were in town. Louise Forehand was gone; her husband, Sess, was patiently holding the fort, waiting for her or their remaining daughter to return before shipping out again himself. He helped me move back into my room, which had been temporarily occupied by three Hungarian women until they had shipped out together in a Three. Moving took no great effort; I didn't own anything anymore, except what I had just bought in the commissary.

The only permanent feature was Shicky Bakin, unfailingly friendly and always there. I asked him if he had heard from Klara. He had not. "Go out again, Bob," he urged. "It is the only thing to do."

"Yeah." I did not want to argue it; he was incontestably right. Maybe I would. . . . I said, "I wish I weren't a coward, Shicky, but I am. I just don't know how I can make myself get into a ship again. I don't have the courage to face a hundred days of fearing death every minute."

He chuckled, and hopped off the chest of drawers to pat my shoulder. "You don't need so much courage," he said, flapping back to the chest. "You only need courage for one day: just to get in the ship and go. Then you don't have to have courage anymore, because you don't anymore have a choice."

"I think I could have done it," I said, "if Metchnikov's theories about the color codes had been right. But some of the 'safe' ones are dead."

"It was only a statistical matter, Bob. It is true that there is a better safety record now, and a better success record, too. Only marginal, yes. But better."

"The ones that died are just as dead," I said. "Still —perhaps I'll talk to Dane again."

Shicky looked surprised. "He's out."

"When?"

"Around when you left. I thought you knew."

I had forgotten. "Wonder if he found the soft touch he was looking for."

Shicky scratched his chin with his shoulder, keeping himself balanced with lazy wing strokes. Then he hopped off the chest and fluttered over to the piezophone. "Let's see," he said, and punched buttons. The locator board jumped into view on the screen. "Launch 88-173," he read. "Bonus, $150,000. That's not much, is it?"

"I thought he was going for something bigger."

"Well," said Shicky, reading, "he didn't get it. Says here he came back last night."

Since Metchnikov had halfway promised to share his expertise with me, it made sense for me to talk to him; but I wasn't feeling sensible. I got as far as checking out that he had returned without a find and with nothing to show for his efforts but the bonus; but I didn't go to see him.

I didn't do much of anything, in fact. I hung around. Gateway is not the most amenity-filled place to live

Classifieds.

AREN'T THERE any English-speaking nonsmokers on Gateway to fill out our crew? Maybe you want to shorten your life (and our life-support reserves!) but we two don't. 88-775.

WE DEMAND prospector representation on Gateway Corporation Board! Mass meeting tomorrow 1300 Level Babe. Everyone welcome!

SELECT FLIGHTS tested, whole-person way from your dreams. 32-page sealed book tells how, $10. Consultations, $25. 88-139.

in the universe, but I found things to do. It beat the food mines. Each passing hour brought me an hour closer to the time when the xenotech's report would arrive, but I managed not to think about that most of the time. I nursed drinks in the Blue Hell, making friends with the tourists, the visiting cruiser crews, the returnees, the new fish that kept coming up from the sweltering planets, looking, I guess, for another Klara. None showed up.

I read over the letters I had written her on the trip back from Gateway Two, and then I tore them up. Instead I wrote a simple, short note to apologize and tell her that I loved her and took it down to radio it off to her on Venus. But she wasn't there! I had forgotten how long the slow Hohmann orbits took. The locator office identified the ship she had left on easily enough; it was a right-angle orbiter, which spent its whole life changing deltas to rendezvous with plane-of-the-ecliptic flights between the planets. According to the records, her ship had made a rendezvous with a Mars-bound freighter, and then a Venus-bound high-G luxury liner; she had presumably transferred to one of them, but they didn't know which, and neither one of them would reach its destination for a month or more yet.

I sent duplicate copies to each ship, but there wasn't any answer.

The closest I came to a new girlfriend was a Gunner Third from the Brazilian cruiser. Francy Hereira brought her around. "My cousin," he said, introducing us; and then, privately, later, "You should know, Rob, that I do not have family feelings about my cousins." All the crews got shore leave on Gateway from time to time, and while, as I have said, Gateway wasn't Waikiki or Cannes, it beat the bare bones of a combat vessel. Susie Hereira was very young. She said she was nineteen and was supposed to be at least seventeen to be in the Brazilian Navy at all, but she didn't look it. She did not speak much English, but we did not need much language in common to drink at the Blue Hell; and when we went to bed we discovered that although we had very little conversation in a verbal sense we communicated beautifully with our bodies.

But Susie was only there one day a week, and that left a great deal of time which needed destroying.

I tried everything: a reinforcement group, group-hugging, and working out loves and hostilities on each other. Old Hegramet's lecture series on the Heechee. A program of talks on astrophysics, with a slant toward earning science bonuses from the Corporation. By careful budgeting of my time I managed to use it all up, and decision was postponed day by day.

I do not want to give the impression that destroying time was a conscious plan in my mind; I was living from day to day, and each day was full. On a Thursday Susie and Francy Hereira would check in, and the three of us might have lunch at the Blue Hell. Then Francy would go off to roam by himself, or pick up a girl, or take a swim in Lake Superior, while Susie and I would retire to my room and my dope sticks to swim on those warmer waters of my bed. After dinner, some sort of entertainment. Thursday was the night the astrophysics lectures took place, and we would hear about the Hertzsprung-Russell diagram, or red giants and dwarfs, or neutron stars, or black holes. The professor was a fat old girl-grabber from some jerk-water college near Smolensk, but even through the dirty jokes there was poetry and beauty in what he talked about. He dwelt on the old stars that gave birth to us all, spitting silicates and magnesium carbonate into space to form our planets, hydrocarbons to form ourselves. He talked about the neutron stars that bent the gravity well around them; we knew about them, because two launches had killed themselves, sheared into rubble, by entering normal space too close to one of those hyperdense dwarfs. He told us about the black holes that were the places where a dense star had been, now detectable only by the observable fact that they swallowed everything nearby, even light; they had not merely bent the gravity well, they had wrapped it around themselves like a blanket. He described stars as thin as air, immense clouds of glowing gas; told us about the prestars of the Orion Nebula, just now blossoming into loose knots of warm gas that might in a million years be suns. His lectures were very popular; even old hands like Shicky and Dane Metchnikov showed up. While I listened to the professor I could feel the wonder and beauty of space. It was too immense and glorious to be frightening, and it was not until later that I would relate those sinks of radiation and swamps of thin gas to *me*, to the frail, frightened, pain-sensitive creation that was the body I inhabited. And then I would think about going out among those remote titans and . . . my soul curled up inside me.

After one of those meetings I said good-bye to Susie and Francy and sat in an alcove near the lecture room, half hidden by the ivy, and despondently smoked a joint. Shicky found me there, and halted just in front of me, supporting himself on his wings. "I was looking for you, Bob," he said, and stopped.

The grass was just beginning to hit me. "Interesting lecture," I said absently, reaching for the good feeling that I wanted from the joint and not really very interested in whether Shicky was there or not.

"You missed the most interesting part," said Shicky.

It occurred to me that he was looking both fearful and hopeful; there was something on his mind. I took another hit, and offered him the joint; he shook his head. "Bob," he said, "I think there is something worth having coming up."

"Really?"

"Yes, really, Bob! Something quite good. And soon."

I was not ready for this. I wanted to go on smoking my joint until the temporary thrill of the lecture had worn off, so that I could go back to destroying the days. The last thing I wanted was to hear about some new mission that my guilt would make me want to sign on for, and my fear would abort.

Shicky caught the shelf of ivy and held himself up by it, looking at me curiously. "Bob-friend," he said,

Dearest Father, Mother, Marisa
and Pico-João,

Please tell Susie's father that
she is very well and is regarded
with favor by her officers. You can
decide for yourselves whether to
tell him that she has been seeing
much of my friend Rob Broadhead. He
is a good man and a serious one, but
he is not a fortunate one. Susie has
applied for leave to go on a mission, and if the captain grants it
she speaks of going with Broadhead.
We all speak of going but, as you
know, we do not all do it, so perhaps it is not to be worried about.

This must be very short; it is almost docking time, and I have a 48
for Gateway.

                     With all love,

                          Francescito

"if I can find something out for you will you help me?"

"Help you how?"

"Take me with you!" he cried. "I can do everything but go in the lander. And this mission, I think, is one where it does not so much matter. There is a bonus for everyone, even for someone who must remain in orbit."

"What are you talking about?" The grass was hitting me now; I could feel the warmth behind my knees and the gentle blur all around me.

"Metchnikov was talking to the lecturer," Shicky said. "I think from what he said that he knows of a new mission. Only—they spoke in Russian, and I did not understand very well. But it is the one he has been waiting for."

I said reasonably, "The last one he went out on wasn't much, was it?"

"This is different!"

"I don't think he would really cut me in on anything good—"

"Certainly not, if you don't ask."

"Oh, hell," I grumbled. "All right. I'll talk to him." Shicky beamed. "And then, Bob, please—take me with you?"

I stubbed out the joint, less than half smoked; I felt as though I wanted what was left of my wits about me. "I'll do what I can," I said, and headed back for the lecture room just as Metchnikov was coming out.

We had not spoken since he had returned. He looked as solid and broad as ever, and his fringe of chin whiskers was neatly trimmed. "Hello, Broadhead," he said suspiciously.

I didn't waste words. "I hear you've got something good coming up. Can I go along?"

He didn't waste words, either. "No." He looked at me with frank dislike. Partly that was what I had expected from him all along, but I was pretty sure part of it was because he had heard about me and Klara.

"You are going out," I persisted. "What is it, a One?"

270

He stroked his whiskers. "No," he said reluctantly, "it isn't a One. It's two Fives."

"*Two* Fives?"

He stared at me suspiciously for a moment, and then almost grinned; I did not like him when he smiled, it was always a question in my mind what he was smiling about.

"All right," he said. "You want in, you can have it, for all of me. It's not up to me, of course. You'll have to ask Emma; she's doing a briefing tomorrow morning. But she might let you go. It's a science mission, with a minimum million-dollar bonus. And you're involved."

"I'm involved?" That was something out of an unexpected direction! "Involved how?"

"Ask Emma," he said, and brushed past me.

There were about a dozen prospectors in the briefing room, most of whom I knew: Sess Forehand, Shicky, Metchnikov, and a few others I'd drunk with or gone to bed with, one time or another. Emma wasn't there yet, and I managed to intercept her as she was coming in.

"I want to go out on this mission," I said.

She looked startled. "You do? I thought—" But she stopped there, without saying what it was she thought.

I followed up: "I have as much right to go as Metchnikov does!"

"You sure as hell don't have as good a record as he does, Bob." She looked me over carefully, and then she said, "Well, I'll tell you how it is, Broadhead. It's a special mission, and partly you're responsible for it. That boner of yours turns out to be interesting. I don't mean wrecking the ship; that was stupid, and if there was any justice in the universe you'd pay for it. But dumb luck is almost as good as brains."

"You got the report from Gateway Two," I guessed.

She shook her head. "Not yet. But it doesn't matter. We routinely programmed your mission into the computer, and it found some interesting correlations.

The course pattern that took you to Gateway Two—Oh, hell," she said, "come on inside. You can sit through the briefing, at least. It'll explain everything, and then—we'll see."

She took my elbow and pushed me ahead of her into the room, which was the same one we had used for a classroom—how long before? It seemed like a million years. I sat down between Sess and Shicky, and waited to hear what it was she had to say.

"Most of you," she started off, "are here by invitation—with one or two exceptions. One of the exceptions is our distinguished friend Mr. Broadhead. He managed to wreck a ship near Gateway Two, as most of you know. By rights we ought to throw the book at him, but before he did that he accidentally turned up some interesting facts. His course colors were not the regular ones for Gateway Two, and when the computer compared them it came up with a whole new concept of course setting. Apparently only about five settings are critical for destination—the five that were the same for the usual Gateway Two setting, and for Broadhead's new one. What the other settings mean we don't know. But we're going to find out."

She leaned back and folded her hands. "This is a multiple-purpose mission," she said. "We're going to do something new. For openers, we're going to send two ships to the same destination."

Sess Forehand raised his hand. "What's the point of that?"

"Well, partly to make sure it *is* the same destination. We're going to vary the noncritical settings slightly . . . the ones we *think* are noncritical. And we're going to start the two ships thirty seconds apart. Now, if we know what we're doing, that means you'll come out about as far apart as Gateway travels in thirty seconds."

Forehand wrinkled his brow. "Relative to what?"

"Good question," she nodded. "Relative, we think, to the Sun. The stellar motion relative to the Galaxy —we think—can be neglected. At least, assuming that your destination turns out to be inside the Galaxy, and not so far away that the galactic motion has a markedly different vector. I mean, if you came out on the opposite side, it would be seventy kilometers a second, relative to the galactic center. We don't think that's involved. We only expect a relatively minor difference in velocity and direction, and—well, anyway, you should come out within somewhere between two and two hundred kilometers of each other.

"Of course," she said, smiling cheerfully, "that's only theoretical. Maybe the relative motions won't mean anything at all. In that case, the problem is to keep you from colliding with each other. But we're sure—pretty sure—that there will be at least some displacement. All you really need is about fifteen meters—the long diameter of a Five."

"How sure is pretty sure?" one of the girls asked.

"Well," Emma admitted, "reasonably sure. How do we know until we try?"

"It sounds dangerous," Sess commented. He did not seem deterred by it. He was only stating an opinion. In this he was unlike me; I was very busy ignoring my inner sensations, trying to concentrate on the technicalities of the briefing.

Emma looked surprised. "That part? Look, I haven't come to the dangerous part yet. This is a nonaccept destination for all Ones, most Threes, and some Fives."

"Why?" someone asked.

"That's what you're going there to find out," she said patiently. "It happens to be the setting the computer picked out as best for testing the correlations between course settings. You've got armored Fives, and both accept this particular destination. That means you have what the Heechee designers figured was a good chance to handle it, right?"

"That was a long time ago," I objected.

"Oh, sure. I never said otherwise. It *is* dangerous —at least to some extent. That's what the million is for."

She stopped there, gravely considering us, until someone obliged by asking, "What million?"

"The million-dollar bonus each one of you gets

A NOTE ON SIGNATURES

Dr. Asmenion. So when you're looking for signs of life on a planet, you don't expect a big neon sign that says "Aliens Live Here." You look for signatures. A "signature" is something that shows something else is there. Like your signature on a check. If I see that, I know it shows that you want it paid, so I cash it. Not yours, of course, Bob.

Question. God hates a smart-assed teacher.

Dr. Asmenion. No offense, Bob. Methane is a typical signature. It shows the presence of warm-blooded mammals, or something like them.

Question. I thought methane could come from rotting vegetation and all that?

Dr. Asmenion. Oh, sure. But mostly it comes from the guts of large ruminants. Most of the methane in the Earth's air is cow farts.

when you come back," she said. "They've appropriated ten million dollars out of Corporation funds for this. Equal shares. Of course, there's a good chance that it will be more than a million each. If you find anything worthwhile, the regular pay scales apply. And the computer thinks this is a good prospect."

"Why is it worth ten million?" I asked.

"I don't make these decisions," she said patiently. And then she looked at me as a person, not part of the group, and added, "And by the way, Broadhead. We're writing off your damage to the ship. So whatever you get is yours to keep. A million dollars? That's a nice little nest egg. You can go back home, buy yourself a little business, live the rest of your life on that."

We looked at each other, and Emma just sat there, smiling gently and waiting. I don't know what the others were thinking about. What I was remembering was Gateway Two and the first trip, wearing our eyes out at the instruments, looking for something that wasn't there. I suppose each of the others had washouts of their own to remember.

"Launch," she said at last, "is day after tomorrow. The ones who want to sign, come see me in my office."

They accepted me. They turned Shicky down.

But it wasn't as easy as that, nothing ever is; the one who made sure Shicky was not going to go along was me. They filled up the first ship quickly: Sess Forehand, two girls from Sierra Leone, and a French couple—all English-speaking, all briefed, all with previous missions. For the second ship Metchnikov signed as crew chief right away; a gay couple, Danny A. and Danny R., were his first picks. Then, grudgingly, he agreed to me. And that left one opening.

"We can take your friend Bakin," Emma said. "Or would you prefer your other friend?"

"What other friend?" I demanded.

"We have an application," she said, "from Gunner

Third Susanna Hereira, off the Brazilian cruiser. She has their permission to take leave for this purpose."

"Susie! I didn't know she'd volunteered!"

Emma studied her punch card reflectively. "She's very well qualified," she commented. "Also, she has all her parts. I am referring," she said sweetly, "to her legs, of course, although as I understand it you have some interest in her other parts as well. Or would you care to go gay for this mission?"

I felt an unreasoning rush of anger. I am not one of your sexually uptight people; the thought of physical contact with a male was not frightening in itself. But —with Dane Metchnikov? Or one of his lovers?

"Gunner Hereira can be here tomorrow," Emma commented. "The Brazilian cruiser is going to dock right after the orbiter."

"Why the hell are you asking me?" I snarled. "Metchnikov's crew chief."

"He prefers to leave it to you, Broadhead. Which one?"

"I don't give a damn!" I yelled, and left. But there is no such thing as avoiding a decision. Not making a decision was in itself decision enough to keep Shicky off the crew. If I had fought for him, they would have taken him; without that, Susie was the obvious choice.

I spent the next day staying out of Shicky's way. I picked up a new fish at the Blue Hell, fresh out of the classroom, and spent the night in her room. I didn't even go back to my own room for fresh clothes; I dumped everything and bought a new outfit. I knew pretty well the places where Shicky might look for me—the Blue Hell, Central Park, the museum—and so I stayed away from all those places; I went for a long, rambling wander through the deserted tunnels, seeing no one at all, until late that night.

Then I took a chance and went to our farewell party. Shicky would probably be there, but there would be other people around.

He was. And so was Louise Forehand. In fact, she seemed to be the center of attention; I hadn't even known she was back.

Dear Voice of Gateway:

Last month I spent £58.50 of my hard-earned money to take my wife and son to a "lecture" by one of your returned "heroes," who gave Liverpool the dubious honour of a visit (for which he was well paid, naturally, by people like me). I didn't mind that he was not a very interesting speaker. It was what he flaming well said that drove me right up the flaming wall. He said we poor sods of earthlings had just no idea of how dicey things were for you noble adventurers.

Well, mate, this morning I drew out the last pound in the savings account so the wife could get a lung patch (good old melanomic asbestosis CV/E, you know). The kid's tuition comes due in a week, and I haven't a clew where it⁺s coming from. And after spending eight-to-twelve this morning waiting by the docks for a chance to shift some cargo (there wasn't any) the foreman let me know I was redundant, which means tomorrow I don't even have to bother to show up to wait. Any of you heroes care to pick up a bargain in surplus parts? Mine are for sale—kidneys, liver, the lot. All in good condition, too, or as good as nineteen years on the docks can be expected to leave them, except for the tear glands of the eyes, which are fair wore out with weeping over the troubles of your lot.

> H. Delacross
> "Wavetops"
> Flat B bis 17, 41st Floor
> Merseyside L77PR 14JE6

She saw me and waved to me. "I struck it rich, Bob! Drink up—I'm buying!"

I let someone put a glass in one hand and a joint in the other, and before I took my hit I managed to ask her what she'd found.

"Weapons, Bob! Marvelous Heechee weapons, hundreds of them. Sess says it's going to be at least a five-million-dollar award. *Plus* royalties . . . if anyone finds a way to duplicate the weapons, anyway."

I let the smoke blow out and washed out the taste with a swallow of white lightning. "What kind of weapons?"

"They're like the tunnel diggers, only portable. They'll cut a hole through anything. We lost Sara allaFanta in the landing; one of them put a hole in her suit. But Tim and I are whacking up her share, so it's two and a half mil apiece."

"Congratulations," I said. "I would have thought the last thing the human race needed was some new ways to kill each other, but—congratulations." I was reaching for an air of moral superiority, and I needed it; because as I turned away, there was Shicky, hanging in air, watching me.

"Want a hit?" I asked, offering him the joint.

He shook his head.

I said, "Shicky, it wasn't up to me. I told them—I didn't tell them not to take you."

"Did you tell them they should?"

"It wasn't up to me," I said. "Hey, listen!" I went on, suddenly seeing an out. "Now that Louise has hit, Sess probably won't want to go. Why don't you take his place?"

He backed away, watching me; only his expression had changed. "You don't know?" he asked. "It is true that Sess has canceled out, but he has already been replaced."

"By whom?"

"By the person right behind you," said Shicky, and I turned around, and there she was, looking at me, a glass in her hand and an expression I could not read on her face.

"Hello, Bob," said Klara.

I had prepared myself for the party by a number of quick ones in the commissary; I was ninety-percent drunk and ten-percent stoned, but it all whooshed out of me as I looked at her. I put down the drink, handed the joint to someone at random, took her arm, and pulled her out into the tunnel.

"Klara," I said. "Did you get my letters?"

She looked puzzled. "Letters?" She shook her head. "I guess you sent them to Venus? I never got there. I got as far as rendezvous with the plane-of-the-ecliptic flight, and then I changed my mind. I came right back on the orbiter."

"Oh, Klara."

"Oh, Bob," she mimicked, grinning; that wasn't much fun, because when she smiled I could see where the tooth was missing that I had knocked out. "So what else have we got to say to each other?"

I put my arms around her. "I can say that I love you, and I'm sorry, and I want to make it up to you, and I want to get married and live together and have kids and—"

"Jesus, Bob," she said, pushing me away, gently enough, "when you say something you say a lot, don't you? So hold it for a while. It'll keep."

"But it's been *months!*"

She laughed. "No fooling, Bob. This is a bad day for Sagittarians to make decisions, especially about love. We'll talk about it another time."

"That crap! Listen, I don't believe in any of that!"

"I do, Bob."

I had an inspiration. "Hey! I bet I can trade with somebody in the first ship! Or, wait a minute, maybe Susie would trade with you—"

She shook her head, still smiling. "I really don't think Susie would like that," she said. "Anyway, they bitched enough about letting me switch with Sess. They'll never stand still for another last-minute change."

"I don't care, Klara!"

MISSION REPORT

Vessel 3-184, Voyage 019D140. Crew
S. Kotsis, A. McCarthy, K. Metsuoko.

Transit time out 615 days 9 hours.
No crew reports from destination.
Spherical scan data inconclusive as
to destination. No identifiable
features.

No summary.

Extract from log: "This is the
281st day out. Metsuoko lost the
draw and suicided. Alicia voluntarily suicided 40 days later. We
haven't yet reached turnaround, so
it's all for nothing. The remaining
rations are not going to be enough
to support me, even if you include
Alicia and Kenny, who are intact in
the freezer. So I am putting everything on full automatic and taking
the pills. We have all left letters.
Please forward them as addressed, if
this goddamned ship ever gets
back."

Mission Plan filed proposal that a
Five with double life-support rations and a one-person crew might be
able to complete this mission and
return successfully. Proposal tabled
on grounds of low priority: no evi-
dent benefit from repeating this
mission.

"Bob," she said, "don't rush me. I did a lot of thinking about you and me. I think we've got something that's worth working for. But I can't say it's all straight in my head yet, and I don't want to push it."

"But, Klara—"

"Leave it at that, Bob. I'll go in the first ship, you go in the second. When we get where we're going we'll be able to talk. Maybe even switch around to come back together. But meanwhile we'll both have a chance to think about what we really want."

The only words I seemed to know I seemed to be saying over and over again: "But, Klara—"

She kissed me, and pushed me away. "Bob," she said, "don't be in such a hurry. We've got all the time there is."

27

"Tell me something, Sigfrid," I say, "how nervous am I?"

He is wearing his Sigmund Freud hologram this time, truculent Viennese stare, not a bit *gemütlich*. But his voice is the same gently sad baritone: "If you are asking what my sensors show, Bob, you are quite agitated, yes."

"I thought so," I say, bouncing around the mat.

"Can you tell me why?"

"No!" The whole week has been like that, marvelous sex with Doreen and S. Ya., and floods of tears in the shower; fantastic bidding and play at the bridge tournament, and total despair on the way home. I feel like a yo-yo. "I feel like a yo-yo," I yell. "You've opened up something I can't handle."

"I think you underestimate your capacity for handling pain," he says reassuringly.

282

"Fuck you, Sigfrid! What do you know about human capacity?"

He almost sighs. "Are we back to that again, Bob?"

"We bloody well are!" And funnily, I feel less nervous; I've got him into an argument again, and the peril is reduced.

"It is true, Bob, that I am a machine. But I am a machine designed to understand what humans are like and, believe me, I am well designed for my function."

"Designed! Sigfrid," I say reasonably, "you *aren't* human. You may *know,* but you don't *feel.* You have no idea what it feels like to have to make human decisions and carry the load of human emotion. You don't know what it feels like to have to tie a friend up to keep him from committing murder. To have someone you love die. To know it's your fault. To be scared out of your mind."

"I do know those things, Bob," he says gently. "I really do. I want to explore why you are feeling so turbulent, so won't you please help me?"

"No!"

"But your agitation, Bob, means that we are approaching the central pain—"

"Get your bloody drill out of my nerve!" But the analogy doesn't throw him for a second; his circuits are finely tuned today.

"I'm not your dentist, Bob, I'm your analyst, and I tell you—"

"Stop!" I know what I have to do to get him away from where it hurts. I haven't used S. Ya.'s secret little formula since that first day, but now I want to use it again. I say the words, and convert him from a tiger to a pussycat; he rolls over and lets me stroke his tummy, as I command him to display the gaudier bits from some of his interviews with attractive and highly quirky female patients; and the rest of the hour is spent as a peepshow; and I have got out of his room one more time intact.

Or nearly.

28

Out in the holes where the Heechee hid, out in the caves of the stars, sliding the tunnels they slashed and slid, healing the Heechee-hacked scars. . . . Jesus, it was like a Boy Scout camp-out; we sang and frolicked all the nineteen days after turnaround. I don't think I ever felt that good in my life. Partly it was release from fear; when we hit turnaround we all breathed easier, as you always do. Partly it was that the first half of the trip had been pretty gritty, with Metchnikov and his two boyfriends in a complicated triple spat most of the time and Susie Hereira a lot less interested in me on shipboard than she had been as a once-a-week night out on Gateway. But mostly, I think, for me anyway, it was knowing that I was getting closer and closer to Klara. Danny A. helped me work out the figures; he'd taught some of the

Classifieds.

INTERESTS HARPSICHORD, Go, group sex. Seek four likeminded prospectors view toward teaming. Gerriman, 78-109.

TUNNEL SALE. Must sell holodisks, clothes, sex aids, books, everything. Level Babe, Tunnel Twelve, ask for DeVittorio, 1100 hours until it's all gone.

TENTH MAN needed for minyan for Abram R. Sorchuk, presumed dead, also ninth, eighth, and seventh men. Please. 87-103.

courses on Gateway, and he may have been wrong but there wasn't anybody around righter so I took his word for it: he calculated from the time of turnaround that we were going something like three hundred light-years in all—a guess, sure, but close enough. The first ship, the one Klara was in, was getting farther and farther ahead of us all the way to turnaround, at which point we were going something over ten light-years a day (or so Danny said). Klara's Five had been launched thirty seconds ahead of us, so then it was just arithmetic: about one light-day. 3×10^{10} centimeters per second times 60 seconds times 60 minutes times 24 hours . . . at turnaround Klara was a good seventeen and a half billion kilometers ahead of us. It seemed very far, and was. But after turnaround we were getting closer every day, following her in the same wormhole through space that the Heechee had drilled for us. Where my ship was going, hers had gone. I could feel that we were catching up; sometimes I fantasized that I could smell her perfume.

When I said something like that to Danny A. he looked at me queerly. "Do you know how far seventeen and a half billion kilometers is? You could fit the whole solar system in between them and us. Just about exactly; the semimajor axis of Pluto's orbit is thirty-nine A.U. and change."

I laughed, a little embarrassed. "It was just a notion."

"So go to sleep," he said, "and have a nice dream about it." He knew how I felt about Klara; the whole ship did, even Metchnikov, even Susie, and maybe that was a fantasy, too, but I thought they all wished us well. We were all wishing all of us well, constructing elaborate plans about what we were going to do with our bonuses. For Klara and me, at a million dollars apiece, it came to a right nice piece of change. Maybe not enough for Full Medical, no, not if we wanted anything left over to have fun on. But Major Medical, at least, which meant really good health, barring something terribly damaging, for another thirty

286

or forty years. We could live happily ever after on what was left over: travel; children! A nice home in a decent part of—wait a minute, I cautioned myself, a home where? Not back anywhere near the food mines. Maybe not on Earth at all. Would Klara want to go back to Venus? I couldn't see myself taking to the life of a tunnel rat. But I couldn't see Klara in Dallas or New York, either. Of course, I thought, wish racing far ahead of reality, if we really *found* anything the lousy million apiece might be only the beginning. Then we could have all the homes we wanted, anywhere we liked; and Full Medical, too, with transplants to keep us young and healthy and beautiful and sexually strong and—

"You really ought to go to sleep," said Danny A. from the sling next to mine; "the way you thrash around is a caution."

But I didn't feel like going to sleep. I was hungry, and there wasn't any reason not to eat. For nineteen days we had been practicing food discipline, which is what you do on the way out for the first half of the trip. Once you've reached turnaround you know how much you can consume for the rest of the trip, which is why some prospectors come back fat. I climbed down out of the lander, where Susie and both the Dannys were sacked in, and then I found out what it was that was making me hungry. Dane Metchnikov was cooking himself a stew.

"Is there enough for two?"

He looked at me thoughtfully. "I guess so." He opened the squeeze-fit lid, peered inside, milked another hundred cc of water into it out of the vapor trap, and said, "Give it another ten minutes. I was going to have a drink first."

I accepted the invitation, and we passed a wine flask back and forth. While he shook the stew and added a dollop of salt, I took the star readings for him. We were still close to maximum velocity and there was nothing on the viewscreen that looked like a familiar constellation, or even much like a star; but it was all beginning to look friendly and good to me.

A NOTE ON PIEZOELECTRICITY

Professor Hegramet. The one thing we found out about blood diamonds is that they're fantastically piezoelectric. Does anybody know what that means?

Question. They expand and contract when an electric current is imposed?

Professor Hegramet. Yes. And the other way around. Squeeze them and they generate a current. Very rapidly if you like. That's the basis for the piezophone and piezovision. About a fifty-billion-dollar industry.

Question. Who gets the royalties on all that loot?

Professor Hegramet. You know, I thought one of you would ask that. Nobody does. Blood diamonds were found years and years ago, in the Heechee warrens back on Venus. Long before Gateway. It was Bell Labs that figured out how to use them. Actually they use something a little different, a synthetic they developed. They make great communications systems, and Bell doesn't have to pay anybody but themselves.

Question. Did the Heechee use them for that?

Professor Hegramet. My personal opinion is that they probably did, but I don't know how. You'd think if they left them around they'd leave the rest of the communications receivers and transmitters, too, but if they did I don't know where.

To all of us. I'd never seen Dane so cheerful and relaxed. "I've been thinking," he said. "A million's enough. After this one I'm going back to Syracuse, get my doctorate, get a job. There's going to be some school somewhere that'll want a poet in residence or an English teacher who's been on seven missions. They'll pay me something, and the money from this will keep me in extras all the rest of my life."

All I had really heard was the one word, and that I had heard loud and surprising: "Poet?"

He grinned. "Didn't you know? That's how I got to Gateway; the Guggenheim Foundation paid my way." He took the pot out of the cooker, divided the stew into two dishes, and we ate.

This was the fellow who had been shrieking viciously at the two Dannys for a solid hour, two days before, while Susie and I lay angry and isolated in the lander, listening. It was all turnaround. We were home free; the mission wasn't going to strand us out of fuel, and we didn't have to worry about finding anything, because our reward was guaranteed. I asked him about his poetry. He wouldn't recite any, but promised to show me copies of what he'd sent back to the Guggenheims when we reached Gateway again.

And when we'd finished eating, and wiped out the pot and dishes and put them away, Dane looked at his watch. "Too early to wake the others up," he said, "and not a damn thing to do."

He looked at me, smiling. It was a real smile, not a grin; and I pushed myself over to him, and sat in the warm and welcome circle of his arm.

And nineteen days went like an hour, and then the clock told us it was almost time to arrive. We were all awake, crowded into the capsule, eager as kids at Christmas, waiting to open our toys. It had been the happiest trip *I* had ever made, and probably one of the happiest ever. "You know," said Danny R. thoughtfully, "I'm almost sorry to arrive." And Susie, just beginning to understand our English, said:

"*Sim, ja sei,*" and then, "I *too!*" She squeezed my

hand, and I squeezed back; but what I was really thinking about was Klara. We had tried the radio a couple of times, but it didn't work in the Heechee wormholes through space. But when we came out I would be able to talk to her! I didn't mind that others would be listening, I knew what it was that I wanted to say. I even knew what she would answer. There was no question about it; there was surely as much euphoria in her ship as in ours, for the same reasons, and with all that love and joy the answer was not in doubt.

"We're stopping!" Danny R. yelled. "Can you feel it?"

"Yes!" crowed Metchnikov, bouncing with the tiny surges of the pseudo-gravity that marked our return to normal space. And there was another sign, too: the golden helix in the center of the cabin was beginning to glow, brighter every second.

"I think we've made it," said Danny R., bursting with pleasure, and I was as pleased as he.

"I'll start the spherical scan," I said, confident that I knew what to do. Susie took her cue from me and opened the door up to the lander; she and Danny A. were going to go out for the star sights.

But Danny A. didn't join her. He was staring at the viewscreen. As I started the ship turning, I could see stars, which was normal enough; they did not seem special in any way, although they were rather blurry for some reason.

I staggered and almost fell. The ship's rotation did not seem as smooth as it should be.

"The radio," Danny said, and Metchnikov, frowning, looked up and saw the light.

"Turn it on," I cried. The voice I heard might be Klara's. Metchnikov, still frowning, reached for the switch, and then I noticed that the helix was a brighter gold than I had ever seen it, straw-colored, as though it were incandescently hot. No heat came from it, but the golden color was shot through with streaks of pure white.

"That's funny," I said, pointing.

NavInstGdSup 104

Please supplement your Navigation
Instruction Guide as follows:

Course settings containing the
lines and colors as shown in the attached chart appear to have a definite relation to the amount of fuel
or other propulsion necessity remaining for use by the vessel.

All prospectors are cautioned that
the three bright lines in the orange
(Chart 2) appear to indicate extreme
shortage. No vessel displaying them
in its course has ever returned,
even from check flights.

I don't know if anyone heard me; the radio was pouring out static, and inside the capsule the sound was very loud. Metchnikov grabbed for the tuning and the gain.

Over the static I heard a voice I didn't recognize at first, but it was Danny A.'s. "Do you feel that?" he yelled. "It's gravity waves. We're in trouble. Stop the scan!"

I stopped it reflexively.

But by then the ship's screen had turned and something was in view that was not a star and not a galaxy. It was a dimly glowing mass of pale-blue light, mottled, immense, and terrifying. Even at the first glimpse I knew it was not a sun. No sun can be so blue and so dim. It hurt the eyes to look at it, not because of its brightness. It hurt inside the eyes, up far into the optic track; the pain was in the brain itself.

Metchnikov switched off the radio, and in the silence that followed I heard Danny A. say prayerfully, "Dearest God! We've had it. That thing is a black hole."

29

"With your permission, Bob," says Sigfrid, "I'd like to explore something with you before you command me into my passive display mode."

I tighten up; the son of a bitch has read my mind. "I observe," he says instantly, "that you are feeling some apprehension. That's what I would like to explore."

Incredible, I feel myself trying to save his feelings. Sometimes I forget he's a machine. "I didn't know you were aware that I've been doing that," I apologize.

"Of course I'm aware, Bob. When you have given me the proper command I obey it, but you have not ever given me the command to refrain from recording and integrating data. I assume you do not possess that command."

"You assume good, Sigfrid."

"There is no reason that you should not have access to whatever information I possess. I have not attempted to interfere until now—"

"Could you?"

"I do have the capacity to signal the use of the command instruction to higher authority, yes. I have not done that."

"Why not?" The old bag of bolts keeps on surprising me; all this is new to me.

"As I have said, there is no reason to. But clearly you are attempting to postpone some sort of confrontation, and I would like to tell you what I think that confrontation involves. Then you can make your own decision."

"Oh, cripes." I throw off the straps and sit up. "Do you mind if I smoke?" I know what the answer is going to be, but he surprises me again.

"Under the circumstances, no. If you feel the need of a tension reducer I agree. I had even considered offering you a mild tranquilizer if you wish it."

"Jesus," I say admiringly, lighting up—and I actually have to stop myself from offering him one! "All right, let's have it."

Sigfrid gets up, stretches his legs, and crosses to a more comfortable chair! I hadn't known he could do that, either. "I am trying to put you at your ease, Bob," he says, "as I am sure you observe. First let me tell you something about my capacities—and yours—which I do not think you know. I can provide information about any of my clients. That is, you are not limited to those who have had access to this particular terminal."

"I don't think I understand that," I say, after he has paused for a moment.

"I think you do. Or will. When you want to. However, the more important question is what memory you are attempting to keep suppressed. I feel it is necessary for you to unblock it. I had considered offering you light hypnosis, or a tranquilizer, or even a fully human analyst to come in for one session, and any or all of those are at your disposal if you wish them. But I have observed that you are relatively comfortable in discussions about what you perceive as objective reality, as distinguished from your internalization of reality. So I would like to explore a particular incident with you in those terms."

I carefully tap some ash off the end of my cigarette. He's right about that; as long as we keep the conversation abstract and impersonal, I can talk about anybloodything. "What incident is that, Sigfrid?"

"Your final prospecting voyage from Gateway, Bob. Let me refresh your memory—"

"Jesus, Sigfrid!"

"I know you think you recall it perfectly," he says, interpreting me exactly, "and in that sense I don't suppose your memory needs refreshing. But what is interesting about that particular episode is that all the main areas of your internal concern seem to converge there. Your terror. Your homosexual tendencies—"

"Hey!"

"—which are not, to be sure, a major part of your sexuality, Bob, but which give you more concern than is warranted. Your feelings about your mother. The immense burden of guilt you lay on yourself. And, above all, the woman Gelle-Klara Moynlin. All these things recur over and over in your dreams, Bob, although you often do not make the identification. And they are all present in this one episode."

I stub out a cigarette, and realize that I have had two going at once. "I don't see the part about my mother," I say at last.

"You don't?" The hologram that I call Sigfrid von Shrink turns toward a corner of the room. "Let me show you a picture." He raises his hand—that's pure theater, I know it is—and in the corner there appears a woman's figure. It is not very clear, but it is young, slim, and is in the act of covering a cough.

"It's not a very good resemblance to my mother," I object.

"Isn't it?"

"Well," I say generously, "I suppose it's the best

you can do. I mean, not having anything to go on except, I guess, my description of her."

"The picture," says Sigfrid gently enough, "was assembled from your description of the girl Susie Hereira."

I light another cigarette, with some difficulty, because my hand is shaking. "Wow," I say, with real admiration. "I take my hat off to you, Sigfrid. That's very interesting. Of course," I go on, suddenly feeling irritable, "Susie was, my God, only a child! Apart from that I realize—I realize now, I mean—that there are some resemblances. But the age is all wrong."

"Bob," says Sigfrid, "how old was your mother when you were little?"

"She was very young." I add after a moment, "As a matter of fact, she looked a lot younger than she was even."

Sigfrid lets me hang there for a moment, and then he waves his hand again and the figure disappears, and instead we are suddenly looking at a picture of two Fives butted lander-to-lander in midspace, and beyond them is—is—

"Oh, my God, Sigfrid," I say.

He waits me out for a while.

As far as I am concerned, he can wait forever; I simply do not know what to say. I am not hurting, but I am paralyzed. I cannot say anything, and I cannot move.

"This," he begins, speaking very softly and gently, "is a reconstruction of the two ships in your expedition in the vicinity of the object SAG YY. It is a black hole or, more accurately, a singularity in a state of extremely rapid rotation."

"I know what it is, Sigfrid."

"Yes. You do. Because of its rotation, the translation velocity of what is called its event threshold or Schwarzschild discontinuity exceeds the speed of light, and so it is not properly black; in fact it can be seen by virtue of what is called Cerenkov radiation. It was because of the instrument readings on this and other aspects of the singularity that your expedition was

A NOTE ON NUTRITION

Question. What did the Heechee eat?

Professor Hegramet. About what we do, I would say. Everything. I think they were omnivores, ate anything they could catch. We really don't know a thing about their diet, except that you can make some deductions from the shell missions.

Question. Shell missions?

Professor Hegramet. There are at least four recorded missions that didn't go as far as another star, but went clear out of the solar system. Out where the shell of comets hangs out, you know, half a light-year or so away. The missions are marked as failures, but I don't think they are. I've been pushing the Board to give science bonuses for them. Three seemed to wind up in meteorite swarms. The other came out at a comet, all hundreds of A.U. out. Meteorite swarms, of course, are usually the debris of old, dead comets.

Question. Are you saying the Heechee ate comets?

Professor Hegramet. Ate the things comets are made out of. Do you know what they are? Carbon, oxygen, nitrogen, hydrogen—the same elements you ate for breakfast. I think they used comets for feedstocks to manufacture what they ate. I think one of those missions to the cometary shell is sooner or later going to turn up a Heechee food factory, and then maybe we won't have anybody ever starving anywhere anymore.

awarded a ten-million-dollar bonus, in addition to the agreed-upon sum which, along with certain other lesser amounts, is the foundation of your present fortune."

"I know that, too, Sigfrid."

Pause.

"Would you care to tell me what else you know about it, Bob?"

Pause.

"I'm not sure I can, Sigfrid."

Pause again.

He isn't even urging me to try. He knows that he doesn't have to. I want to try, and I take my cue from his own manner. There is something in there that I can't talk about, that scares me even to think about; but wrapped around that central terror there is something I can talk about, and that is the objective reality.

"I don't know how much you know about singularities, Sigfrid."

"Perhaps you can just say what you think it is that I ought to know, Bob."

I put out the current cigarette and light another one. "Well," I say, "you know and I know that if you really wanted to know about singularities it's all in the data-banks somewhere, and a lot more exactly and informatively than I can say it, but anyway . . . The thing about black holes is they're traps. They bend light. They bend time. Once you're in you can't get out. Only . . . Only . . ."

After a moment Sigfrid says, "It's all right for you to cry if you want to, Bob," which is the way that I suddenly realize that that's what I'm doing.

"Jesus," I say, and blow my nose into one of the tissues that he always keeps handy right next to the mat. He waits.

"Only I did get out," I say.

And Sigfrid does something else I had never expected from him; he permits himself a joke. "That," he says, "is pretty obvious, from the fact that you're here."

"This is bloody exhausting, Sigfrid," I say.

"I am sure it is for you, Bob."

"I wish I had a drink."

Click. "The cabinet behind you," says Sigfrid, "that has just opened contains some rather good sherry. It isn't made from grapes, I'm sorry to say; the health service doesn't go in for luxuries. But I don't think you'll be aware of its natural-gas origins. Oh, and it is laced with just a dollop of THC to soothe the nerves."

"Holy Christ," I say, having run out of ways of expressing surprise. The sherry is all he says it is, and I can feel the warmth of it expanding inside me.

"Okay," I say, setting the glass down. "Well. When I got back to Gateway they'd written the expedition off. We were almost a year overdue. Because we'd been *almost* inside the event horizon. Do you understand about time dilation? . . . Oh, never mind," I say, before he can answer, "that was a rhetorical question. What I mean is, what happened was the phenomenon they call time dilation. You get that close to a singularity and you come up against the twin paradox. What was maybe a quarter of an hour for us was almost a year by clock time—clock time on Gateway, or here, or anywhere else in the non-relativistic universe, I mean. And—"

I take another drink, then I go on bravely enough:

"And if we'd gone any farther down we would have been going slower and slower. Slower, and slower, and slower. A little closer, and that fifteen minutes would have turned out to be a decade. A little closer still, and it would have been a century. It was *that* close, Sigfrid. We were almost trapped, all of us.

"But I got out."

And I think of something and look at my watch. "Speaking of time, my hour's been up for the last five minutes!"

"I have no other appointments this afternoon, Bob."

I stare. "What?"

Gently: "I cleared my calendar before your appointment, Bob."

I don't say "Holy Christ" again, but I surely think

it. "That makes me feel right up against the wall, Sig-frid!" I say angrily.

"I am not forcing you to stay past your hour, Bob. I am only pointing out that you have that option if you choose."

I mull that for a while.

"You are one brassbound ringding of a computer, Sigfrid," I say. "All right. Well, you see, there was no way we could get out, considered as a unit. Our ships were caught, well inside the point of no return, and there just ain't no way home from there. But old Danny A., he was a sharp article. And he knew all about the loopholes in the laws. Considered as a unit, we were stuck.

"But we weren't a unit! We were two ships! And each of them came apart into two other ships! And if we could somehow transfer acceleration from one part of our system to the other—you know, kick part of us deeper into the well and at the same time kick the other part up and out—then *part* of the unit could go free!"

Long pause.

"Why don't you have another drink, Bob?" says Sigfrid solicitously. "After you finish crying, I mean."

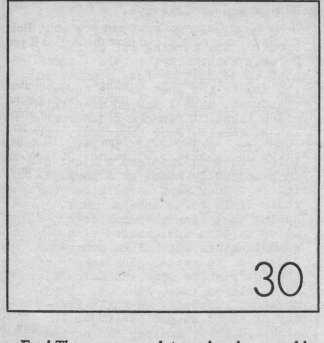

30

Fear! There was so much terror jumping around inside my skin that I couldn't feel it anymore; my senses were saturated with it; I don't know if I screamed or babbled, I only did what Danny A. told me to do. We'd backed the two ships together and linked up, lander-to-lander, and we were trying to manhandle gear, instruments, clothes, everything that moved out of the first ship into whatever corners we could find of the second, to make room for ten people where five were a tight fit. Hand to hand, back and forth, we bucket-brigaded the stuff. Dane Metchnikov's kidneys must have been kicked black-and-blue; he was the one who was in the landers, changing the fuel-metering switches to blow every drop of hydrox at once. Would we survive that? We had no way of knowing. Both our Fives were armored, and we didn't ex-

Dear Voice of Gateway:

On Wednesday of last week I was crossing the parking lot at the Safeway Supermarket (where I had gone to deposit my food stamps) on the way to the shuttle bus to my apartment, when I saw an unearthly green light. A strange spacecraft landed nearby. Four beautiful, but very tiny, young women in filmy white robes emerged and subjected me helpless by means of a paralyzing ray. They kept me prisoner on their craft for nineteen hours. During that time they subjected me to certain indignities of a sexual nature which I am honorbound not to reveal. The leader of the four, whose name was Moira Glow-Fawn, stated that, like us, they have not succeeded in fully overcoming their animal heritage. I accepted their apology and agreed to deliver four messages to Earth. Messages One and Four I may not announce until the proper time. Message Two is a private one for the manager of my apartment project. Message Three is for you at Gateway, and it has three parts: 1, there must be no more cigarette smoking; 2, there must be no more mixed schooling of boys and girls at least until the second year of college; 3, you must stop all exploration of space at once. We are being watched.

Harry Hellison

Pittsburgh

péct to damage the Heechee-metal shells. But the contents of the shells would be us, all of us in the one of them that went free—or we hoped would go free—and there wasn't really any way to tell whether we could come free in the first place, or whether what would come free would be nothing but jelly, anyway. And all we had was minutes, and not very many of them. I guess I passed Klara twenty times in ten minutes, and I remember that once, the first time, we kissed. Or aimed at each other's lips, and came close enough. I remember the smell of her, and once lifting my head because the musk oil was so strong and not seeing her, and then forgetting it again. And all the time, out of one viewscreen or another, that immense broad, baleful blue ball hung flickering outside; the racing shadows across its surface that were phase effects made fearful pictures; the gripping grab of its gravity waves tugged at our guts. Danny A. was in the capsule of the first ship, watching the time and kicking bags and bundles down to the lander hatch to pass on, through the hatch, through the landers, up to the capsule of the second ship where I was pushing them out of the way, any which way, just to make room for more. "Five minutes," he'd yell, and "Four minutes!" and *"Three minutes, get the goddamn lead out!"* and then, "That's it! All of you! Drop what you're doing and come on up here." And we did. All of us. All but me. I could hear the others yelling, and then calling to me; but I'd fallen behind, our own lander was blocked, I couldn't get through the hatch! And I tugged somebody's duffelbag out of the way, just as Klara was screaming over the TBS radio, "Bob! Bob, for God's sake, get up here!" And I knew it was too late; and I slammed the hatch and dogged it down, just as I heard Danny A.'s voice shouting, *"No! No! Wait. . . ."*

Wait. . . .

Wait for a very, very long time.

We sometimes get squashed, and we sometimes
    get burned,
And we sometimes get shredded to bits,
And we sometimes get fat on the Royalties
    Earned,
And we're always scared out of our wits.
        We don't care which—
Little lost Heechee, start making us rich!

31

After a while, I don't know how long, I raise my head and say, "Sorry, Sigfrid."

"For what, Bob?"

"For crying like this." I am physically exhausted. It is as if I had run ten miles through a gauntlet of mad Choctaws pounding me with clubs.

"Are you feeling better now, Bob?"

"Better?" I puzzle over that stupid question for a moment, and then I take inventory, and, curiously enough, I am. "Why, yeah. I guess so. Not what you'd call *good*. But better."

"Take it easy for a minute, Bob."

That strikes me as a dumb remark, and I tell him so. I have about the energy level of a small, arthritic jellyfish that's been dead for a week. I have no choice but to take it easy.

NOTICE OF CREDIT

To ROBINETTE BROADHEAD:

1. Acknowledgment is made that
your course setting for Gateway II
permits round-trip flights with a
travel-time saving of approximately
100 days over the previous standard
course for this object.

2. By decision of the Board, you
are granted a discovery royalty of
1 percent on all earnings on future
flights using said course setting,
and an advance of $10,000 against
said royalty.

3. By decision of the Board, you
are assessed one-half of said royalty and advance as a penalty for
damage to the vessel employed.

Your account is therefore CREDITED
with the following amount:
Royalty advance (Board Order
A-135-7), less deduction
(Board Order A-135-8): $5,000
Your present BALANCE is: $6,192

But I do feel better. "I feel," I say, "as if I let myself feel my guilt at last."

"And you survived it."

I think that over. "I guess I did," I say.

"Let's explore that question of guilt, Bob. Guilt why?"

"Because I jettisoned nine people to save myself, asshole!"

"Has anyone ever accused you of that? Anyone but yourself, I mean?"

"Accused?" I blow my nose again, thinking. "Well, no. Why should they? When I got back I was kind of a hero." I think about Shicky, so kind, so mothering; and Francy Hereira holding me in his arms, letting me bawl, even though I'd killed his cousin. "But they weren't there. They didn't see me blow the tanks to get free."

"*Did* you blow the tanks?"

"Oh, hell, Sigfrid," I say, "I don't know. I was going to. I was reaching for the button."

"Does it make sense that the button in the ship you were planning to abandon would actually fire the combined tanks in the landers?"

"Why not? I don't know. Anyway," I say, "you can't give me any alibis I haven't already thought of for myself. *I* know maybe Danny or Klara pushed the button before I did. But I was reaching for mine!"

"And which ship did you think would go free?"

"Theirs! Mine," I correct myself. "No, I don't know."

Sigfrid says gravely, "Actually, that was a very resourceful thing you did. You knew you couldn't all have survived. There wasn't time. The only choice was whether some of you would die, or all of you would. You elected to see that somebody lived."

"Crap! I'm a murderer!"

Pause, while Sigfrid's circuits think that over. "Bob," he says carefully, "I think you're contradicting yourself. Didn't you say she's still alive in that discontinuity?"

"They all are! Time has stopped for them!"

"Then how could you have murdered anybody?"

"What?"

He says again, "How could you have murdered anybody?"

". . . I don't know," I say, "but, honestly, Sigfrid, I really don't want to think about it anymore today."

"There's no reason you should, Bob. I wonder if you have any idea how much you've accomplished in the past two and a half hours. I'm proud of you!"

And queerly, incongruously, I believe he is, chips, Heechee circuits, holograms and all, and it makes me feel good to believe it.

"You can go any time you want to," he says, getting up and going back to his easy chair in the most life-like way possible, even grinning at me! "But I think I would like to show you something."

My defenses are eroded down to nothing. I only say, "What's that, Sigfrid?"

"That other capability of ours that I mentioned, Bob," he says, "the one that we've never used. I would like to display another patient, from some time back."

"Another patient?"

He says gently, "Look over in the corner, Bob."

I look—

—and there she is.

"Klara!" And as soon as I see her I know where Sigfrid got it; from the machine Klara was consulting back on Gateway. She is hanging there, one arm across a file rack, her feet lazily floating in air, talking earnestly; her broad black eyebrows frown and smile, and her face grins, and grimaces, and then looks sweetly, invitingly relaxed.

"You can hear what she's saying if you want to, Bob."

"Do I want to?"

"Not necessarily. But there's nothing in it to be afraid of. She loved you, Bob, the best way she knew how. The same as you loved her."

308

NOTICE OF CREDIT

To ROBINETTE BROADHEAD:

   Your account is CREDITED with the
following amounts:
Guaranteed bonus for
Mission 88-90A and
88-90B (survivorship
total): $10,000,000
Science bonus awarded by
Board: 8,500,000
Total: $18,500,000
Your present BALANCE is: $18,506,036

I look for a long time, and then I say, "Turn her off, Sigfrid."

In the recovery room I almost fall asleep for a moment. I have never been so relaxed.

I wash my face, and smoke another cigarette, and then I go out into the bright diffuse daylight under the Bubble, and it all looks so good and so friendly. I think of Klara with love and tenderness, and in my heart I say good-bye to her. And then I think of S. Ya., with whom I have a date for that evening—if I'm not already too late for it! But she'll wait; she's a good scout, almost as good as Klara.

Klara.

I stop in the middle of the mall, and people bump up against me. A little old lady in short-shorts toddles over to me and says, "Is something wrong?"

I stare at her, and don't answer; and then I turn around and head back for Sigfrid's office.

There is no one there, not even a hologram. I yell, "Sigfrid! Where the hell are you?"

No one. No answer. This is the first time I've ever been in the room when it wasn't set up. I can see what is real and what was hologram now; and not much of it is real. Powder-metal walls, studs for projectors. The mat (real); the cabinet with the liquor (real); a few other pieces of furniture that I might want to touch or use. But no Sigfrid. Not even the chair he usually sits in. "Sigfrid!"

I keep on yelling, with my heart bubbling up in my throat and my brain spinning. "Sigfrid!" I scream, and at last there is a sort of a haze and a flash and there he is in his Sigmund Freud suit, looking at me politely.

"Yes, Bob?"

"Sigfrid, I did murder her! She's gone!"

"I see that you're upset, Bob," he says. "Can you tell me what it is that's bothering you?"

"Upset! I'm worse than upset, Sigfrid, I'm a person who killed nine other people to save his life! Maybe not 'really'! Maybe not 'on purpose'! But in their eyes I killed them, as much as in mine!"

"But Bob," he says reasonably, "we've been all over this. She's still alive; they all are. Time has stopped for them—"

"I know," I howl. "Don't you understand, Sigfrid? That's the point. I not only killed her, *I'm still killing her!*"

Patiently: "Do you think what you just said is true, Bob?"

"*She* thinks it is! Now, and forever, as long as I live. It isn't years ago that it happened for her. It's only a few minutes, and it goes on for all of my life. I'm down here, getting older, trying to forget, and there's Klara up there in Sagittarius YY, floating around like a fly in amber!"

I drop to the bare plastic mat, sobbing. Little by little, Sigfrid has been restoring the whole office, patching in this decoration and that. There are piñatas hanging over my head, and a holopic of Lake Garda at Sirmione on the wall, hoverfloats, sailboats, and bathers having fun.

"Let the pain out, Bob," Sigfrid says gently. "Let it all out."

"What do you think I'm *doing?*" I roll over on the foam mat, staring at the ceiling. "I could get over the pain and the guilt, Sigfrid, if *she* could. But for her it isn't over. She's out there, stuck in time."

"Go ahead, Bob," he encourages.

"I *am* going ahead. Every second is still the newest second in her mind—the second when I threw her life away to save my own. I'll live and get old and die before she lives past that second, Sigfrid."

"Keep going, Bob. Say it all."

"She's thinking I betrayed her, and she's thinking it *now!* I can't live with that."

There is a very, very long silence, and at last Sigfrid says:

"You are, you know."

"What?" My mind has gone a thousand light-years away.

"You are living with it, Bob."

"Do you call this living?" I sneer, sitting up and wiping my nose with another of his million tissues.

"You respond very quickly to anything I say, Bob," says Sigfrid, "and therefore sometimes I think your response is a counterpunch. You parry what I say with words. Let me strike home for once, Bob. Let this sink in: you *are* living."

". . . Well, I suppose I am." It is true enough; it is just not very rewarding.

Another long pause, and then Sigfrid says:

"Bob. You know that I am a machine. You also know that my function is to deal with human feelings. I cannot *feel* feelings. But I can represent them with models, I can analyze them, I can evaluate them. I can do this for you. I can even do it for myself. I can construct a paradigm within which I can assess the value of emotions. Guilt? It is a painful thing; but because it is painful it is a behavior modifier. It can influence you to avoid guilt-inducing actions, and this is a valuable thing for you and for society. But you cannot use it if you do not feel it."

"I *do* feel it! Jesus Christ, Sigfrid, you know I'm feeling it!"

"I know," he says, "that now you are letting yourself feel it. It is out in the open, where you can let it work for you, not buried where it can only harm you. That is what I am for, Bob. To bring your feelings out where you can use them."

"Even the bad feelings? Guilt, fear, pain, envy?"

"Guilt. Fear. Pain. Envy. The motivators. The modifiers. The qualities that I, Bob, do not have, except in a hypothetical sense, when I make a paradigm and assign them to myself for study."

There is another pause. I have a funny feeling about it. Sigfrid's pauses are usually either to give me time to let something sink in, or to permit him to compute some complex chain of argument about me. This time I think it is neither of them. He is thinking, but not about me. And at last he says, "So now I can answer what you asked me, Bob."

"Asked you? What was that?"

"You asked me, 'Do you call this living?' And I answer: Yes. It is exactly what I call living. And in my best hypothetical sense, I envy it very much."

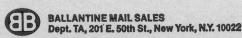